FANGS
AND
FUDGE

FANGS
AND
FUDGE

Melissa Nicole

Shattered Glass
— PUBLISHING —

Published by Shattered Glass Publishing.

Cover design by Trif Designs
© Depositphotos.com
Proofread by The Proof Posse (Jackie, Dawn, Heather, Mirjam, and Roxanne)

ISBN 978-1-63869-039-9 (eBook Edition)
ISBN 978-1-63869-046-7 (Paperback Edition)

Version 2024.06.05

To the ride or die friend we all need in our lives.

CHAPTER ONE

I DROVE THROUGH THE GATE OF BLUR'S EMPLOYEE PARKING LOT and glanced at the back entrance. Despite barricading myself in the upstairs office less than twenty-four hours ago, I wasn't nervous about returning to work. Work was normal, and normal was good. Necessary even. Just like the party tray of gourmet cupcakes buckled into the seat beside me.

Doc, Blur's manager, exited the building as I was removing my precious cargo. With his typical meticulously brushed-back hair and trimmed beard, I could almost believe Blur hadn't been attacked last night and it was business as usual. Only the smudge of dirt on his sleeve gave away the fact that he was pitching in to help repair the damage caused by the vampire-thralled people.

"Need a hand, Everly?" he asked.

The box wasn't heavy, and I could easily manage on my own, but I knew Doc liked to help. Plus, the cupcakes were for my coworkers. I'd already eaten mine earlier while with Cross.

"Sure," I said, straightening.

Doc's light blue gaze swept over my face, and I thought I

saw a hint of a frown when I handed off the box. I didn't question it. After all, I'd just spent the morning chatting with a vampire and was now walking into a den of werewolves. Both had good noses and didn't like smelling one another.

"How's everything going inside?" I asked as I locked my aging compact car.

"Good. Almost cleaned. Shepard was thinking of opening tonight to see how many patrons show up."

I held the employee door open for Doc. "I can't imagine people *not* showing up. How many times have you had to tell the people in line we weren't taking any more patrons because it got too late?"

"That was before the attack," he said, pausing so I could stow my purse in my locker.

"The attack" had been approximately thirty minutes of heart-pounding terror when humans under vampire compulsion had stormed Blur and attacked anyone in sight. Vena and I had escaped unscathed, thanks to Shepard's sturdy office desk and Vena's quick thinking.

"Word spreads fast when it involves vampires," Doc continued. "Shepard thinks the humans will stay clear of this place for a while."

Had we not found Miles, Vena's brother, tied to a chair several hours ago and learned that vampires were the reason for his kidnapping, I could have told myself that vampires weren't a problem, too. Unfortunately, that wasn't an option anymore. Unlike the rest of humanity, I now knew the truth.

"I'm betting my fellow humans line up even faster. Right now, Blur is like a daytime drama. People will want to gawk and talk about what happened. It doesn't matter if coming here is dangerous or not."

"Humans lack common sense," Doc said, not unkindly.

Since I lived with Vena and had to deal with her common sense glitches daily, I grinned at his comment and followed him through the door to the main bar.

"Oh, I think we have common sense. We just choose not to listen to it too often," I said as I looked around.

What had been a complete disaster the night before wasn't so horrible now.

The floor that Pam, one of the waitstaff, had coated with soda spray the night before looked recently mopped. The tables were already cleared and cleaned, and Gunner, one of Shepard's youngest crew members who did whatever was needed, was sweeping up broken glass from the top right section while Shepard mopped the lower section.

"Wow, you made fast progress," I said. "And I think I brought too many cupcakes. Where's everyone else?"

"Out patrolling," Doc said as he set the box on the bar. "And you can never have too many sweets."

I held a hand over my heart. "You're speaking my love language, Doc."

He grinned. The silver streaking his temples didn't detract from his muscled build or good looks; it added to them.

"Stop flirting with Everly and clean up the glass behind the bar," Shepard said. I glanced at him and saw he'd abandoned his mop and was headed our way.

"On it," Doc said with a knowing smirk.

I felt him leave my side, but I didn't look. I was too focused on Shepard. He moved with a grace that didn't quite match his muscled size. That was only part of what made women stop and stare, though. The other part was the gorgeous mane of dark blonde hair that framed his face and accentuated his intense light grey gaze. His stubborn, chiseled chin was currently dipped low as he studied me.

"You were downtown for a while. Problem with your phone?" he asked.

I shook my head as he reached me.

"Just a problem with my sweet tooth. There was a bakery nearby." I arched a brow at him. "Which you know from watching on that tracking app, right?"

He grinned a little, which completely changed how he looked. Boyish and handsome and definitely not someone I should be looking at for too long.

Turning, I flipped back the lid on the box Doc had deposited on the bar.

"I brought some for everyone. They're addictively good."

When Shepard stepped close to me, I thought he would take a cupcake, but instead, he frowned as he studied my face. His gaze lingered on my forehead.

"Why do you smell like vampire?" he asked.

Since I'd been with Cross less than an hour ago, I didn't doubt Shepard could smell him. However, I wasn't about to admit our meeting to Shepard.

"It must be from the same vampire this morning." Which was true since Cross had been there when we'd found Miles as well.

Shepard leaned in, his dark blonde hair wisping against mine as he softly inhaled. "You're right. It's the same vampire."

Shepard placed a kiss on my forehead. "Don't worry, Everly. We're going to clean out the vampires. Help is already on its way."

He straightened away from me as my heart stuttered from

the kiss. It wasn't the first time he'd done it, but I still wasn't used to it.

Resisting the urge to clear my throat or fidget, I focused on his words.

"Help?" I asked. "What kind of help?" I couldn't imagine anyone who would want to deal with creatures that could kill and compel.

"Nothing for you to worry about. Just expect to see new faces here soon. If you have any concerns, let me know." He reached over, moving closer for a moment as he grabbed a cupcake. "Thank you for these."

"No problem. What should I clean?"

Shepard glanced around the bar area and then over to the seating sections. "How about working in the VIP section? It wasn't hit as hard as the rest of the bar, but I want attention to detail, and I trust that you'll do it best."

With a nod, I grabbed cleaning supplies on my way to the second floor. Other than a few overturned chairs, questionable liquid on the glass wall overlooking the main club, and a few broken liquor bottles at the VIP bar, it wasn't too bad. I knew I'd have it back to perfection in an hour or two.

As I worked, I periodically checked my phone, making sure I didn't miss any calls or messages from Vena or Miles. Since one of Blur's bouncers was watching over Miles, I wasn't too concerned about him leaving and getting into trouble. But I still feared the effects of him being fed on by vampires. And Vena...well, I was always worried about her, especially since she was supposed to be hiding the disgusting scrotum map and titleless book.

It only took an hour to restore the VIP section. Once I

finished, I sat in a chair and opened the tracking app on my phone.

Vena was still at her parents' house—a source of research information for treasure hunts. I hated it when she stayed there too long.

"Tracking Vena?" Shepard asked.

I tipped my head back, looking up at him as he peered down at my phone.

A smile played on his lips. "Worried about her?"

"Always."

He gave a knowing nod. "I can help keep an eye on her as well." He sat down next to me and held out his phone. "Put her on my tracking app."

Vena would hate if Shepard was tracking her, too, but after what happened to Miles, I was afraid Vena would have the same fate or worse, especially with her treasure hunting.

I entered her ID into Shepard's phone and sent her a text, warning her that she was going to get a notification and it was for Shepard. As I'd anticipated, she had something to say about it.

Vena: No. I do not need a watchdog.

Me: Please play nice with your boss.

Vena: You play nice enough for the both of us.

Me: Don't make me pull the parental card.

Vena: You wouldn't... *wow emoji*

"Do I even want to know what you're texting back and forth?" Shepard asked dryly.

"I'm trying to get her to accept your request to track her. She's being a little stubborn."

"Tell her there's a five-hundred-dollar sign-on bonus and another one hundred monthly to keep it active."

I glanced up at him. "I'm not sure if I should be impressed that you know her well enough to know money would sway her or offended that you think money can get you your way?"

His smile melted my insides a little.

"I'm smart enough to know money motivates some people and only use it when I'm trying to protect those I care about."

"Good answer," I said, typing out the text.

He glanced down at his phone and chuckled.

"She's accepted me. Talk her into accepting Anchor, too."

"You mean in the app, right?"

Shepard's gaze lost some of its humor. "There are worse things than saying yes to a wolf, wouldn't you agree?"

"That's not what I meant," I said quickly. "There is absolutely nothing wrong with werewolves. I think they're great and nice. I haven't met one yet who isn't amazingly good-looking."

Someone downstairs barked out a laugh, and I felt my face flush.

"What I *did* mean," I continued, "is that I don't want Anchor's heart bruised by Vena. She's flirty and fun and not ready to be serious yet. I've already warned her, and I've told her to cut it out. I love her, but Vena is like a wrecking ball. She comes in hard and fast, and sometimes people get hurt."

Shepard reached out to brush a thumb over the fading cut on my cheek.

"She doesn't sound like a good friend."

"Ah, that's where you're wrong. Once she's set her loyalty, there's no shaking it. She doesn't just jump two feet into her own trouble but mine as well. She has saved me more times than I can count. And not because she was the one who got me into trouble. At least, not the majority of those saves. Vena is my no-questions-asked yes-man. She'll bring the shovel and a chair for me to sit on while she cleans up my mistakes."

"So she's the person you trust most in this world?"

"Absolutely."

"I see. I'll warn Anchor as well then...unless you'd rather have someone else stay at your house until we have the vampire infestation cleaned up."

"No. Anchor's great," I said quickly.

His distractibility, when it came to Vena, would come in handy since Cross had no plans to stay away. Especially not when I had over two million dollars of his money in my bank account, and he still needed my help to find somewhere to live.

"Good," Shepard said. "Anchor will be there tonight, then."

"How long do you think the vampire infestation will take to clean up? I'm not hinting you should rush or anything. I'm just wondering if Vena and I should maybe condense into one room so Anchor can have his own." I wasn't actually thinking anything of the sort. I just wanted to know how long Anchor was going to be staying with us.

"Anchor stays on the couch. It should only take a few weeks. Definitely not worth the effort of moving all your things."

I nodded and looked around the VIP section one last time to make sure I didn't miss anything.

"Do you want me to let Vena know we're working tonight?" I asked.

"If you're sure you're up for it. I was thinking of opening the doors at seven."

Seven was much later than usual, but a short shift during prime hours didn't sound like a bad thing.

"See you at seven, then."

8

I sent Vena a quick text and went down to the main bar where I looked at the empty cupcake box.

Buzz winked at me as he cleaned a glass. "Don't worry. We shared."

"As in three for me and one for everyone else kind of sharing?"

He chuckled. "You would have heard fighting if any of us tried that. Thanks for the cupcakes, Everly."

I waved goodbye and went to collect my things.

At home, I saw a familiar truck sitting at the curb behind Miles' car and waved to Tank. He nodded and watched me let myself into the house.

I didn't exactly mind the extra eyes on me. Not after what had happened to Miles.

Dropping my things on the couch, I checked the message from Vena saying she was on her way back and then sent Miles a text.

Me: Did you eat? Have you sent your proof of life pictures to Vena?

Miles: Yes and yes. I ordered a pizza and tried to invite my guard in. He declined the invite and my offer to have a slice.

Me: Sierra drugged Gunther. I'm betting they're going to be careful about taking pizza and booze from strangers for a while.

Yet, as I typed that last message, I realized they'd had no problem eating the cupcakes I'd brought. Even after smelling vampire on me.

Miles: Geez. Now I feel twice as bad. I'll have to find a way to pay them back. Let me know if you have any ideas.

I went to the kitchen and started making two sandwiches.

Vena arrived just as I was settling in to watch the latest episode of *The Other House* that had aired last night.

"How'd everything go at your parents'?" I asked.

She placed a pile of leather-bound books on the coffee table next to our sandwiches. She kicked back on the couch and snagged a plate.

"Good. The map and book are in a spot Miles will never find. And I brought back a few books for research."

Mid-bite, I choked. "Research? Vena, I swear you better mean research for an upcoming university class and not treasure hunting."

"I already told you I'd pick up a few books for Miles to keep him entertained and out of trouble." When I narrowed my eyes at her, she added, "Safe books. I will even go through them first to make sure they won't trigger him. Everything will be fine."

Her attempt to soothe only made me more nervous, even though I knew Miles would never be okay without something to research.

"What books did you get?"

"Information on vampires. I want to know a little more about them myself."

"Because Miles was fed on?"

She nodded. "And the compelling aspect. We should know these things anyway, given our recent encounters, don't you agree?"

I knew she was talking about Cross.

"Let's not poke our noses where they don't belong," I said, not wanting to throw any shade on Cross. He had done nothing but help us. Yes, he was considered a dangerous supernatural, but so was Shepard, and I trusted him. "Let's just watch *The Other House* and relax until we go to work."

"Shepard's really opening already?"

I nodded as I chewed the last of my sandwich. "Blur wasn't as bad as I thought it would be. Just needed cleaning and a few repairs."

Vena flipped through the book. "I was hoping for more time off."

"I doubt there will be a huge crowd. Some of our regulars will be too afraid to come."

"What about the nosey people who want to see the crime scene?"

"As long as they tip well, I don't care." I nudged her. "I'm starting the show."

Vena glanced up at the TV for a second before her gaze returned to the book. She flipped through the pages and tsked. "Isn't there a glossary in this thing? Do they expect me to read it from front to back to get the information I'm looking for?"

"I don't know, but it looks like there is going to be drama in the house," I said, watching as the show teased an upcoming fight scene. "I normally don't like fighting, but they're all glistening and muscle-bulging."

Vena peeked up from the book and was entranced by a shirt being ripped from the hottie. "Damn," she breathed, book forgotten.

I smiled, knowing "research" was no longer a priority. While I did want to find answers regarding any side effects from a vampire feeding, Vena and I could use a little mindless entertainment for an hour. We deserved that much, at least.

Unfortunately, the hour flew by, and my escape from reality ended on a cliffhanger.

"I hate when they do that," I said, taking our plates to the kitchen.

"It's so you are eager for the next episode."

"I'd be eager either way," I said. "The guys in this season are mouthwatering."

"Anchor is that mouthwatering. He'd make great babies."

"Stop," I warned.

"Anchor's not even here to hear me," Vena said.

Perhaps watching *The Other House* wasn't the best idea before a shift. It was hard enough getting her to curb her hormones around Anchor without the added pre-shift eye candy.

"I asked Shepard how long he thought we'd have Anchor on our couch," I said as I put our dishes in the sink. "He thought a few weeks."

"You won't hear any complaints from me," Vena said.

"You're forgetting what having them around means. No getting into trouble."

She groaned. "You mean no hunting."

"Probably."

"So we need the vampires gone and Anchor, that delicious hunk of puppy chow, off our couch. Good thing I have some light reading to help that along." I heard the books thump down on the dining room table and shook my head.

"Good thing," I echoed.

I used the spare time before work to research and write up a spin on a cannoli cupcake I wanted to try making before we both had to change for work and head in early.

Buzz was waiting by the back door when we pulled into the employee parking.

"Shepard called everyone in," he said as we got out of the car. "There's already a line in front."

A meow from under the dumpster drew my attention, and I squatted down in my pencil skirt to look at the black cat.

"It didn't go home yet?" I asked as I peered at the familiar cat.

"If it's a stray, that might be its home," Buzz said.

It did that weird one-eye-at-a-time blink that cats managed, and I straightened to glance at Vena.

"We should call animal control," she said. "If it's not fixed, you're going to have a whole lot more cats."

"I'll tell Shepard," Buzz said, holding the door open for us. "The thing smells like vampire, though. Probably some feeder's pet, considering last night. We're hoping someone will come to claim it."

"Ah," Vena said.

That was it. Just "ah."

Meanwhile, my insides were doing an "ew" squeal and flail. The feeders who'd been at Juicy and the people who'd attacked Blur last night hadn't exactly been in their right minds.

"I really hope no one comes," I said as we headed to our lockers to store our things.

"Even if someone does, we have nothing to worry about, Ev. Not here. Not with this staff."

We left the employee area, and I spotted Shepard leaning against the sink with his arms crossed.

"Vena's right," he said. "What happened last night won't happen again. You have my word. We'll have extra security around the bar by nine." He pushed away from the sink and clasped my arms, his thumbs brushing over the sleeves of my white button-up.

"But if anything feels off, tell me. I'm here for you." He glanced at Vena. "Both of you."

She nodded and waited until he walked out of the kitchen to give me an exaggerated wink and the sign for a blow job.

Griz, the head chef, caught Vena in mid-stroke and smirked. Normally a stoic man in his kitchen domain, his brown eyes twinkled with amusement.

"What is wrong with you?" I said, smacking her arm. "You need treatment."

"Spa treatment? I wouldn't mind a happy-ending massage from a certain someone."

"More like electrotherapy treatment. Take it down a notch."

She grinned unrepentantly as we made our way through the main bar and upstairs to the employee meeting room. Pam gave us a nervous smile when she entered.

"Next time, I'm hiding like you two did. Buzz said it took Shepard an hour of mopping to get the soda off the floor."

"Don't worry about it," I said. "Shepard's not mad. Buzz just likes teasing."

Thomas proved me right when he came in with a serving tray and a grin.

"Check it out. Buzz got my serving tray engraved."

He flipped it over to show us the words, "Would you like another round?"

"Get it?" he asked.

"Buzz isn't as funny as he thinks he is," Vena said.

Adrian was the last one to join us before Shepard entered.

"Thank you all for keeping level heads last night. Because

of you, all the customers got out without any injuries, and there was no major damage to Blur. I appreciate everyone agreeing to come in tonight for a fast re-opening."

"What about Sierra?" Thomas asked. "Did she no-show again?"

While Vena, the werewolves, and I knew Sierra had been mind-controlled by a vampire into kidnapping Miles, no one else did.

Shepard shook his head. "She's a little rattled and needs some time off. She should be back in a month, hopefully."

"Drama queen sympathy move," Thomas muttered under his breath.

Shepard ignored him and swung his gaze to Vena. "That means you're on your own tonight if you're up for it."

"Absolutely."

"Good. Then you're stage left lower. Everly can take stage left upper so she's close if you need anything. Adrian, lower right. Pam, upper right. Thomas, you're on VIP.

"I have some friends coming in from out of town later. They're going to help out for a bit just to make sure we don't have any repeats of last night. I'll introduce everyone after we close. Any questions?"

We all shook our heads.

"All right. Let's have a good night."

CHAPTER TWO

LET'S HAVE A GOOD NIGHT.

Sure, *Shepard* could say that. But he'd stationed Vena way too close to Anchor, which meant I was on double duty, watching to ensure Vena didn't need help and to ensure she kept her comments, suggestive eyes, or body parts to herself.

With the DJ playing wall-thumping beats, the dance floor swarmed with dancers.

I noticed familiar faces of our regular guests and some that seemed to be looking for evidence of the attack the prior night. Their gazes swept along the black walls that twinkled with lights, the rich purple booths and chairs, and up to the ceiling with the purple accent lighting.

After they couldn't find anything to gawk at, they turned their attention back to drinks and music.

"Everly." A dwarf who sat in my section waved me down.

When I stepped over to him and his friends, I asked, "The usual or something different?"

"An Effervescence as usual," he said. Before I could leave

with the order, he touched my arm. "Are you okay? We heard about the attack."

"Everything is fine."

"Everything looks fine, but how are you?"

I smiled at him, hoping to put him at ease. "No worse for wear. No injuries. We were lucky Shepard and his crew got everything under control as quickly as they did. Were you here during the attack?"

He shook his head. "We had left a little before then. When I heard the news, I felt terrible about it. If we were here, we would have lent a hand."

I was glad they hadn't been. I would have felt guilty if anything had happened.

Patting him on the shoulder, I said, "Don't worry about it. I'll grab your drinks. Should I order the lamb skewers for you, too?"

He grinned and rubbed his thick hands together. "You know us too well, Everly. Two orders, please."

"Perfect. I'll be right back with the drinks."

As I walked to the bar, I checked on my other tables. I then blocked Anchor's view of Vena as she bent down to pick up a cocktail napkin she "accidentally" dropped in front of him. He gave me a grateful smile.

After that, I went to the bar to wait for my order and took a moment to catch my breath.

"How's it going in your section?" Buzz asked as he worked on my drinks.

"Fine. People are checking the place out for evidence of the attack, but with nothing to see, it's back to business as usual."

"Good to hear. Shepard will be relieved."

While I knew Shepard worried about his employees, he

always seemed like a rock when it came to the business. I scanned the room for him.

"He's in the kitchen," Buzz said, interpreting my search correctly. "Griz got slammed with orders and needed help."

Back-of-the-house help reminded me of Gunther, the one responsible for washing the dishes at Blur, and I felt guilty. I hadn't been able to talk to him after he'd gotten whammied by Sierra's drug concoction this morning.

"How is he? Gunther, I mean?" I asked.

"He's fine."

"I didn't see him when I came in."

Buzz grinned. "He was running late. I like that you worry about us, Everly. But you don't need to." He leaned over the bar, his face close to mine, and said in a low voice, "Did you forget wolves heal fast?"

A hand jutted between our faces. I followed the hand over to find Shepard scowling at Buzz.

Buzz backed up with a smirk on his face to finish mixing the drinks I needed, and I watched Shepard place a second plate of lamb skewers on my drink tray.

"Your order is ready."

That was a little too fast, and I wondered if he made my order before anyone else's.

"Thanks."

He nodded, gave Buzz a warning glance, which made Buzz smirk again, and returned to the kitchen.

I picked up the tray and carried it to my section. The dwarves eyed the lamb skewers with a hunger that I typically reserved for bakery.

As I placed the last drink on the table, I asked, "Is there anything else I can get you?"

Before they could answer, a commotion at the door drew our attention. Thankfully, it wasn't a mob of crazy people. Just a group of men who gave fae men a run for their money in the looks department.

If their sun-kissed hair and skin didn't draw the eye, the excessive muscle display sure did.

During my time working at Blur, I'd grown used to muscles–ones hidden by button-up shirts and modestly fitted jeans. The muscles on the group at the door were barely concealed with t-shirts and snug denim that left nothing to the imagination.

My gaze drifted to the lead man's not-so-hidden bulge, and I felt a stab of panic.

Shepard had warned us that more help was coming, but I hadn't expected the help to look like the rest of the werewolves I knew.

Scanning Blur's crowd and noting over half the patrons were also staring at the men, I finally spotted Vena. She was standing next to her table, her mouth slightly open as she stared at the newcomers. Or, more specifically, at the leader's enormous bulge.

As I watched, a slow smile tugged at her lips.

"Excuse me," I said, grabbing a napkin from the dwarves' table and balling it up.

My makeshift "don't get us fired" projectile bounced off the side of Vena's head. She turned toward me, grinning like the horny idiot she was.

"Did I just get pregnant?" she mouthed, using both hands to check her stomach.

I rolled my eyes at her and gave her a get-to-work look.

Pretending like I hadn't just lobbed a napkin at my coworker, I smiled at my table, asked if they needed anything, and moved to another table closer to the door.

By the time I made my way to the stairs, Shepard was speaking with the newcomers and pointed to the stairs leading to the VIP section. Relieved they'd be out of Vena's eyesight, I watched Shepard lead them away.

"Why are samples only a thing for food?" Vena asked two inches from my ear, scaring the daylights out of me.

"Cut it out. Don't you have work to do?"

"Yes. But please tell me you'll be ready to discuss that dear-god vision we just had once we're on our way home."

Knowing Vena would not let this go, I turned her toward her section. "In vivid detail. I promise. Now go."

She grinned as I pushed her toward her tables.

Focusing on my own section, I smiled, delivered food and drinks, and forgot all about Shepard's special guests.

When the DJ switched to Blur's overhead music, which was easier on the ears and signaled the end of the night, I let out a relieved breath and started clearing the vacated tables. The lingering patrons paid their tabs and made their way to the exit. Once they were out, Army locked the door, and the music was turned down even more.

"This is a sweet place," a voice said in the relative hush.

I looked up from the table I was clearing and saw Shepard leading the group downstairs. Our gazes locked, and he gave me a slight smile. It felt reassuring.

"We've worked hard to build a reputation in the D.C. area," Shepard said. "The drinks and food play a part, but it's the atmosphere and the staff that make it."

"Understood," the chestnut-haired man said. It was the same man who'd made Vena's tongue roll out like a red carpet.

I understood why, though. His tight clothes left nothing to the imagination. He was big all over.

When they reached the bottom, Shepard called everyone over.

"Due to last night's disruption, I've invited a few friends from the west coast to give us a hand. I promise I won't cut anyone's hours. They're in addition to our regular staff to ensure we continue running smoothly," Shepard said, his gaze sweeping across the servers and landing on me.

"This is Everly," he said, motioning to me.

I nodded at the men.

"She's been serving at Blur the longest," Shepard continued. "If I'm not around and you have a question, ask her."

The comment stunned me even though I tried to hide it. Yes, I was the server with the most tenure. But Doc was Shepard's right hand and managed the bar staff, all of whom had worked longer at Blur. So why point the new people to me?

"To her left," Shepard continued, "is Vena, Thomas, Adrian, and Pam."

"Nice to meet you all," the chestnut-haired man with the prominent sausage display said. "My friends call me MC."

"Stands for Man Candy," Vena whispered.

I wanted to die as every non-human set of eyes swung to us. The heat flooding my face had to be giving me third-degree burns. Why did the floor never crack open when it needed to?

MC slowly smiled at Vena and looked at the man to his right. "This is Ink, LA, Hollywood, Thruster–" Vena made a choked noise "–Riff, Diego, Demo, Hero, and Jaws."

Their nicknames, while unusual, sort of fit each of them and would help me keep them all straight.

MC had a Mega Cruller. Hollywood wore sunglasses and stylish clothes. Jaws actually looked like he could bite someone's arm off. Riff looked like he was pulled from a rock band. Ink was covered in tattoos. LA was a photoshopped masterpiece. Thruster had a package to rival MC's, but I really hoped that wasn't why he was called "Thruster." Diego looked beautifully Hispanic. Demo sported a scar on his upper lip. It didn't detract from his looks at all. And Hero's nickname had to come from his resemblance to Captain America.

"Welcome to Blur," I managed with a weak smile for all of them.

"Thanks," MC said, his gaze shifting from me to Vena.

Had she just purred?

I grabbed her arm. "We better finish the cleanup so Gunther isn't stuck doing dishes until dawn."

Everyone else moved to their sections as I bodily dragged Vena back to her tables.

Instead of scolding her, which I knew everyone would hear, I picked up my phone and sent her a rapid text while standing a foot away.

Me: WTH is wrong with you? Anchor was standing right there! Did you even notice? You know he likes you and will be spending tonight on the couch. Don't break hearts, Vena. It's a rule.

Her eyes lost some of their lust-glaze as she read.

Vena: I'm sorry. You're right. I'll make it better. I promise.

Vena: But you can't fully blame me. If MC wedged that

impressive cum cannon into those tight pants, he wanted to be noticed.

Vena: How big do you think it is? 9 inches?

Vena: I'm betting a solid 9. And the girth! That could destroy a girl. Just think of the ride, though, right?

And the lust-glaze was back.

Me: Anchor.

Vena: You're right. I bet he'd look just as big in jeans that tight. I'll check tonight.

Shaking my head in defeat, I pocketed my phone and returned to my section.

As I cleaned, I kept an eye on the newcomers. Some mingled with Buzz as he closed down the bar. A couple of guys followed Shepard back to the office. But MC lingered, leaning against the stair rail, his focus aimed directly at Vena. After a moment of watching her, he pushed off from the rail and walked over. She was bent at the waist, ass up in the air as she fished something from under a booth table.

When she righted herself, she turned to find him only a step away. I thought I'd have to hurdle the half wall that separated my section from hers, but she appropriately retreated a step and gave him a polite smile.

"Did you need something?" she asked.

"Looks like you have a heavy tray," he said. "Can I carry it to the back for you?"

Expecting her to turn even a helpful request into a sexual innuendo, I braced myself.

"It's okay," she said. "I can carry my own tray."

Stunned, I stared at my best friend of over a decade. Had my two-second lecture actually sunk in? None of my lectures ever really sank in when it came to her libido, and yet, her eyes didn't stray to MC's muff mallet. Not even once.

Anchor appeared behind MC and swooped in to take the tray. He shot MC a warning look and said, "I got this."

MC raised a brow, but judging from his smirk when Anchor walked away, MC considered the warning more of a challenge.

Vena returned her attention to cleaning, and MC drifted to the bar with the others. As long as Vena didn't start flirting with MC, I knew that we wouldn't have any issues.

After we closed our sections and clocked out, Buzz walked us to our car.

"How was everything tonight?" he asked.

"Good," I said. "We made some decent tips for a short shift."

"Buzz, how long are the new guys staying?" Vena asked randomly.

"As long as it takes."

She opened her mouth to ask another question but stopped when she saw a black cat near our car.

"I swear, you're still a cat magnet," she said with a side glance at me.

"Let it go, Vena. That was years ago."

"It feels like just yesterday that I was grounded for a week for a crime I didn't commit."

"Do I want to know?" Buzz asked.

"I wanted a cat really bad and thought I could sneak one home and keep it in my room without my parents knowing."

"And you blamed it on Vena?" he asked.

I flashed him a mischievous smile. "Vena was always

getting into trouble. It was more believable. Besides, I didn't think my parents would call her parents."

Vena snorted. "They did, and you still have a thing for cats."

I shrugged and looked at the black cat.

"Don't even think about it," Buzz said. "That thing still reeks like a vampire." He attempted to shoo it away with his foot. Instead, the cat stepped around him and wrapped itself around my leg, purring like a racecar engine.

It looked so much like the cat we'd seen at Juicy, which would explain why it smelled like vampire to Buzz. But, even if it did belong to a vampire, that didn't make it a bad cat. And if it did belong to someone at Juicy, that meant it was homeless now.

I reached down and petted the poor thing.

"Do you think it's hungry?" I asked.

"Do not feed it," Buzz said.

"It's not the cat's fault it smells like vampire," I said. Another thought hit me as I recalled Cross' initial dining habits. "Do you think a vampire was feeding on it?"

"Don't," Buzz warned.

"Don't what?" I asked.

"Get attached."

"I'm not. What I am is empathetic. It's homeless and hungry, Buzz."

I glanced at Vena, who was suspiciously quiet, for backup. But she was edging toward her car door.

"It's also an animal that can hunt to feed itself," Buzz said. "It's fine."

When he saw his argument hadn't convinced me, he gently pulled me to my feet and steered me to my car door.

"Go home. Anchor will follow in a minute. Wait in your car until he gets there. Got it?"

I nodded and got in with a slight pout. Buzz watched as I started the engine and made sure I wouldn't run over the cat as I drove out of the lot.

"I should have known he wouldn't be a cat guy," I said, half under my breath.

"I can't hold it in anymore!"

Her abrupt yell made me jump.

"What?"

"Now that we're in the car with no ears, can I please talk about them?"

"Them?" I asked, confused.

"Those delicious California-wrapped morsels of juiciness. I mean, our Blur guys are hot, but damn. Did you see the size of those baby-batter bazookas? And the way they held themselves... There's something about a guy who knows he's hot that makes him hotter."

"And probably more egotistical, too."

"I'm not around for his ego. I'm around for the ride on his mommy-maker. And those are some seriously large springs to bounce on."

I rolled my eyes. "If you're so excited to go bouncing, what was up with that cool rejection of MC's offer to carry your tray?"

"Even though you think I don't listen to you, I do. You were right. Anchor was right there watching everything. Unless I want to break his cute little puppy heart, I need to respect his feelings for me."

"And?" I said, knowing there was more.

"And," she huffed, "MC was coming on too strong. Not my thing."

I grinned. "Of course it isn't. You're a hunter. You need to chase down what you want, or it wouldn't be nearly as valuable to you."

"You know it. I think Anchor knows it, too. His playing hard to get is driving me insane. I really need to buy him some tighter jeans so I can compare sizes. You know...wolf research. Are east coast species as well equipped as the west coast species? It's a valid research question."

"I dare you to send that research question to Miles," I said with a snigger.

Vena laughed with me. "It would be a good distraction."

"Probably an unwanted one. But speaking of distractions, you might need to create a few."

"You've come to the right girl. Who, what, where, why, and when?"

"Cross isn't going away until he can be financially independent of me–"

"Stop your cussing," Vena scolded.

"And," I said, speaking over her, "Anchor isn't going away until the vampires are gone. That means you're going to need to run interference any time Cross' scent might be in the house."

The wicked grin on her face was unsettling.

"You know you've just invited me to sit bare-assed on our sofa."

I sighed. "I'll be sure to ask Cross not to sit on or touch anything in the house."

"He was in your bed," Vena reminded me.

"You will *not* go anywhere near my bed while naked."

She said nothing. She didn't need to. Her grin said enough.

When we reached the house, we waited as instructed for Anchor, who was only a few minutes behind us. He waved and went to unlock the door and check the house. He didn't signal it was all clear but jogged over to our car.

Vena rolled down her window.

"Hey, handsome," she said with a grin. "Everly just told me clothing could be optional in the common areas. You ready for a good time?"

That big, agile hunk of a man stumbled over his own feet and caught himself on the car door.

"What?" he rasped.

I watched his eyes dilate as he stared at her.

"Anchor," I said, leaning forward in my seat to draw his attention. "Don't let her mess with your head. Is the house clear?"

He looked down and shook his head slightly. I wasn't sure if he was trying to clear his thoughts or telling us the house wasn't safe.

"Uh." He cleared his throat. "Your room faintly smelled like vampire. It's, uh, probably left over from this morning. I mean, uh...if you napped?"

"Today's been a crazy long day," I said, neither confirming nor denying.

"What about my room?" Vena asked. "Did you smell anything interesting in there?"

His gaze pinned hers, dilating again.

"Yeah."

She grinned slowly. "Under my pillow?"

He swallowed hard and nodded.

I started rolling up her window on them. Anchor quickly backed up a step, and Vena turned to grin at me.

"You're worse than a cat in heat. Don't make me get out the spray bottle," I said.

"Hey, I can't help it if all men want a taste of V."

The old, overused joke from high school had me narrowing my eyes.

"Vena, you just broke our high school pact. You know what this means."

"Come on," she whined. "You set me up. I couldn't *not* use it."

"You could have taken the higher ground and chose not to. You've lost all V privileges for one whole month."

She scrambled out of the car after me.

"I take it back. I'm sorry. I slipped, and it fell out."

I ignored her pawing at my arm and walked past a confused Anchor.

"I'm showering first," I said over my shoulder.

They quietly followed me inside and didn't say anything as I grabbed some clean pajamas from my room and claimed the bathroom for the next fifteen minutes.

When I returned to my bedroom, my bed was stripped of its sheets. Vena's door, opposite mine on the other end of the hallway, was open, and her lights were off. I could hear the washer running on the other side of the kitchen but nothing else.

Curious, I drifted out to the dining room. From there, I could see Vena standing in front of Anchor in the living room. Fine tremors ran through his body as she slowly dragged a single finger up his arm.

"I'm glad you kept them," I heard her say. "A lot of thought of you went into them."

He groaned and closed his eyes.

"Vena," I said.

She jerked her hand back and hurried toward me.

"Just making sure he had everything he needs for a comfortable night on the couch."

She disappeared into the bathroom, and I heard the water turn on.

"What did she do?" I asked Anchor.

He swallowed hard and shook his head, and I sighed.

"She gave you her underwear, didn't she?"

He sat heavily on the couch and hung his head into his hands, confirming my suspicion.

Whether hunting or dating, my best friend loved walking on the wild side.

CHAPTER THREE

I BLINKED MY EYES OPEN TO SUNLIGHT THAT DANCED ALONG PALE skin and auburn locks of hair.

Shit.

My gaze met Cross' amused one.

"What are you doing here?" I asked softly. "There is a wolf on the other side of the door."

"Your watchdog left at the first ray of light," Cross said as his fingers brushed my cheek, a thumb grazing the bottom of my lip.

The touch was distracting and displayed a degree of affection I hadn't known we'd reached.

"Quite eagerly, too," Cross added as if he wasn't turning my world upside down with his current level of attention. "Nearly sprinted from the house."

I cleared my throat and tried to focus. "Good. It'd be better if you didn't cross paths." Then, I groaned when I realized I'd have to de-vampire the house again.

"We need to find you a place to live," I said.

"I was just going to suggest that," he said. "There'd be no interference from the mutts that keep lingering here, then."

"They aren't interfering with anything. They're trying to keep us safe."

I carefully dislodged Cross' touch and set his hand on my blanket with a pat.

He smirked.

Before I could leave the bed, he caught my wrist and leaned forward to kiss my forehead. The same spot he'd kissed the day before when I met him by my car. The same spot Shepard had kissed.

"Better," he said.

Rather than asking what he meant and possibly hearing something I wasn't ready to hear, I got out of bed and grabbed shorts and one of my favorite print shirts.

"Cupcakes are muffins that believe in miracles," Cross read the shirt over my shoulder.

His lips were precariously close to my neck, making me want to shiver. But not in a bad way. I trusted Cross and considered him a friend. A really good-looking friend who I'd seen shirtless in the shower.

As soon as I had the thought, my mind shied away from it, and I focused instead on how I hadn't really been keeping up on my end of the deal to help him in today's world. He had the money and the clothes, but he really needed a place to stay.

If he continued showing up here, I'd never get rid of Anchor, and I'd have to deal with Vena and her V.

"Start thinking about where you'd like to live," I said. "We'll start looking at options today. I don't have to be at work until later this afternoon."

I hurried to the bathroom and locked the door. Not that

locking things seemed to matter when it came to Cross. The man could get into any place he wanted to, and with the way my thoughts had wanted to veer, I was afraid the next place might be my pants.

Think about cupcakes, I said as I scoured my teeth and ran a brush through my blonde hair.

It didn't work.

The cut on my cheek, which I'd earned by falling into Cross' cave almost a week ago, was almost healed. The one on my hand that I'd gotten while at Juicy's three days ago looked just as old, thanks to Cross' help. And the one on my arm from the morning before looked the same.

I could remember the feel of his lips on my skin. The light suction as he drank from me.

Three times now. What did that mean? Was that why I liked him?

"What's taking so long?" Vena asked as she knocked on the door. "And why was I greeted by a vampire on our couch instead of my plaything?"

Dressed, I opened the door.

"First, Anchor isn't a toy. And second, he fled at dawn because of your jacked-up hormones."

"You're a bit cranky this morning. Is the Crimson Tide coming in?"

"No. This has nothing to do with that and everything to do with you teasing Anchor until he had to run away."

Vena slipped her arms around me, hugging me like she would a teddy bear. "But if he hadn't run, he would have met Cross, right? See how good I am? I'll make breakfast. How's that?"

"Bad. I don't want burnt food."

33

"I only burn things because I start thinking about something else. I promise I'll stay focused."

"How about if I make breakfast, and you help Cross find a few homes we can look at today?"

"Today?"

I nodded. "Yes. He needs a place, and you need a distraction."

The front door opened.

We hurried to the dining room and found Cross bending down to pick up something off the ground outside. When he turned, he was holding a black cat by the scruff of its neck. His expression as he stared at it was pure revulsion.

"Don't eat it," I said, hurrying to grab the cat.

"I prefer my food clean and not–" he leaned in a little and sniffed at it "–digging around garbage cans."

I took the cat from him. It started purring the instant it was in my arms.

"I think this is the same cat from Blur," I said. It was hard to tell since black cats tended to look alike, but my gut feeling told me it was the same cat. "You're hungry, aren't you?"

Cross moved to take it back, but I turned toward the kitchen.

"Everly, there is something concerning about that cat," he said as he followed me.

"The fact that he's homeless and hungry?"

"No. His scent."

"Yeah, Buzz already mentioned it smells like a vampire."

"The same vampire scent I found at Juicy. Everly, you do not want his vampire to track him to your house."

"If he was going to track him, he would have done so by now."

Cross moved faster than I could see, stealing the cat from my arms and moving to the back door to toss it outside. The cat yowled as it landed safely, and I scowled at Cross.

"Did you not learn your lesson, Everly?" he asked, frowning back at me. "Vampires will track their possessions. Simply because the creature roams does not mean it is not a kept pet."

"I'm siding with Cross on this one," Vena said before I could retort. "We've had too many run-ins with vampires to take in a vampire's stray. That's just asking for it."

"You don't know it belongs to a vampire. One might have just stopped to pet it."

Vena gave me a disbelieving look before glancing at Cross. "Would a vampire have any issue with feeding on a cat?"

"It's not a preferred source of nourishment. However, you are right that vampires are not overly affectionate and are unlikely to stop to pet a stray cat."

"Fine," I said. "I'll let the poor thing starve on our doorstep."

I went to the kitchen and started fixing our breakfast while Vena leaned against the counter and asked Cross questions about what kind of place he was looking for.

"House or apartment?"

"I have no preference," he said. "I will not spend much time there."

"So, a creepy basement?"

He gave her a dry look.

"Well, I don't know your style."

He looked around our home. "Spacious. Clean. Preferably not close to railroad tracks, but I will overlook the noise as long as it's close to here."

"Here?" she asked. "Why?"

"I still need access to Everly...and my money."

She gave him a considering look.

"Okay. Close to here." She scrolled through her phone as I flipped the cinnamon swirl pancakes I'd made. "There's actually something two blocks over," she said. Two bedrooms, one bath. It's a year lease, which is typical for the area." She stated the rental price, which wasn't horrible considering how much sat in my bank account. "I'll make an appointment to see it."

She drifted out to the living room, and Cross took her place close to me.

"You have a soft heart for animals, don't you?" he asked, watching me.

"Yeah, I do. I always wanted a pet growing up."

"Is that why you favor the wolves?"

I almost laughed.

"No. And I wouldn't say I favor them. They're nice, and they've helped out when there was trouble. Like family," I said, echoing Shepard's words.

Cross made a humming sound.

"Good news," Vena said, coming back to the kitchen. "The landlady is nearby, and we can check it out in an hour."

We quickly ate our breakfast, discreetly dropped off Miles' car, and went to see the place. Like our house, it wasn't much. The landlady, an older woman who looked like she was in her seventies, eyed the three of us.

"You all living together?" she asked. "You're not swingers, are you?"

Vena nearly died on her choked laugh.

"No," I said. "We're friends."

"Hm. So, who's living here?" she asked.

I opened my mouth to say it would be Cross and realized the rental couldn't go under his name. She'd likely want his information to do a background and credit check.

"I'll be the primary resident."

She looked me over then glanced at Cross.

"That mean he's going to be staying over a lot?"

"When was the roof last replaced?" Vena asked, looking up at the shingles. "It looks pretty old."

Properly distracted, they started talking about the house, and Vena very politely drove the conversation to indicate that it wouldn't work for us. When all three of us were in the car again, Vena shook her head.

"We're going to have a hard time with rentals, I think," she said. "If the landlords see you staying there night after night, they're going to want you on the lease."

"Which means Cross would need an ID of some sort," I said, already understanding her line of thought.

"The best solution is to have your sugar mama buy you a house," Vena said with a grin at Cross.

She went back to her phone and searched for nearby homes for sale. We drove past almost a half a dozen, but none of them looked worth the money.

"He has the funds to fix them up, though," Vena pointed out.

I glanced at Cross. "It's your call, but if it were my money, I wouldn't do it. You'd be sticking in more money than it's worth in these neighborhoods. It'd be different if we were looking closer to downtown."

"How far away is downtown?" he asked.

"With how fast you can move, does it really matter?" Vena

asked. She talked him into checking out places closer to downtown until we worked our way close enough to a restaurant she liked.

"I'm hungry. You should buy us lunch for all the help we've given," she said. "You know how Everly likes her sweets."

I almost snorted at her attempt to wheedle him until he agreed.

"You don't need to buy us lunch. We can just go home and–"

"Is that how friends treat each other? Rejection and abandonment?" Vena asked with a shake of her head at me. "Cross needs us to show him around. When was the last time you went to a restaurant, Cross? You probably want to see how it's done, right?"

He looked at me. "Vena is correct. There is much I still do not know."

I glanced between the two of them and gave in. "Where do you want to go for lunch?"

Vena wrapped her arm around me. "I know the perfect place."

The perfect place ended up being a five-star restaurant that she knew we couldn't afford.

"You're taking advantage of the situation," I whispered to her as she pulled me to the front door.

"When will we ever get the chance to come here? And remember the dessert selection you were drooling over on their website only a few months ago? *Chocolat au crumble de fraises, la madeleine au truffle*, black diamond lush, *luxe--*"

"Stop. You had me at *chocolat*. But Cross has to agree to the prices first. It's not fair to take advantage of him like this."

When I turned, I found him standing nearly on top of us.

"You heard that?" I asked.

He nodded. "You are not taking advantage of me, Everly. If the food here calls to you, I am willing to accommodate your desires."

Vena yanked me inside and over to a man who sneered at my t-shirt. But then his gaze lit when he saw Cross, who, after his recent makeover, looked like a cologne ad with his fitted suit, shirt collar unbuttoned, and styled auburn hair cut short on the sides.

He really did look amazing.

Vena snapped her fingers in front of my face. "Come on. The snooty guy is seating us."

Cross placed his hand on my lower back, guiding me to the table near the window that overlooked the bustling downtown street. From the view, I saw boutique shops and more restaurants. All high-end. Vena and I were so out of place.

Picking up the menu, sans prices, I looked for something that might not cost as much. Maybe a side salad and a glass of water.

Vena had other plans. She ordered the Gruyère and Crab Palmers, Beef Spiedini, and Kobe Steak with Matsutake Mushrooms.

When the server left with our order, I kicked her under the table.

"What?" she asked.

"Kobe steak? Matsutake mushrooms? Do you realize how much those cost?"

"No. But I ordered water instead of a drink."

Cross reached across the table and placed his hand on mine. "It's okay, Everly. Allow me to repay you for all the help you've given me."

"See?" Vena said. "He's thanking us. Be grateful."

"I said I was repaying Everly," Cross said. "Which is why you'll share your meal with her since she only ordered a side salad."

"Because you've already repaid me. If not for you, Vena and I would still be trapped at that club or wouldn't have found Miles. Actually, I think Vena and I are still in your debt."

Vena picked up her phone.

"Let's get back to finding you a place to live," she said, eyeing Cross. "That way, I can earn my lunch. I'm sure there are a lot of condos in the area."

"Condos?" he questioned.

"Like an apartment, but you own it," I said.

While Vena scrolled through her phone, tsking and muttering under her breath about steak, I wondered what kind of place would suit Cross. He seemed like a private kind of guy who wouldn't appreciate a condo or apartment next to a bunch of people. And a house seemed too domestic for him.

"Cross, is there anything you want to do with your time? Hobbies? A business? It might help us narrow down the search."

"There are a few things I'd like to do with my time," he said with the barest of smirks aimed directly at me. Heat sizzled down to my toes. "But, no. There is nothing in this new world that holds my attention except for a fleeting curiosity."

"What did you use to do before?"

He smirked again, and I had a feeling it was nothing that I wanted to know about.

"I did own one thing that nearly made my unlimited time bearable," he said.

"What was it?"

"A gentleman's club."

Vena glanced up. "Is that code for strip club? You know... with naked female entertainers?"

Cross shook his head. "No, it was for drinks, smoking, and gambling. A club member could acquire a room to sleep, if he should want, and an occasional courtesan might accompany the gentleman to the room for a shared evening."

"Prostitution isn't legal in D.C.," Vena said.

"I have no interest in prostitutes or courtesans," he said. "I'm merely answering Everly's question. I used to distract myself from the endless passage of time with the discreet management of a gentleman's club."

"How long ago was that?" I asked.

His gaze held mine as he answered. "Sixteen ninety-three."

Vena swore under her breath and, forgetting her phone, leaned in to ask, "How old are you?"

"Thirty-two."

She snorted and returned to her phone search.

"There are a number of condos in the downtown area, but I'm not sure you'll like having neighbors paying attention to when you're coming and going. And whatever company you keep. What's your budget?"

He glanced at me, and I shook my head slightly. "I have no idea what you want to spend."

"I'll pay whatever is necessary to secure a permanent residence near here but with fewer neighbors interested in my business."

Vena tapped her fingers on the table. "We'll come up with something. I'll broaden my search under the assumption that you don't mind parting with another coin."

He nodded, and the waiter arrived with the first course.

Vena stared at Cross as he lifted his spoon to try the soup he'd ordered.

"I didn't think you'd actually eat it," she said.

"Like sleep, it's unnecessary. However, sitting and watching my dining companion eat would have made her uncomfortable. Are you enjoying the salad, Everly? Would you prefer my soup?"

I wasn't sure if he was asking to get rid of the soup or because he felt bad I'd only ordered the salad. Either way, if he was willing to part with it, I was willing to eat it. I quickly nodded and almost moaned at the decadence of the French onion soup.

While we ate, he asked questions about dining out, favorite spots, what made them our favorites, and when most people dined. It was a relaxing conversation that didn't seem overly vampire-y, just curious.

Cross offered me his plate when the main course arrived. Like Vena, he'd ordered a steak. I accepted half, which had Vena smirking.

"Don't let her fool you, Cross. She's not just saving you money. She's saving room for dessert. You've seen how she is. She craves sugar as much as you crave–"

I kicked her under the table, and Cross smiled slightly.

When the waiter returned, Cross ordered every dessert they currently offered.

I was in heaven until it was time to stand and walk. My stomach hurt, and I knew I'd suffer from my gluttony at work later. But I had so many ideas to add to my pastry notebook, thanks to his generosity.

Before we made it to the door, Cross stopped me.

"You have another watchdog. I will leave you here and speak with you again in the morning."

"Feel free to use that fancy new phone she got you," Vena said. "It'd make our lives easier, and I wouldn't need to keep traumatizing Anchor."

Cross shot her a look then disappeared.

"Like you'd stop traumatizing Anchor," I said. "You had your underwear under your pillow before we even got home last night."

She grinned unrepentantly as we left together.

"Will you look at that," Vena said softly, glancing around the street. "Mr. California is here."

I followed her gaze and saw MC leaning against a building across the street. He still wore the jeans that prominently displayed his beaver basher.

He nodded to us, and I offered a smile back.

"I'm pretty sure that's not what MC stands for," I said quietly, hoping the sound of traffic would drown out our conversation.

"Half the fun is trying to guess," Vena said. "Muff-munching Champion? Maximum Capacity? That could apply to anything that tries to accommodate what he's packing."

"If you spend too much time guessing, he might think you're interested," I warned her.

"It's hard not to be interested in his super-sized muscled self. Just think of the workout."

I elbowed her as I wrapped my arm around hers and continued to the car.

"Remember the trouble we just got out of, and try not to throw us back into more."

"Fine. You're right. It's still early yet," she said. "Let's stop and check on Miles. Maybe he'll have some alternative housing ideas."

Her phone buzzed with a message on the way to the car, and she made a happy sound when she read it.

"My parents are extending their trip by a few days. No specifics, but more time is good."

"Why?"

"Seriously? We're sandwiched between wolves and vampires, Miles was already kidnapped by one, and we have the other staying on our couch at night. Do you really think my parents won't notice something's up when they're back?"

I made a face, knowing she was right. The extra days would give us time to make sure Miles was okay or get him help. It wouldn't help with our other problem, though.

I loved her parents. They were great and super supportive of their kids. However, they also frequented the Shadow Trade as much as Miles and loved to pop in for unannounced visits. The likelihood of them running into Cross or a wolf guard was pretty high. Especially if Cross and the wolves were following us. Something I'd thought we would avoid because of the tracking app. Shepard had used it yesterday. Why send someone today?

"Do you think it's weird that MC was outside of the restaurant?" I asked once we were in the car.

She shrugged. "Not really. They came here to help Shepard and his pack, right? But, now that you mention it, Shepard is overly protective of you. I would have thought he'd send Anchor or Doc. Maybe Buzz."

As I pulled into traffic, I glanced back in the mirror and saw MC still leaning against the wall. He hadn't moved, but he was still watching us as he grew smaller with distance.

"I got it!" Vena said.

"Got what?"

"Remember how Cross said he owned a club."

I nodded, not wanting to think about the courtesans. "What about it?"

"He said he liked it because it distracted him from his long, boring life."

"And?"

"He can be a club owner again. Juicy's available, right?"

"No. That's a horrible idea." I shivered, remembering getting trapped there and the bloody aftermath. "Shepard said they'd destroyed the place to ensure the vampires wouldn't come back. Plus, can you imagine the clean up? No way."

"Cross won't care about blood and bodies. He's the one that made the mess, anyway."

She was right. But he'd only made the mess because he'd had to come and save us.

"I bet we could get that building cheap," she said. "No one would want to go in there after that bloodbath, and when Cross buys the place, I can get a finder's fee."

I rolled my eyes at her. "You forget one thing."

"What?"

"Shepard said Juicy is under his watch now. He'd never let Cross stay there."

Vena frowned. "But it's a perfect place. He can have his club on the first floor, and he can live on the top floor. He'll be so busy with renovations and starting the club up that we won't have to see fangs ever again. It's a win-win."

It was my turn to frown. "Unless he has papers to make himself a legal citizen, he'll still need me. The building would be under my name. I'd be the one responsible for permits and business registration and–"

"I'll talk to Shepard about Juicy tonight," she said.

"Are you even listening, Vena? No. No Juicy. No talking to Shepard. I don't want him to know about Cross. Shepard's on a mission to get rid of all the vampires. It won't matter to him that Cross isn't like the others. I'm not throwing Cross to the wolves like that."

"Just by being near you, he's already involved with the wolves because you are."

I didn't want to think about it now. "Let's go see Miles. Maybe he can help us think of a place for Cross. It will give him something to do. He's got to be bored by now."

As we drove to Miles' apartment, Vena spoke more about the building Juicy had been in and its potential.

"Maybe you should rethink treasure hunting as your career and go into real estate," I said.

"I just see the value in it."

I parked outside of Miles' apartment building and glanced at the vehicles, not spotting anyone I knew.

A message buzzed on my phone from Shepard.

Shepard: I see you're at Miles' place. Problem?

Me: Nope. Just stopping to check in on him. Where's his guard? Truck's empty.

Shepard: Inside watching for signs of unusual behavior. Call me right away if you think there is any.

CHAPTER FOUR

"Is Shepard being a stalker again?" Vena asked.

"He's not stalking; he's worried. There's a difference," I said.

She made a doubtful sound. "You should have never given him access to track you. It's never too late to revoke it."

I shook my head at her and got out of the car.

"Behave. Miles has company inside."

Vena gave me a look but didn't say anything else as we walked up the sidewalk. Near Miles' door, I braced myself, ready for when the freaky fairy jumped out of the bushes at me. However, it didn't.

Had it moved on?

Vena knocked before letting herself in.

Miles glanced up from the kitchen table where the blue fairy sat in a pile of silverware, looking like it was in heaven.

"Um, are you okay?" Vena asked him. "Why is there a fairy on your spoons?"

"I'm making friends," he said. "They're a source of information I'd never get from books. It's a whole new way to research that I'd overlooked."

"You're not supposed to research, remember?" Vena gently scolded.

He waved away Vena's concern. "The only thing I'm researching is how to communicate with my fine fairy friend here."

The fairy beamed at him, and I fought not to make a face.

"Everly mentioned that the fairy was the reason you found me," he said.

Vena, Miles, and the fairy looked at me expectantly.

"It was. Which is why I gave it a dime as a token of my appreciation. Thank you," I said with a nod toward the little blue beast.

It didn't beam at me like it did Miles, though.

"But how did you communicate with it?" he asked.

"A lot of pantomiming and frustration on its part when I didn't understand right away."

Vena made a sympathetic sound. "She sucks at Pictionary, too."

The fairy pantomimed belly laughing. I wasn't amused and looked around Miles' apartment, not noting any hulking werewolf bodyguard. However, the bathroom and bedroom doors were closed.

"Why are you trying to communicate?" I asked, looking at Miles again.

"Like I said, it's another potential way to research. In the future, of course."

The toilet flushed in the bathroom.

"Company?" she asked Miles.

"Yeah, of the furry variety, which I don't mind at all. Not a fan of the fanged variety." He gave me a look that I couldn't quite decipher. Surely, he wasn't against my connection with

Cross, too. Without Cross, Miles would still be tied to a chair in Sierra's house.

The door opened, robbing me of any ability to use my questionable pantomiming skills to ask what his deal was.

"Hey, Buzz," I said. "Are you on day duty?"

"For now. We're rotating so we don't get too lax in security," he said, sitting on Miles' sofa. "What brings the two of you here?"

"Checking to see how crazy Miles is after his time as a feeder," Vena said bluntly. "And as unlikely as this sounds, trying to talk to a fairy to gain information isn't crazy. He would have done this before the kidnapping if he'd known."

I nodded. "The fairy was helpful."

"How did you know it could be?" Buzz asked.

I flashed him a smile. "I pay attention. You know that."

He nodded. "I do. But I know for a fact that you don't like fairies."

The tiny blue monstrosity left its shiny silverware kingdom and darted at me.

Vena saved me with a palm to my face.

"Hey, no going for the eyes," she said. "That's why she doesn't like fairies. How would you like it if every human you saw came after you with a flyswatter? Would you like humans?"

A beat of silence followed.

"Well, that's just rude," she said.

Since I couldn't see, I could only imagine what the fairy had done to warrant that remark.

"Come now, my friend," Miles said. "In my line of work, I need to welcome all my guests equally. Let's consider this neutral territory in the future. Why don't you lounge in my silverware a little longer while I walk them out?"

Vena slowly uncovered my face.

"Your hand smells like chocolate," I said when I looked at her smirking face.

"For you, baby, I can smell like anything."

Buzz chuckled.

"I can see why Anchor's been having a hard time with you."

Vena's focus lasered in on Buzz. "When you say hard, do you mean difficult or *hard?*"

Buzz laughed again, goading Vena.

"Did Anchor tell you about the gift I left him?"

It was my turn to cover her face. Her overactive mouth, specifically.

"And I think we're done here," I said. "Thanks for keeping an eye on Miles, Buzz."

"Fang-goo!" Vena said from behind my hand. Her eyes went wide, and she started to snort.

"If you snot on me, you're cleaning the bathroom for a month," I warned. "Bye, Miles. We'll come back soon with some books Vena got for you."

He waved to us as he spoke softly to the fairy perched in his silverware drawer.

Once outside, I released Vena's yap-trap.

"Do you really want to announce to the world that you crossed a line with Anchor?" I whispered.

"Pfft. Line-schmine. He liked it."

"He bolted at first light."

"Because he knew he was close to cracking." She made a humming sound. "That man has no idea how good I am at hunting. I'll have his pleasure treasure in my hands before he knows it."

I shook my head. "Get in. We need to get ready for work. And no teasing him tonight, or we'll end up with someone else on our couch."

She rolled her eyes but didn't argue.

VENA and I saw Ink standing near the employee entrance when we parked in Blur's back lot. I knew it was him from the tattoos covering his arm and neck and disappearing under his white t-shirt.

His gaze tracked us as we got out of the car and walked toward him.

"On security duty?" Vena asked Ink.

He gave a nod. "Looks like you're down a couple guys, so I'm helping out back here."

"Down a couple guys?" I questioned. "Are they sick? Or did Shepard send them somewhere else?"

"I'm not sure," he said. "Shepard and MC are talking about it in the office."

Vena leaned in with a smile. "Can you hear what they're saying?"

"Not from out here."

Vena tugged me past Ink and inside. "Hurry up so we can ask Anchor."

"We're here to work, Vena. Let Shepard and MC sort everything out. If they need us, they'll let us know."

"But you always drag us here early. We have plenty of time."

I glanced at the dish station and didn't see Gunther as we headed to the lockers.

The night before, he had been slammed with work and didn't leave with the rest of us. I really hoped he wasn't coming in late again. In the past, he had gotten into trouble for drinking. Shepard would be livid if Gunther did that after what happened with Sierra.

Pulling Vena with me to the main floor, I reminded her, "Ten minutes is not that early to get ready for a shift before opening."

"As long as we're clocked in by the time Shepard gives us our stations, what does it matter?"

"Think of work as treasure hunting," I said. "You can't just run off into the woods. You have to prepare first."

Vena's nose wrinkled. "You sound like Miles. Fine. Let's get ready for work. But I'm asking Anchor later."

We stored our things in the lockers and put on our aprons. As we left the kitchen and made our way to the VIP stairs, Vena's gaze swept through the bar area.

"Where is Anchor?" she asked. "I see almost everyone else."

"He might have been pulled for a different assignment," I said.

Shepard entered the meeting room after the rest arrived.

"Good evening, everyone," he said and glanced at his list. "Everly VIP section, Vena upper stage left, Adrian lower stage left, Thomas upper stage right, Pam lower stage right."

I debated whether I should ask to trade with Adrian. If I was in the VIP section, it'd be harder to keep an eye on Vena. Not that she needed help with her section. She was a pro at it. But she needed to be corralled occasionally, especially when it came to Anchor. Yet I supposed if Anchor was somewhere else, she couldn't get into much mischief.

"If anyone needs help tonight, find Buzz," Shepard said. "If there is an emergency, call me."

"Are you going to be offsite?" Pam asked.

"I'll be in and out," he said. "Just do your best. I'm using some of the new guys as security and bouncers. Doc will oversee them. I'll help wherever needed."

As everyone left, I stayed behind. Not only was my VIP section close, but I wanted to talk to Shepard.

He glanced at me. "Is anything wrong, Everly?"

"I was about to ask you the same thing."

"Nothing to worry about."

"So, Gunther is okay? He's not in trouble, is he?"

Shepard stepped closer. "What makes you ask that?"

"I just wanted to make sure he's okay. He's not at his station."

Shepard inhaled a breath and stared at me funny. Did he smell Cross? I took a shower before my shift to make sure there were no lingering scents.

Shepard's face cleared, but his eyes strayed to my forehead. Before I registered him moving closer, his lips pressed against my forehead.

"Uh, Shepard?"

He exhaled against my skin then backed away.

"Everything is fine, Everly," he said. "Gunther and Anchor didn't come into work today, but they've been working hard. They're probably asleep somewhere and forgot to set the alarm."

His words said one thing, but the tension in his expression said something else. Even without the worry reflecting in his gaze, I would have been concerned. Anchor was never late. He never missed a shift. Neither had Gunther, not even after Sierra had drugged him. Sure, he'd reeked like alcohol a few times, but he never ghosted his shifts.

I opened my mouth to ask but closed it again realizing Shepard would have said more if he'd wanted to. So, I nodded and left the office.

As soon as I had my station ready for the shift to start, I went to the top of the stairs to check on Vena below.

With my bird's-eye view, I saw the way she paused to look at MC as he took his place at the bottom of the stairs. He caught her looking at him and nodded at her, sending a flirty smile her way.

Instead of smiling back, she lifted her gaze to me. I could see the whirlwind of questions in her gaze, I shook my head slightly, warning her not to do or say whatever she was thinking about doing or saying.

I loved Vena like crazy. She was my ride-or-die girl till the end. And she was wicked smart. But I also knew she had a tendency to jump first and think later. Considering recent events, I needed her to be more of a thinker and less of a jumper.

She sighed visibly and turned back to straightening her tables.

MC looked up with a slight frown until he saw me. I received the same nod and flirty smile that Vena had. I returned both, but without the flirt. After, I checked with Detroit, who was manning the VIP bar. He was dark and handsome as always, but even he had a crease on his brow. That didn't stop him from giving me a friendly wink when he realized I was studying him.

Once the doors opened, I barely had time to glance over the railing at Vena. The three times I did manage to check, she was laughing with customers and taking orders. Seeing her handling her own section without any problems and seeming to enjoy it, relieved me. After all, that was the whole point of talking her into working at Blur. To give her another option to earn money other than treasure hunting.

By the time the last call was announced, my feet were tired, and I was ready for the shift to end. Detroit helped me clear my tables as soon as they emptied and carried the full bin of dishes downstairs.

I peeked over the railing again and saw MC offering to take Vena's tray. She shook her head, giving him a polite smile as she walked around him. MC watched after her, and I could almost hear his thoughts.

But she'd called me Man Candy. What gives with the cold shoulder now?

I almost felt sorry for him. He wasn't the first guy to fall for Vena's fun-loving and flirty ways, and I doubted he'd be the last.

Hurrying back to my tables, I finished straightening my chairs and went downstairs. MC had moved off to help Pam clear her tables, and Thomas was clearing his and Adrian's while Adrian washed and straightened the cleared ones. Vena was finishing wiping down her last table.

"Not a bad night," Shepard said as I sat at the bar to wait for her.

"Sales-wise or...?"

He smiled slightly. "All around. Vena kept up with her tables. The floor was packed. The sales barely reflected what happened a few days ago. And we didn't need Doc to remove any patrons."

"So, not a bad night," I repeated with a smile.

He grinned and nodded as he wiped down the soda gun nozzles.

I unloaded my tip money and started counting it. Vena sat beside me.

"Damn, girl, look at you being rich. Oh, wait..." She placed a neat stack of bills on the bar. "One. Ah-ah-ah! Two. Ah-ah-ah!"

I rolled my eyes at Shepard. "I'm dead on my feet, and she has enough energy to be The Count. The universe does not divvy up energy as fairly as we do tip money."

Vena snorted. "I give them ten percent just like you."

The rest of the servers joined us as we cashed out our tips. Vena reached over the bar and stole some olives, and Buzz playfully swatted her hand. The others didn't comment when Vena and I lingered after they called out their goodbyes. Buzz followed them into the kitchen with the last tray of dirty glasses.

"So..." Vena said when it was just Shepard behind the bar. "Is Anchor meeting us at the house, or is someone else volunteering as tribute?"

Shepard stopped wiping down the bar and kept his gaze down for a moment. When he looked up, I saw his concern.

"Anchor and Gunther are missing. Gunner checked both their places. Neither was there today. The last time we saw Gunther was when he left here last night, and Anchor sent me a message when he left your place just before dawn this morning. He disappeared after that."

Vena flushed and looked down at her hands. Shepard inhaled, and I wondered what guilt smelled like to him.

"I'm sure Anchor's fine," I said. "He probably just needs some time to relax."

"I'm hoping that's the case with both of them," Shepard said.

But we all knew even if that was the case, they would have checked in with Shepard.

"If you're looking for a volunteer to watch over the girls tonight, I'm up for it," MC said, joining us.

"I think they'd prefer a familiar face," Shepard said with a glance at me.

I nodded, and Shepard grabbed his phone.

"If you don't mind waiting a few more minutes, everyone will be coming here to talk about tonight's patrols. I'll have Doc go with you then."

Buzz yelled for Shepard from the kitchen, loud enough that Vena and I heard.

"Stay with them," Shepard said to MC before taking off.

"What's going on?" Vena asked, looking at MC.

He shook his head. "I can't see through walls, babe."

"No, but you can hear through them," she said.

MC smirked. "Sounds like Gunther showed up looking like someone handed him his tail."

Vena and I were off our stools at the same time.

MC caught Vena's arm.

"Shepard wants you to stay here."

"I don't 'sit' or 'stay' very well," she said, tugging her arm free. "It's not in my genes."

MC didn't try to stop us again as we rushed through the kitchen door, almost knocking into Ink.

"You two shouldn't be in here," Ink said. He didn't try to make us leave, though, as we stepped around him to look at Gunther.

He was sitting on a chair from the locker room and looked pale as hell beneath all the blood smearing his face. Bite marks covered his neck. Shepard, who'd been speaking to him, looked up at us.

"What happened?" I asked.

"Vampire," Gunther breathed. "He used me until sunup then left."

The way he said "used" and the hitch in his voice left nothing to my imagination.

Shepard set a hand on Gunther's shoulder. The man shuddered at the touch, and tears trailed down his cheeks.

"It took all day to heal enough to walk here. He gave me a message for you, Shepard. He said, 'We were here well before any mutt called D.C. home. Stay out of our business, and we'll stay out of yours.'"

Fury radiated from Shepard and every other wolf present. Whoever abused Gunther would not be let off easy. Which made me wonder why the vampire had taken Gunther. The message could have been delivered without hurting Gunther. It was like the vampire had *wanted* to provoke the pack. But why? Did they think the pack was responsible for the vampire deaths at Juicy?

"Was Anchor with you?" Vena asked shakily.

Gunther looked at Shepard. "Anchor's missing?"

Shepard nodded.

Gunther shook his head as a fresh wash of tears trailed down his cheeks. "He wasn't there."

Vena made a small pained sound, and I wrapped an arm around her waist.

"Where did the vampire take you?" Shepard asked.

"It was the hotel down the road. I was caught off guard last night. There was no one in the lot when I left. Someone came up behind me before I got to my car. They stuck me with something." He lifted his hand as if he wanted to rub his neck then let it fall back to his lap without touching the mangled mess.

"Can you tell us anything else?" Shepard asked. "Did the vamp talk on the phone? Did anyone...join him?"

The employee door opened. The twins, Tank and Boulder, walked in.

"Army and Griz are backtracking the blood trail," Tank said.

"Good. Take a team, and find the leech that did this," Shepard said. "When you find him, don't make a move until I send backup. This time, we'll wipe out what's left of Juicy's nest."

"I'll have my guys do a little scouting as well," MC said.

"Thank you," Shepard said, running a hand through his hair as he visibly attempted to contain his rage.

Doc walked in behind Tank and Boulder.

"Doc, you'll take over for Anchor tonight," Shepard said. "Make sure Everly and Vena get home safely."

Doc nodded.

"Where is Anchor?" Vena asked again, her voice shaking.

Shepard shook his head. "I wish we knew."

I looked uneasily between Vena and Shepard. "They wouldn't have taken two of your men to deliver one message, right?"

Before Shepard could respond, Jaws came into the room.

"There are two police officers at the front door. They want to talk to you, Shepard."

CHAPTER FIVE

SHEPARD'S GAZE SWUNG FROM JAWS TO GUNTHER, THEN TO ME.

"Can you stay with him while I talk to the police?" he asked.

"Of course."

He left the room with Jaws. I glanced at MC and Doc. Neither made a move toward Gunther. Was it because Shepard looked at me when he'd asked for someone to stay with him?

Releasing Vena, I went to the sink, grabbed a clean towel, and wet it with Blur's hot-to-the-point-it-hurts water.

"Here," I said, handing it to Gunther. "You might want to clean off your face."

"I'd rather have a drink," Gunther said, taking the cloth.

"I'll get you something better," Doc said. "I'll be right back." He paused and looked at me. "Don't leave without me."

"I won't," I said.

He walked out the door while Gunther wiped most of the blood off his face then his neck. The number of holes peppering his throat made me cringe.

"Let me get another one," I said.

"Thanks," he rasped.

From the corner of my eye, I saw Vena edge closer to the main-floor door. She wanted to know what was being said on the other side of those doors. If I were honest with myself, so did I.

"MC, can you wet another towel? They're a little too hot for me to handle."

"Sure." He went to get a fresh one, and I glanced at Vena as she crept toward the door and slipped out to the service area.

I focused on Gunther and how he was scrubbing at his neck.

"That's not going to help it heal," I said, touching the back of his hand. "But a new shirt might help you feel better. Do you want one?"

He nodded as he took the new cloth from MC.

"There are spare white t-shirts in locker zero. Would you mind getting one?" I asked.

MC nodded and left.

When Gunther took off his shirt, I wanted to cry with him. There were bites everywhere, and someone had written "my boy toy" and "I love furry friends" on his chest in permanent marker.

He scrubbed the new cloth over his skin.

"MC, grab my purse from locker 7, too, please," I said without raising my voice.

He returned with the shirt and purse. When he saw the writing on Gunther's chest, his lip curled, and anger burned in his eyes.

"I'll get another wet towel," he said, walking to the sink.

I took a makeup wipe from my purse and gently pulled Gunther's hands away from his chest.

"You'll make it worse. Let me," I said.

He closed his eyes and shuddered non-stop as I gently used the makeup wipe to remove the marker. When I finished, I took the new cloth from MC and wiped away more of the blood.

"It's gone now," I said to Gunther. "You can open your eyes."

He took the shirt I offered and slipped it on. Then he just sat there and stared at the floor.

Whoever had done that to Gunther was a monster, reminding me that Cross was the exception to vampires, not the norm. Miles had been so lucky with his kidnapping.

Vena slipped back into the kitchen and came to stand beside me moments before Doc entered.

"Here. Drink this. It'll take a few minutes to kick in, but once it does, it'll knock you out for a day."

"Thanks," Gunther said, tipping back the small vial.

"Shepard'll take you home. He said he'll be here in a minute, okay?"

Gunther nodded, and Doc looked at MC. "Mind staying with him?"

"Not at all."

He nodded to Vena and me as we left with Doc.

She didn't say anything until we were on the main road home and knew our escort wouldn't hear.

"You're not going to believe this shit," she said.

"What?"

"The police were called to the hotel and saw the bloodbath in the room Gunther had been in. They saw the video surveillance that showed him leaving the hotel and tracked him to Blur. They didn't want to question him, though.

63

Because they *know* there are vampires in D.C. Just like they know there are werewolves in D.C. Specifically, in Blur.

"They came to ask if Gunther was okay, Ev. And they wanted to know what Shepard planned to do about the attack on one of his men. Do you know what Shepard said?

"He said that he and his people are going to hunt down every last vampire and kill them all. And he told the police to pull all the permits and licenses on Juicy. Shepard told the police what to do, and they *listened*. Do you know why?

"Because he's the damn pack alpha, Ev. And the police came into Blur already knowing that."

I focused on driving for a second while I let that news settle in my mind.

"Wow."

"That's it? Wow? What the fuck did we get ourselves into?" Vena said. "This is what happens when you strive for full-time employment. That shit just isn't safe."

I rolled my eyes at her and saw her excitement and humor fade.

She let out a shaky breath. "Was Anchor taken like Gunther because of me, Ev? If I hadn't been so adamant about going to Juicy, maybe the vampires wouldn't have retaliated."

"No. No way. Whatever happened isn't your fault. And Anchor isn't Gunther. He's observant and stronger. In fact, I bet he wasn't even taken at all. He probably just needed to go for a run because he's crushing hard for you."

She nodded, but I knew she didn't believe me any more than I believed myself.

When we arrived home, Doc went in first, checking to make sure it was safe. After his sweep, we were allowed inside. He closed the door behind us and locked it.

I showed him where the bathroom and towels were located then grabbed a blanket and pillow for him.

"Don't go to any trouble for me," Doc said. "This is luxury compared to some of the places I've stayed."

I wanted to ask him more about that, but my head was already too full of stuff I didn't want to know, and my energy was drained. I just wanted a hot shower and my bed.

As if knowing my thoughts, he said, "Take a shower, and go to bed. You'll feel better in the morning."

But would I? I had so many unanswered questions, topped with new information that made me question more.

Before I could head to the bathroom, Doc picked up a book from the coffee table. "Is there a reason you're reading up on vampires?"

Vena swooped in to collect her stack of books and snatched the one out of Doc's hand. "With all of their recent activity, a girl can't be too careful."

"We have your back," Doc said. "You don't need to worry. Gunther was taken because he wasn't paying attention and was alone. You stick with us, and you'll be fine."

Vena didn't let go of the books. Instead, she said goodnight and headed to her room.

Doc glanced after her, but I patted his arm. "Don't worry about her. Get some sleep. If you want anything to eat or drink, help yourself to the kitchen."

"I'll be fine, Everly."

I nodded and headed to my bedroom to get my pajamas. On my way to shower, I knocked on Vena's door and peeked inside.

"Do you need the bathroom first?" I asked.

She shook her head, not taking her eyes off the open book that sat in her lap. "You go ahead."

I wanted to ask her what she was up to, but it was Vena, and she was the type who needed answers when life failed her. Having Anchor missing was a major failure.

"Make sure to sleep," I said.

"I will."

Closing the door, I claimed the bathroom and got ready for bed while my mind raced. Anchor was missing. Gunther had been abused in numerous ways by a vampire most certainly associated with the vampires who'd controlled Juicy. And Shepard was the alpha wolf of D.C.

Cross needed to know what was happening.

I toweled off too quickly and had to fight to get my pajamas on over damp skin. Covered, I left the bathroom and called to Doc that it was free then closed myself in my bedroom.

When I grabbed my purse to fish out my phone, I found a note from MC tucked inside. He had written his phone number down in case I needed him for anything. The message said to give the number to Vena as well.

Placing it on the nightstand, I resumed my search and found my phone with a chocolate wrapper stuck to the screen. I plucked it off with a frown. Had I eaten it, or had Vena snarfed my chocolate again?

Focus, Everly. Chocolate isn't the problem.

I typed a message to Cross.

Me: One of the guys from Blur was taken by a vampire. He was able to get back to Blur, but he was fed on and is in bad shape. The vampire gave him a message that made it sound like the vampires are staking their territory in D.C. Do you know anything about it?

As I waited for Cross' response, I tucked myself under the covers. My fingers trembled.

After seeing Gunther, who could blame me for the fear I felt? Just imagining what he had gone through made my insides churn. While I knew vampires and wolves were enemies, the attack had gone beyond violent. It was as if the vampire took pleasure in the assault. And that kind of person scared me more than any other.

My phone buzzed with a message.

Cross: I haven't heard anything. Who was taken?

Me: His name is Gunther.

Cross: I will check into it. Are you safe?

Me: I'm at home. Doc is here with us.

Cross: Good. If you need anything, call me.

Me: Can you check into one more thing? Anchor is missing as well. No one knows where he is. I'm afraid he might have been taken by the vampires too.

Cross: I'll check on him as well. I'll be in touch tomorrow.

Me: Thank you.

It looked like he was replying to my text, but after a moment, the little dots went away. I placed the phone on my nightstand and turned off the lights.

DREAMS I COULDN'T QUITE REMEMBER TEASED the back of my mind as the morning light prodded me awake. I curled deeper under my covers, not wanting to get out of bed and face a new day. I wanted a vacation from summer break already, and it had barely even started.

Where were the nights out laughing, drinking, and having fun? Where were the days spent on the beach in our bikinis? Vena and I should have gone with Piper and Robyn to Europe.

But no, Vena and I had wanted to make money, not spend it. She'd wanted to hunt, and I'd wanted to serve at Blur. Where had everything gone so wrong?

I realized my mood was spiraling and shook my head. This kind of thinking wasn't going to solve anything. If I wanted a better life, I needed to put some effort into making it one.

Sitting up, I reached for my phone and saw a message from almost an hour ago.

Cross: There are three wolves lurking around your home, and the one on your couch hasn't left yet. Regretfully, I'm unable to wake you this morning. Call me.

The text was followed by three pictures. One of Ink leaning against a tree by the tracks. One of Thruster sitting in a beat-up car at the end of the block. And another of Jaws on our neighbor's front porch with his feet up on her railing like he lived there.

Me: I can't call if Doc's still on the couch. He'll hear. Did you find anything?

Cross: Yes. It seems your friends have started a war. I prefer to discuss the details in person.

Me: Where should we meet and when?

Cross: I found a bakery outside of downtown D.C. that I think you'll like.

He sent me the address and asked if an hour would work. Since I wasn't sure if Vena was up yet, I asked for two then got out of bed.

Vena's door was still closed when I left my room. Rather

than knock, I shuffled to the kitchen to make coffee for both of us. It was already made and waiting in the pot.

I backed up enough to look at the couch.

"Doc?" I called softly.

He sat up abruptly, and I jumped a little.

"I wasn't sure if you were still here or not. Anchor usually knocks on my bedroom door and leaves at dawn."

"Oh. Sorry about that."

"It's not a problem. Did you sleep well?"

"I didn't sleep."

"Oh. Was the couch too–"

He shook his head. "Everything was fine. Just staying alert and paying attention."

"Okay. Thanks for the coffee, then."

Someone knocked on the front door. Doc was off the couch and answering before I could say anything.

MC's gaze swept the room, spotted me, and kept searching until he finally looked at Doc.

"I brought donuts to go with the coffee. Figured you'd be hungry."

Doc looked at me, and I shrugged. He'd stayed awake the whole night on the couch. Why would I object to MC bringing donuts for him?

Doc let MC in, and I drifted to the dining room to inspect the donut selection. Standard gas station cake donuts weren't anything special and didn't call to me. Probably because I knew I'd be meeting Cross at a bakery.

"Thanks," Doc said, taking one and devouring a third of it in one bite.

"Any chance I could get a cup?" MC said, nodding at the cup of coffee I held.

"You can have this one."

I handed it off and went back to the kitchen to pour Vena another cup. Ignoring the two men wolfing down donuts, I slipped into Vena's dark room and shut the door behind me.

"Time to wake up," I said. "I have coffee."

A slight rustle came from the bed.

"Gimme," Vena mumbled.

"I'm going to open a curtain."

She moaned, and I heard another rustle. Likely, she'd burrowed under the covers. Pulling the blackout curtain aside confirmed it.

"MC stopped by with donuts for Doc if you want one," I said while eyeing the stack of books on the nightstand. Bookmarks stuck out from various pages, proving she'd stayed up and read.

"Not hungry," she said.

"Probably because you haven't had your coffee. Come on, Vena. Emerge a butterfly already."

The covers flipped back, and she glared at me. Her hair was tangled around her head, adding to the very non-butterfly effect she had going on.

"That's a lot of sexy right there," I said, holding out the cup. She sat up and took a large gulp of her morning kickstart.

While she focused on that magical elixir of life, I pulled out my phone and showed her the text conversation with Cross. She nodded and got out of bed.

"Better?" I asked.

"Not really. Has there been any word from Anchor?"

I shook my head, and she nodded toward her phone on the nightstand. Her recent texts were all to Anchor, asking if he was okay, asking if she'd gone too far, apologizing. I put the phone down and hugged her, beginning to see that regardless of her flirting history with men, she'd been more serious with Anchor than I'd realized.

"I'm sure he's fine," I said.

"Yeah, I'm sure you're right."

I left her to finish waking up and went to get ready. When I emerged from the bathroom, Vena's bedroom door was open, and I heard her voice from the kitchen.

"It's okay," Vena said. "I'm not hungry right now."

"I can get you something else if you don't want donuts," MC said. "I just thought you might want something a little sweet to start your day."

"I'm more of a savory person. Everly is the sweet one."

"Does anyone need coffee?" I asked, interrupting the conversation before either of them could take the savory comment to a that's-what-she-said place. Even though Vena was worried about Anchor, her mouth could still flirt. "I can make another pot."

"I'm good, Ev," Vena said as she placed her cup down. "I'll get ready. Then we can go."

"Go?" MC asked. "Where are you going?"

"Errands," I said.

"I can drive," he said. "It's safer if one of us is with you."

I shook my head. "No, it's okay. I made a deal with Shepard. And we'll be around other people."

MC's slight frown eased. "Okay. Well, let me know if you need anything."

"I will. You and your guys should get some rest."

"My guys?"

Not wanting to rat out Shepard and his overprotectiveness, I smiled and said, "Everyone who's losing sleep running around looking for vampires in the dead of night. Just get some rest. Vena and I will be okay."

Glancing at Doc who sat at the table, I asked, "Have you heard how Gunther is doing?"

"He's still out cold but healing well. He won't work for a few nights but should be back by Wednesday."

"If you see him, tell him I'll bake him whatever treat he wants."

"I will."

Doc stood and clapped MC on the shoulder. "Time to go."

MC glanced between Doc, me, and down the hall. "Yeah. Okay. Everly, I'm serious. Let me know if you need anything."

"I will."

I locked the door after they left and began to tidy the kitchen as I waited for Vena. By the time the coffee pot was sparkling and the cups were put away, Vena emerged.

She peeked through the house.

"They're gone," I said.

She let out a breath. "Good. The house was getting a little too small with the wolves in here."

Checking the time, I said, "I guess I didn't need to say we'd meet Cross in two hours. I just didn't know how long it would take to get out of here without followers."

"That's okay. We can stop by Miles'. He hasn't texted yet today, and I want to bring him the books."

"Based on all the marked pages, you must have been up all night, reading."

"Close, but it was worth it," she said. "I'll tell you what I found on the ride over."

By the time I pulled onto the road, Vena was opening books and spreading them on her lap.

"There are a few things I read that concern me.

"Basically, what we saw Cross do with the pawnshop guy was compelling. It's a mental nudge to get the person to do something that doesn't go against who they are. There are no lasting effects to being compelled, and it doesn't require a feeding. However, if there are feedings with the compelling, the vampire can form a bond with the feeder called a thrall. It's more permanent, and it's more dangerous. The feeder's personality changes. They want to please the vampire and will do anything to that end even if it's something they wouldn't normally do. It's like being mentally-enslaved.

"That's what happened to Sierra. Considering that Miles and Gunther have been fed on, there's a serious risk they could be thralled too. Even you, Ev. Cross has tasted your blood several times already. And just because he hasn't compelled you yet doesn't mean he won't in the future. The connection is there and lasts for a long time. Unfortunately, there are only a few ways to break it, and none of them are easy or without risk."

"Cross wouldn't enslave me, Vena."

When she remained silent, I glanced at her.

"What?"

"He scared me with the way he compelled both me and Sierra without even looking at us."

"Is eye contact necessary?"

"Typically. But honestly, Cross is less terrifying than the thought that Miles might be under the thrall of a vampire as sadistic as the one who took Gunther. Which is why I want to break any potential connection Miles might have."

"Okay. How do we break it?"

"Either the vampire or the feeder would have to die. I

doubt we'd be able to kill a vampire without help, especially not after the sun charm-cleavage fiasco that scorched your girls and my mom's chair."

"You shouldn't have bought the sun charm in the first place."

Ignoring me, she said, "The second way to sever a bond is to wait until it fades. But it takes time, during which the vampire will still have a link to the person and will know how to track them."

"I'm fine with that option for me. I trust Cross. But it doesn't sound like a good option for Miles or Gunther."

"Exactly. Which brings us to the final option. We would need to find an older and more powerful vampire to take over the link."

"Wouldn't that be worse?"

"I thought so, too. But, what if it's a vampire we know?"

"Cross? You just said you barely trust him and that I might be under his influence."

"Listen, we both know it's better him than the vampire that fed off Miles and Gunther. Then the enslavement link can fade, and everyone will be okay."

"Let's say someone is under vampire influence. How would you know if Cross is older and more powerful to take over the link?"

"Yeah. That's the main thing that concerns me right now. I have no doubt that Cross is stronger. Everything in these books proves he is no ordinary vampire."

"Like what?"

She flipped open a book with scribbled notes. "Cross exhibits the normal vampire traits. He's crazy fast, has a heightened sense of smell, eyes that turn black when he feels the call of fresh blood, and he can see perfectly at night." She moved her finger down the printed words. "But then there are things that don't match him. Vampires can't eat human food. We both have seen him eat food. He doesn't seem to need eye contact to compel. And then there is walking around in daylight. No vampire should be able to do it, and yet, Cross hasn't even sent up a smoke signal yet."

She shut the book. "If he can do those things, I think he can break another vampire's bond."

CHAPTER SIX

I glanced at Vena as I came to a stop in front of Miles' place.

"How old is that book?" I asked.

"It was written before the creature reveal."

"So we can assume everything in there was written by humans for humans. You saw Gunther last night. Those bites were already healing. And you heard Shepard's talk with the police. Werewolves are just as much the hunters as the vampires are. Which probably means werewolves won't be as susceptible to vampires as humans." I paused for a moment then added, "Anchor will be fine."

She nodded and reached for the car door as my phone buzzed.

Shepard: Just checking in. Saw you were at Miles'.

I chewed on my lip for a minute and dialed him. He answered on the first ring.

"Is everything all right?" he asked. Urgency and worry laced his words.

"Everything's fine. I'm sorry for calling. I just thought it would be easier than texting."

"You can call me anytime. Sorry if I overreacted."

"It's okay. I understand why. Actually, that's why I wanted to call. I didn't want you to read a text and think I was being ungrateful."

"Ungrateful?"

Vena settled back into her seat to listen to my side of the conversation.

"I know you're worried about us with everything that's going on, but wouldn't it be better to use the manpower available to you to track down the vampires instead of having them babysit us? Four seems a bit much. Again, I'm not complaining. I'm super grateful, but our neighbors might start noticing if really big guys are suddenly loitering on porches in the middle of the night."

Shepard was quiet for too long.

"You know what? Forget I said anything. I trust you, Shepard."

He let out a long breath. "It means a lot to hear you say that. I trust you too, Everly. Which is why I'll make sure you're down to one guard tonight, and you'll call me if anything goes wrong. Or if you just want to talk."

The last bit he added quickly as if an afterthought, and I smiled slightly.

"I appreciate it. Oh, and Miles' place is a stop on the way to check out a new bakery outside of D.C. Just in case you notice us veering west."

"Got it. Thanks for the heads up."

When I hung up, Vena was making kissy faces at me.

"You're ridiculous," I said.

She laughed as we got out of the car. It was a good sound but one that died too quickly as we walked up the sidewalk.

Thankfully, the little blue nemesis was once again absent when we approached the door and knocked.

"Check it out," Vena said. "He actually got a doorbell camera."

"Come in," Miles called.

I looked at the device as she opened the door.

"Nice security addition," she called .

"Thanks. I installed it this morning," Miles said from his place at the table.

I nodded to Boulder, who was watching TV quietly.

"What are you both up to?" I asked.

"Trying not to die of boredom," Miles said. When he turned in his chair, I saw the fairy sitting on the edge of a coffee mug in front of him. It dead-eyed me even though I tried to smile and wave. My insides were cringing hard, and it could probably sense it.

"Brought you the books," Vena said. "Interesting stuff on vampires. I marked a few spots for you." She turned toward Boulder. "Are werewolves immune to vampire influence like being compelled or thralled?"

He shut off the TV. "They are."

She continued to wear her thinky look.

"I'm expecting smoke to start rolling out of her ears any second," Miles said with a smirk at me.

She ignored him.

"The easier food sources are obviously humans then," she said to Boulder.

"They are," he agreed. "And it makes the most sense. Vampires can't control any of the other races like they can humans or gain any information from feedings. Humans have been their preferred food source for centuries. They only deviate when they're up to something."

Vena nodded slowly. "Like revenge."

"Is there something I don't know?" Miles asked.

"No," Vena said. "Nothing. Those books just got me thinking about how much I don't know about vampires–or a lot of other races, for that matter."

"Well, you've come to the right place," he said. "I just so happen to know a bit about everyone."

Vena snorted. "Except for vampires. You didn't know much about them, did you?"

"Knowing about vampires wouldn't have stopped Sierra from kidnapping him," Boulder said, defending Miles.

"I wasn't blaming him for that. I just wish we knew why," Vena said.

"You and me both," Miles said. He motioned me over to the table. "Take a look at this, Ev."

I looked at the note he'd written.

Can I have Cross' contact information? I have questions.

"Interesting," I said as if I was reading an article. "Might need to fact-check that."

"Yeah. No rush."

He folded the paper into a small square and handed it to the fairy. It tore into it with its tiny claws, making the note into confetti.

"Wow. That's impressive," I said.

It gave me a flat stare again, and I dug into my pocket for a dime.

"It's the shiniest one I have," I said.

The fairy darted at me, stole the dime, and disappeared into Miles' cupboard.

"Is it a pet now?" Vena asked.

"You don't want a fairy as a pet," Boulder said. "I promise you nothing good will happen."

Miles just grinned and shrugged. "At least, I won't be bored."

We chatted with Miles and Boulder as we waited for the meet-up with Cross. But Vena kept sneaking glances at the time as if she was actually impatient to see Cross.

After checking the time again, Vena glanced at Miles, who had lured the fairy out of the cupboard with a paperclip.

"Everly and I are going to head out," Vena said to Miles. "We have errands to run before our shift tonight. Make sure you keep sending me those proof of life photos. And that fairy better not be in them. You are not allowed to keep one as a pet, or I'll tell Mom and Dad when they get back."

Miles frowned at her but then smiled at the fairy. "Chompers can come and go as he pleases. He's not a pet."

"Chompers?" she asked.

"If you hold onto one of his treasures too long, he'll bite. But then he's nice again. He even has his own treasure hoard here."

"It's too late," Vena muttered. "He's already a pet owner."

"We'll revisit this pet problem once he's back to researching like normal," I whispered.

I waved to Boulder and Miles and pulled Vena with me out the door, knowing we couldn't do anything to stop Miles' friendship right now. As soon as it closed behind us, she zipped over to the car.

"Can you GPS the bakery?" I asked as I texted Cross we were on the way.

"On it," she said.

By the time I pulled from the curb, she had the coordinates set. Whether from hunger or the fact that my mind needed a break from vampires and the problems they caused, I was already dreaming about the delicious food I would discover at the bakery.

It wasn't until we arrived that I realized Vena had been oddly quiet in her own world. The thinky look in her eyes worried me.

"Are you okay?" I asked when I parked.

"Fine." She pointed outside the window. "Cross is here."

She had her seatbelt unbuckled and had traversed the parking lot before I even got out of the car.

Dressed impeccably in a new suit, Cross eyed her approach as if she were a rabid dog and veered around her to meet me halfway. It was hard not to stare at him. The blue of his jacket really set off the red in his hair.

"I'll grab a table," she called.

Cross eyed her and then me. "Do I want to ask?"

"She read books about vampires and probably has a few questions for you."

"Then I'm not worried."

With a light touch on my lower back, he guided me into the bakery. The warm scents of sugar and cinnamon wrapped around me. I inhaled deeply, finding my happy place.

Vena sat at a table near the window. She waved us over. I gave her the hang-on-one-minute finger, grabbed Cross' hand, and led him to the bakery cases that lined the back portion of the space.

The number of options awed me. Elephant ears larger than my head. Texas donuts, which looked like super-sized, frosted cake donuts. Large squares of various tortes. Slices of pies. Large cookies.

There were so many selections that I wasn't sure where to look first.

Cross dipped his mouth to my ear. "Your pulse kicked up when you saw the cases."

I didn't doubt it, but I did doubt if it was entirely due to the selections in front of me. Cross' fingers had intertwined with mine, and he was slowly rubbing his thumb over my skin in a way that made it hard to concentrate on what to pick.

Cross chuckled as he watched me. "Your indecision is adorable. Choose whatever you like."

"That would be one of everything, which wouldn't be smart. I have to work tonight and can't afford a sugar coma."

Under the guise of pointing, I freed my hand from his hold and placed a reasonable order, selecting seven options to share with Vena. Cross helped me carry everything to the table.

Vena barely managed to wait until Cross was seated before leaning forward in her chair.

"If you're not affected by the sun, does that mean you never rest?"

"I can choose to rest whenever I'd like, but it isn't necessary."

"So then, what do you do with your free time?"

"Is there a reason you're asking?"

"Yes. I'm still thinking about where you can live where the hours you keep won't call attention to you." When he didn't say anything, she sighed a little. "And I'm wondering if you'll be able to help look for Anchor."

"I use my free time to observe and learn."

"And shop?" she asked, looking at his new outfit.

He glanced at me. "The same clothier we frequented has opened an account for me. I will need your assistance settling it."

"No problem," I said after swallowing my first bite of a beignet.

The pastry hadn't been bad. Like everything else in the cases, it was larger than average, but it lacked that softness beignets usually had. A nice subtle level of sweetness, though. I glanced at the case, wondering how well they sold as I took one more bite to verify my silent critique.

"Are you unique, or are there more like you?" Vena asked, drawing his attention from me licking my fingers. "I'm wondering if we need daytime guards, too."

"No, you don't need daytime guards. I would prefer you didn't have any at night, either, but I agree with the necessity. At least until we can determine what happened to your easily distracted friend."

"Easily distracted?" I asked, pushing the beignet to Vena.

"The wolf who I saw run from your house the morning prior–Anchor, I believe–reeked of wolf lust and wasn't paying attention to his surroundings."

I nudged Cross with my foot under the table and glanced meaningfully at Vena, who'd looked down at the pastry I'd pushed toward her. He nodded in understanding when I shook my head.

"Yeah, that was Anchor. The one I asked you to look for. Did you find anything?" I asked.

"I returned to Blur and tracked the injured wolf's scent to a nearby hotel. The area was crawling with wolves, by the way."

"Oh, yeah. Shepard called in some backup. They're from California."

"It's a state to the west," Vena said.

Cross shot her a look. "I know."

She shrugged. "I didn't want to assume. It wasn't yet a state when you decided to take a nap."

"You went to the hotel?" I asked, trying to bring the conversation back on track.

"Yes. I persuaded one of the workers to let me into the room, which was still locked for police investigation. One of the scents was very familiar. The scent was on the cat that was at your house the morning prior."

"That proves it," Vena said. "If the cat was at our house the morning Anchor disappeared and at the club where Gunther disappeared, then the vampires took Anchor. But where? And why both Anchor and Gunther?"

Cross shook his head. "I don't think that's the case. I went to Juicy to see if I could find the scent there, but it's being well guarded by wolves and human police.

"While watching, I crossed paths with a newly turned vampire. It seems the humans know a vampire nest has gained a foothold and have made it impossible for the vampires to return to their haven. Which means they're scattered and looking for a new location to regroup.

"My young friend was willing to trade me information for advice on how to feed without killing while they set up a new feeder bar."

I made a gross face, which Cross noticed.

"Apologies."

"It's fine. What did your friend tell you?"

"The brutality that your wolf friend suffered was

sanctioned by D.C.'s current alpha vampire. It was a declaration of war against the wolves. No other wolf was taken. There was no need. Damaging one in such a way is enough to ensure the retaliation they want."

"Then, where's Anchor?" Vena asked before I could ask why they wanted retaliation. "Why would a vampire's cat be at our house the morning he was taken? A cat that we saw at Blur and at Juicy, mind you."

"Understandably suspicious," Cross said. "Perhaps my friend is simply unaware. Or perhaps others are trying to learn what the wolves know about otherworld activity."

"What do you mean?" I asked.

"The fae and the dwarves are not as innocent as they seem. There were reasons the fae, dwarves, vampires, and wolves hid in the shadows for centuries."

I frowned at my triple layer death by chocolate mousse cheesecake and slowly forked my first bite.

"So you think another group might have taken Anchor to figure out what the wolves know since they had gone after the vampire nest?" I asked.

"It's one theory," Cross said.

"But I thought wolves hunted vampires. That's the reason for their existence," Vena said. "At least, that's what all the old books are saying."

I took my bite and groaned at the flavor before slowly sliding the tines from my lips. The texture was perfect and the chocolate layers were well-balanced. While the other desserts had been okay, this one was out-of-the-park amazing.

"Cross is going to forget how to speak if you keep making love to your fork like that," Vena said. "Focus, Ev."

"You shouldn't have brought me here if you wanted me to

focus on anything but how heavenly this tastes and mentally figuring out how to level it up."

"I don't mind," he said with a quirk of his lips.

"I do," Vena said, handing him a pair of her sunglasses.

I glanced at him and saw his eyes flickering between black and brown.

"Sorry," I said, setting down my fork. "Carry on."

"Thank you," he said to Vena, slipping on the gender-neutral shades. "As I was saying, I simply believe we shouldn't make any assumptions regarding where Anchor might be. However, it is safe to assume that Shepard and his people have stirred up some serious trouble. It would be in your best interests to avoid Blur and the wolves as much as possible."

I shook my head. "We can't. Tuition is due in six weeks. We'll need every shift possible between now and then."

"There is no need to concern yourself with money," he said. "I have plenty, and I'd rather see you safe than laboring at a place that could be attacked again. Being around the wolves right now is asking for trouble."

In a way, he was right. But I couldn't take his money, either.

"Shepard will never let anything happen to Vena or me. He protects his employees."

"Just like he protected Gunther and Anchor?" Cross questioned.

Vena choked.

"Apologies," Cross said.

"No, you're right," Vena said. "Ev, maybe you should think about it. Shepard would understand."

"Think of it as pin money," Cross said. "All the women of high society are given pin money for their frivolities."

Vena stared at him, and in her contemptuous expression, I knew she was no longer siding with Cross.

"It's amazing how someone who looks so hot and young can have archaic views falling out of his mouth. You're not helping win over Everly. You're basically telling her you'll give her an allowance so she can toddle off to the candy store."

He reached over the table and took my hand. "Everly, I simply meant that your life has more value than tips at Blur. I have the means to help you. If nothing else, think of it as a reward for guiding me in this new world. Without you, I wouldn't have funds at all."

Vena nodded. "Very true. You're starting to make sense again."

I glanced between both of them. "I'll think about it. But I'm not going to leave Shepard and the others stranded. And I'll still need a job to pay for bills. So, until I figure out a solution, I'll keep working."

Cross frowned as he played with my hand, stretching his fingers along mine. "Then I will stay near Blur in case you need me."

His actions and his words were doing things to my insides.

I shook my head. "The wolves are against all vampires right now. They won't see you as a friend."

"It doesn't matter how they view me. They'd never be able to catch me."

"Your life has value, too, Cross. Don't risk it for no reason. The California pack is here. One-on-one, you might win, but not against two packs."

Vena nodded. "I agree with Ev. Stay away from Blur for now, and focus on getting more information and finding Anchor."

Cross didn't look convinced, but I allowed him to play with my hand a little longer until a text popped up on my phone.

Miles: Don't forget about your research.

Research? It took a moment before I remembered what he was talking about.

"Cross, is it okay if I give Miles your phone number?" I asked. "He wants to ask you a few questions about vampire stuff."

Cross paused for a moment then nodded. "Of course."

Surprisingly, Vena didn't bring up what she'd learned about enslavement links and breaking them. After I found Cross' contact information in my phone, I forwarded it to Miles, and he replied with an emoji of a happy-faced fairy.

We were going to need an intervention once everything settled down again.

I COLLAPSED on the couch before I remembered I had Cross' scent on me. Between playing with my hand at the table and his hand on my back as he walked with me, there had been a lot of touching...even before the unexpected hug when we said goodbye at the car and the kiss on my forehead.

Peeling myself off the couch, I headed to the bathroom to wash and change.

"Vena," I called from the bathroom, "can you research sprays that can remove vampire scents? There has to be a better way than having to shower and change every time. And I'm not sure it's really working. Shepard gave me a funny look last time."

"I'll check, but I doubt there is anything. You might be stuck showering and using perfume every time you see him."

"Shepard hates perfume," I grumbled.

And I hated that I had to hide Cross. He had done nothing wrong. In fact, he had only been helpful, but having to wash off his scent made meeting him feel cheap and dirty. He wasn't a back alley hooker.

By the time I finished my shower, I had a text on my phone from Shepard, asking if I could come in earlier than usual for a quick one-on-one. Usually, those meetings were about personnel changes. Was he replacing Gunther with someone else? Sierra?

"Hey, we need to go in early," I called to Vena. "Shepard wants to talk to me."

"I'm already ready," Vena called back.

I poked my still-wet head around the corner and saw her in the living room with a piece of our leftover bakery from this morning. It was the chocolatey one.

"You better savor every bite of that," I said.

She grinned at me. "Hurry up and do your hair. If you're fast enough, there might be some left."

I had my hair dried and styled in ten minutes. It wasn't fast enough, though. Making a face at her, I fixed myself a quick sandwich and joined her on the couch with my bakery notebooks while she watched *The Other House* reruns.

"Knowing what I know now makes this less enjoyable," she said.

"What do you mean?"

"Well, look at the way he looks at her. It used to be funny. Now I just feel bad. I mean, we know how much he likes her now, you know?"

"You're thinking of how much Anchor likes you."

She nodded. "I have so many regrets. I should have rocked his world while I had the chance. His howl could have rattled windows, I bet."

"You have once again crossed the TMI line."

She latched onto my arm so tightly that I felt the knife she had hidden in her modest cleavage.

"There's no such thing as too much with me, lover," she said with a sultry purr.

"I have regrets, too. I should have let you have your way with Anchor. You're obviously overdue. Now, let go so we can get to work. And you can't just live on cake. I know; I've tried. You should make yourself a sandwich."

She pouted at me. "But they don't taste good when I make them."

Rolling my eyes, I went to the kitchen to fix her a sandwich.

"I really need a day where we're not running around before a shift so I can work on my recipes," I said as I worked.

"You still want to open a shop?" she asked. "Being a business owner doesn't seem any more sedate than a treasure hunter."

"You might have a point there. Won't know until I try, though, right?"

She made grabby hands as soon as I finished and happily followed me out the door to the car.

"Do you think Doc will couch surf again tonight?" she asked as I drove to work.

"Why? Do you want someone else? And no, I'm not talking about Anchor."

"No, Doc's fine. I just don't want MC. He seems nice and everything, but he's coming off a little too intense for me."

"Pfft. Says the girl who's been pushing me at Shepard because of his intensity."

"Completely different vibes," she said, stuffing the last bite of her sandwich into her mouth.

"Shepard knows we prefer someone we're familiar with. He won't send MC."

Yet, a small part of me worried that was the reason Shepard called me in. Was he upset that Doc hadn't managed to sleep at all? Was he upset that I'd noticed how many guards he'd put around the house?

For Vena's sake and my sanity, I really hoped he didn't switch things up.

CHAPTER SEVEN

"You're tapping the steering wheel," Vena said. "What's on your mind?"

"I just wish I knew what Shepard wanted to talk about."

"He probably figured out how much of a distraction I am to his men and is going to fire me. If he does, I'm totally taking up Cross on misogynistic pin money."

"Misogynistic?"

"You know that's exactly what that was."

"He wasn't trying to be, though. And you're not getting fired. You're staying right by my side where I can keep an eye on you. Three kidnappings in a row already. I don't want you to go missing next."

"Pretty sure I won't."

"Just like you were sure nothing bad would happen on the last treasure hunt, right? And what happened?"

"We made a new friend," she said with a smile. "And he's proven very helpful."

"I'm surprised you're still speaking to Cross after seeing what happened to Gunther," I admitted.

"Well, it helps that Cross is old and rich and managed to feed off of the supermarket guy without marking him like Gunther had been marked. And if we're lucky, Cross will kick the bucket while the money is still in your account, and you'll be set for life."

I snorted. "Until I'm audited and have to explain where that money came from. We really need to get it out of there. No more talking about this," I said as I approached the employee parking lot.

Jaws stood by the back door and watched us park.

"You're here early," he said.

"Yep. Shepard asked us to come," I said.

"What for?"

I shrugged. "I'll find out in a few minutes."

Vena and I walked inside, stowed our things, then headed toward the main bar without clocking in. Shepard was there prepping the drink garnishes. When he saw us, he stopped slicing oranges and wiped his hands on a towel.

"I appreciate you coming in," he said. "Vena, would you mind clocking in early and finishing this up while I talk to Everly? And make sure you say hello to everyone who comes in. By name. Loudly."

Vena wasn't dumb. She knew what all that meant. He wanted to tell me something privately that his own people shouldn't hear. And knowing I would confide in her, she willingly jogged back to clock in and winked at me as I followed Shepard up the stairs.

He invited me to sit as soon as he closed the door behind me.

"What's going on?" I asked.

"I wanted to talk about this morning. Doc mentioned that

MC showed up, but he didn't notice anyone else. Who did you notice and where?"

I rattled off names and where they'd been according to the pictures Cross sent.

"How could you see them from the house?" Shepard asked. "I've been there, and your neighbor's house isn't visible from your room."

"Am I being interrogated? Did I do something wrong?" I asked, avoiding having to lie.

"No, no," he said quickly. "Just trying to understand. Did you leave the house last night, Everly?"

"Nope. I was inside from the second we walked through the door with Doc to the second we left to check on Miles."

He inhaled deeply. "I can smell your shampoo and body wash and the lingering scent of vampire, Everly."

I tried to keep my face straight, but there was no controlling the way my pulse spiked, and I knew he heard it too when he tilted his head and studied me.

"I'm worried," he said.

"You don't need to be. I promise."

He nodded slowly and sighed. "The vampires are a huge problem. There are more of them than we thought. They're scattered, which makes it harder to hunt them down. But despite that, I didn't send more men to watch over you. MC did that on his own, and I'll talk to him about it. But I'd like you to consider staying with me for a while."

Shepard was my boss, and he considered me family, but staying at his place seemed too intimate. What if I saw him walking around in his underwear? An image popped into my head, and it wasn't a bad one. Still. Staying with him was going into a territory I wasn't prepared to go.

"I...um, don't think that's a good idea. And we've been safe at my place so far."

His jaw tightened, but he gave a nod. "It's up to you. If you change your mind, let me know. But Everly, if something else happens with the vampires, I might not give you a choice."

I blinked at him.

"You know I'm only looking out for you, right?"

I nodded.

"And I'd never hurt you. You can trust me."

"I know."

"Good." He glanced at the door.

"Is someone here?" I asked.

His gaze returned to me. "No one to worry about. Why don't you get ready for your shift."

I stood and went to open the door. Pausing on the threshold, I glanced back at Shepard.

"I want to make a treat for Gunther tomorrow. Will he be at work or at home?"

"He'll be at home for another day or two."

"Can I take it to his place?"

Shepard nodded. "I'll send you the address. Message me when you're on your way."

"Message you?" I asked. "Is he staying with you?"

"A pack sticks together," MC said from the hall.

Startled, my hand flew to my heart. "I didn't see you there."

He smiled at me. "I didn't mean to scare you."

"It's okay."

"Is there a reason you're here?" Shepard asked MC.

"I heard something about treats and wanted to get in on the action."

"I'll make a batch for you and your guys, too," I said.

"Can't wait."

"Everly, head downstairs and help Vena."

I nodded and swapped places with MC.

"Close the door," Shepard said to MC, his tone fiercer than I thought the situation required.

Once the door was closed, I crept back to listen. It was fine that Shepard wanted to protect me, but being aware of what was happening was its own form of protection as well.

"What were you doing at Everly and Vena's house this morning?" Shepard asked MC.

"Just checking up on them and bringing breakfast."

"That explains you. What about your guys?"

"Safety in numbers."

"Doc could have handled anyone that came. He didn't need your guys, and I didn't assign them to be at her house."

"*Her* house?" MC laughed. "You're as transparent as glass, Shepard. I'm not encroaching on your turf, so stop thinking things are more than what they seem."

"This isn't about turf. This is about you not following orders."

"What order didn't I follow? I patrolled where and when I was scheduled to patrol. What my guys and I do during free time is my business, not yours."

"Not while you're in D.C. As soon as you got off the plane, your business became mine. You're here for a reason. Don't forget it. Follow the orders you're given, and don't do anything else."

"After seeing what they did to Gunther, I'm not sure if I want my guys under your leadership. You've let D.C. go to hell. Under my watch in California, we don't have vampire uprisings. We kill them as soon as we see them."

"Your arrogance doesn't make you a better leader, just a blind one if you think the same thing can't happen to your territory. The vampires have changed how they feed. They've adapted. We need to do the same, or we'll find ourselves back on the edge of extinction. And if you don't like how I'm leading, you know your options. Leave or challenge. Until then, it's my way. Now, get out."

The last words, coldly delivered with an underlying growl, sent me scurrying away from the door and to the VIP bar just as MC stormed out. Pretending to wipe the surface without a rag, I waited until he jogged down the stairs to follow. He'd already disappeared through the kitchen by the time I reached the main floor.

Vena glanced at me. "What was that about?"

I shook my head that now wasn't the time, and she took the hint and continued the bar prep.

Thankfully, that was the peak drama for the evening. Blur's regulars showed up in force and left generous tips for prompt drink service with a smile. Vena seemed to be doing just fine every time I looked her way, too. For the most part, she completely ignored MC, who had taken Anchor's place at the base of the stairs to the VIP section. Not that MC wanted to be ignored. I caught him winking at her. Twice.

Winks delivered across a crowded bar had never worked to win Vena over in the past, and I knew they wouldn't now. However, they could annoy her. She seemed to keep her cool, though, as the night progressed.

By closing, she was too busy gleefully counting her wad of tip money like Scrooge McDuck to be annoyed by anything. I sat by her to count out my money and handed over the percent due to the bartenders.

"Thanks for the fast service tonight," I said to Buzz. "Made a difference."

"Anytime," he said with a nod. "I hear we're seeing you tomorrow. You bringing enough fudge for Gunther to share?"

"You all live together?"

He shrugged. "You live with Vena. My family's just a little bigger."

"Fair enough. How much fudge should I bring?"

"Do not answer that," Shepard said behind me. "Just bring what you want, Everly."

Buzz threw me a sad pout before turning away. Laughing, I went to the lockers with Vena to grab my things.

"I'm going to have to get some more sweetened condensed milk in the morning. You with me?"

"Ugh. Why do you hate me? Of course, I'm with you. You're going to wait until at least nine, right?"

"You know it needs time to set up," I said, nodding to Doc, who was waiting for us.

He walked ahead of us out to the parking lot.

"Fine. Eight o'clock. That's my final offer," Vena said as I unlocked the doors.

Doc was grinning as he got into his little electric car.

"How many do you think can fit in that thing?" Vena asked.

He held up four fingers even though both our doors were closed.

I started up my engine, waved, and pulled out of the lot.

"I bet that's why he went electric. He can hear better," Vena said softly. As soon as we hit the main highway, she turned to me.

"Okay. Spill it. What happened to make Mr. Crybaby storm off before our shift?"

"Mr. Crybaby?" I echoed.

"MC."

I rolled my eyes.

"Hey, it's a work in progress. Now, talk. I know you heard something."

"MC wasn't supposed to have his guys watching our house. Shepard called him out on it and told MC he either obeys his commands or challenges him. Not sure what a challenge is, but it didn't sound good. Oh, and before he talked to MC, Shepard told me he was worried because he could smell vampire on me." I sighed. "Should I just tell him what's going on?"

"I mean, if you do and they kill Cross for being their natural enemies, you'd be rich so..." She shrugged as she grinned at me.

"You are so unhelpful. But good job ignoring MC tonight."

"You have no idea how badly I wanted to see if I could toss a werewolf over my shoulder."

"With the way he was looking at you, he probably would have let you do anything you wanted to him."

"Ew."

I grinned, loving tormenting Vena for a change. We arrived home too soon to continue, though. We waited in the car for Doc to do his thing then went inside. Vena claimed the bathroom first this time, which gave me time to get Doc settled and check my ingredients in the kitchen.

By the time my head hit the pillow, I knew my list and had my alarm set for seven.

A light knock pulled me from my sleep prematurely.

"Ev, it's me," Doc said. "I'm heading out."

I gave a mumble of acknowledgment and sank back to sleep.

"I told her she'd be rich if someone ends up killing you." Vena's words teased my foggy mind. "You know what her answer was? She didn't want to deal with the tax audit. Her laces can't get any straighter, Cross. What do you think she's going to do when she finds you in her bed...again?"

I opened my eyes and stared into Cross' amber ones.

"Good morning," he said with his sexy light accent.

"Morning."

I heard Vena snort and move away from my bedroom.

"Did you sleep well?" he asked.

"I did. Why are–"

He pressed a finger to my lips as he lifted his head from my pillow. His eyes flickered black. Then he leaned in, kissed my forehead, and disappeared out my bedroom window.

I frowned at the now ripped screen and got out of bed.

Seriously, men caused more problems than they solved.

Just as I was leaving my bedroom, someone knocked on our front door.

"Not it," Vena called from the bathroom.

Groaning a little, I went to answer it.

MC stood on the front porch, holding a paper grocery bag.

"Morning, Everly. I heard you needed some more sweetened condensed milk to make fudge for the pack. Since I know I screwed up yesterday with you and Vena and Shepard, I was hoping this could be a peace offering."

Since he'd gotten into trouble for coming to our house when he wasn't told to in the first place, I doubted that coming here to apologize would win him Shepard's forgiveness, but I didn't say so. MC and I both knew he was here because of his misguided infatuation with Vena.

He lifted the bag. "I got seven cans. I wasn't sure how much you needed."

"That's more than enough. Thanks."

I went to accept the bag, but he pulled it back. "It's heavy. I'll set it on the table for you."

He walked past me before I could block him but jerked to a stop. His nostrils flared twice, and he looked at me like I'd grown two heads. I knew exactly what the problem was, but I played dumb for all it was worth.

"Please don't sneeze on me," I said. "I can't afford to be sick."

"Oh. Yeah. No. No sneeze," he said, turning and continuing to the table.

Vena chose that moment to leave the bathroom.

She was wearing her summer pajamas, which were comfortable cotton shorts and a cotton tank top. The way MC was looking at her, though, you would have thought it was lingerie.

"Can I talk to you outside for a moment, Vena?" he asked. "It's important."

She glanced at me, and I could see the 'I'm going to throat punch him' look in her eyes. So I sent back my 'play nice, or you'll be grounded' look.

"Fine. I'll give you two minutes," Vena said, marching toward the door.

He followed, and I saw the way his nostrils flared again when he walked past me.

After the door closed, I watched them for a moment to make sure Vena wouldn't give into her urge to smack him.

Whatever he started saying to her removed some of her defensive edge, though.

Assured that they'd be fine, I went to my room to grab some clothes then went to shower. If I planned on dropping off fudge, I needed to wash off whatever MC had smelled, or Shepard would have another fit, too.

I sighed and heard the bathroom door open.

"Let me guess. He smelled vampire on me. Why is my life so complicated?"

"Do I complicate your life, Everly?" Cross asked from the other side of the curtain.

My eyes rounded, and I poked my head out of the curtain. Cross wasn't just standing in the bathroom. He was inches away from me. His gaze swept over my wet face and dipped to my lips.

"Allow me to uncomplicate it," he said before closing the distance between us.

His lips settled over mine, warm and firm. Desire and anticipation rushed through me against my better judgement. And when his hands cupped my face and he kissed me with a hunger that stole my breath, I knew I was done for.

I grabbed for Cross, wanting more, and lost my balance. His arm snaked around me and pulled me to his chest at the same time he took advantage of my surprised gasp. Stealing his way inside, his tongue stroked against mine. He groaned. The kiss changed, conveying his desperate need. My pulse thundered in my ears as I held on for dear life as I kissed him back.

When he finally pulled away to look at me, I was gasping for air.

"Beautiful," he whispered.

I shivered. "I think that added more complications."

He smiled slightly. "Depends on how you look at it. But I believe I interrupted your bathing. Would you like me to assist you?"

I started to nod then stopped myself. "Wait. No. I'm showering because the werewolves keep smelling you on me."

"Yeah, and that's a problem," Vena said from the other side of the door. "So stop being pervy, and let Everly shower alone. And there better not be any bite marks on her."

Cross' eyes flashed black briefly, and he let out a long-suffering sigh.

"Must you live with her?" he asked. "I swear she was a fishmonger's wife in a past life."

"I must," I said. "Now close your eyes."

When I'd slipped, he'd pulled me against him, so all my nakedness was plastered against his tailored self and was currently hidden from his view. I wanted to keep it that way.

He turned his head and looked at us in the mirror over the sink.

"This is a memory that will stay with me through the ages," he said.

My face flushed.

"Close your eyes or lose them," I warned.

He chuckled and closed his eyes. Then he had the decency to take my hand and help me straighten so I wouldn't slip again.

Once I was behind the curtain, he said, "I will wait for you in the living room."

The door opened and closed again. I did my best to scrub every inch of my front that had been in contact with him.

When I reemerged, dressed and my hair towel dried, he was waiting for me in the living room with Vena.

"MC could smell Cross on you," Vena said. "He pulled me outside because he's worried you're under vampire influence like Sierra is. He told me what to watch for. Obsessive behavior. Flash anger. Disappearing in the middle of the night. Stuff like that." She turned to look at Cross. "We really need you to stop touching Everly."

Ignoring her, Cross watched me sit on the couch.

"Let them worry," he said. "They'll keep you safer because of it."

"Well, when he says it like that..." Vena uncrossed her arms. "Fine. But no biting. I'm serious on that one."

"Don't worry. I fed well last night while looking for your Anchor."

Vena and I both made faces.

"Yes, I found it rather distasteful, too." He shook his head. "The sex games the fae play hold very little interest to my kind, but feeding from her was the only way the fae woman would speak to me."

"Hold up," Vena said. "Did you have sex with a fae last night?"

"No. I fed from her while her partner brought her pleasure."

Vena sat and propped her chin on her hand. "You have my attention. I need details."

"No, she doesn't," I said. "Did you find anything about Anchor?"

"I found the werewolves are not the only ones having trouble with the vampires. It seems the vampires had made a deal with the fae here. In exchange for their occasional services in securing sexually uninhibited humans, the fae would help the vampires hide their presence from the werewolves. However, the vampires have recently stopped keeping their end of the bargain. Which is why the woman was willing to speak to me. The fae are growing hungry again."

Vena and I shared a look. "Hungry? What do you mean?"

Cross smiled slightly. "As I said, there's a reason the races hid in the shadows for so long. The fae are not as innocent or as benevolent as they would have humans believe. They crave human carnal pleasure. They feed off of it. But don't worry. The humans they currently have should last them for several more weeks before they need to be released."

"Damn," Vena said under her breath.

I couldn't agree more and touched my chest where my charm hung.

"Could the fae have taken Anchor?" Vena asked. "You said he smelled like lust."

Cross shook his head. "No. She confirmed that they have no interest in starting a war with the wolves. And that's what would happen if they took a member of Shepard's pack. It would be an act of war."

I stood. "It looks like we have a lot to ask Shepard when we visit Gunther today. I better get started on the fudge."

When Cross headed into the kitchen with me, I eyed him and his suit.

"You might not want to be near me when I make fudge," I said. "I don't try to make a mess, but it happens in a small kitchen."

"I'm not worried."

Digging out ingredients from the cupboard, I made sure I had everything before I started. I'd experimented with fudge a lot in the past, trying to come up with something that had a smooth, creamy texture like a firm ganache. For today, though, I planned to keep it simple.

Once everything was assembled, I measured, poured, heated, and mixed. Cross watched me as if fascinated by the process.

"Why are you watching me like you've never seen anyone bake before?"

"Never anyone as beautiful."

The spoon slipped from my grasp and landed on the floor with a thick spatter of fudge.

He picked it up and handed it to me. "And I had a houseful of servants. The kitchen was not my domain."

I set the spoon in the sink to rinse later. As I dug through the drawer to get a new spoon, I pricked my finger on something sharp and yanked my hand from the drawer with a curse. Before I could grab a towel, blood dripped from the cut and into the mixing bowl.

"No!" I groaned. "I just ruined the fudge."

Cross took my hand, looked at the blood dotting my finger, and brought it to his lips. His tongue swirled over my skin, and heat flashed through me. When he finished his version of vampire first aid and finally let go of my hand, the only sign I had stabbed myself was a thin pink line.

"I'll take this batch of fudge," he said.

Turning to the bowl to escape from his hungry gaze, I mixed in the blood and poured it into a pan to set.

After washing the bowl twice in hot soapy water, I attempted the fudge again.

"Ev, Shepard is texting you," Vena said.

"What does he want?"

"Asking when you'll be at his place."

"Give me two hours so I can make sure the fudge sets. It'll give us enough time to drive there. I might have to shower again, too."

Cross smirked at me. "You make me want to test how good of a sense of smell the mutts have."

"I was just talking about complications, remember?"

"I remember. And I also remember what your lips taste like."

My heart skipped a few beats.

"Behave, or I won't give you the fudge."

He sighed. "I'll give in. For now."

Vena dropped off my phone. "I told Shepard. He said he'll be waiting for us at the main entrance. Sounds like a big place. Maybe we don't need Cross to be your sugar daddy after all."

Cross' eyes flashed black at her. She backed up a step, but not in fear. She grinned at him. "If you want brownie points, go find Anchor."

"I will leave when you leave," he said.

"You just want the blood fudge," Vena said. "Everly, you need to be less accident-prone before he gets addicted to you."

"Too late," he said.

CHAPTER EIGHT

THE THINGS CROSS DID AND SAID WERE MESSING WITH MY HEAD and my libido. Why did he have to look so damn good in a suit?

"Both of you, out," I said. "This kitchen is not big enough."

With Cross standing near me and Vena verbally poking at him, another accidental injury would likely take place, and I wasn't sure I'd survive Cross' miracle tongue-licking so soon.

By the time I had the fudge packed and ready to go, Vena had the map pulled up on her phone.

Cross opened the door for us and had his own batch of fudge tucked under his other arm as we left the house. It didn't stop him from helping me stow the rest of the fudge in the backseat or opening the driver's door for me.

After I sat down, he said, "Call me if you need me. I'll be around."

"You'll be getting more information, you mean," Vena said.

Cross looked at me. "I'll be around."

He closed the door and stepped back as I pulled away.

The navigation routed me north out of the immediate

downtown area toward Rock Creek Park. Vena was quiet until we hit the highway.

"Are we going to talk about shower time with Cross and how he tasted your lips?"

I tapped the steering wheel for a moment.

"Sure. Let's talk about how screwed I am because I have a best friend with a fetish for trouble. It all started with a ring..."

"Hey now. Let's not go pointing ring fingers. The way you blushed when he mentioned kissing means it wasn't horrible."

I sighed, knowing that she wasn't going to let this go. And she shouldn't. I needed to talk to someone about it.

"It wasn't horrible. If I'm being honest with myself and you, I liked it a lot."

"That's good."

"Is it, Vena? He's a vampire. His eyes go black at the mention of blood."

"Hey, I was watching when he stuck your finger into his mouth. He didn't vamp out."

I shook my head. "It feels like I'm playing with fire with him. And I don't want to get burned."

"Makes sense. You've always been the play-it-safe type."

I made a face at her for making me sound like a prude. "Whatever."

"Just have some fun, Everly. We're young. We're single. Why can't we let our hips mingle?"

"Okay, that sounded wrong on too many levels to even address." And yet, I was glad she'd said it. Knowing that she supported whatever decision I might make helped me feel better about it.

"Since we both know you don't filter well, when we get to

wherever it is we're going, I'll do the talking, and you just look pretty."

Vena snorted. "You gave me the easy job."

We arrived at a wooded lot adjacent to the park. The extra drive through the two open gates was edged by a nice walking path.

"Are we sure this is the right place?" Vena asked, leaning forward to look up at the sky through the canopy above the road.

"You're the one who entered the address," I said.

Ahead, the road split. The one to the left disappeared behind the left most three-story building with a double-door entrance at the top of a set of stairs. The road to the right curved in front of all three of the buildings and ended in a large parking area.

I took the right and parked.

"It looks like a hotel or a nicer version of our dorms," Vena said.

"A little," I agreed, getting out.

I was in the process of taking out the extra-large container of fudge from the back seat when the doors of the center building opened. Shepard strode out with a welcoming smile on his face.

"Everly. Vena. Did you find the place all right?"

"Yeah," Vena said. "This is your house?"

He chuckled as he reached us, but that sound died as he stopped beside me to take the container. Without even hiding what he was doing, he leaned in and smelled me.

When he pulled back and met my gaze, I was expecting some comment about smelling like vampire again. Instead, he glanced at Vena.

"It's not only my home but the home for all of the D.C. area pack. We stick together so we can take care of one another. Come on. I'll show you around."

Vena arched a brow at me behind his back as he led us into the building he'd left. I shrugged, not sure why he hadn't said anything but grateful for it.

The entry gave off a hotel lobby vibe with a small area off to one side that held a reception-type desk. He nodded to the women there and continued leading us down the hall.

"We have a kitchen back here," he said. The room was spacious and connected with another larger area that looked like a lounge and dining room combined.

"If we leave the fudge here, everyone will find it," Shepard said. "We can take a plate to Gunther."

The second he had the lid off, a little boy came racing in and silently gave Shepard puppy eyes. Shepard ruffled the boy's hair with a grin.

"I'm not falling for your trap again, Lucas. Go ask your mum, or she'll be handing me my tail at dinnertime."

The boy growled with an underlying whine and ran off again.

"You like kids?" Vena asked.

"I love kids," Shepard said. "They're the heartbeat of our future."

"Nice," she said. "Women like an invested family man."

I elbowed Vena when his back was turned, fixing a plate for Gunther. She grinned at me.

"Safe," she mouthed.

I rolled my eyes at her and watched Shepard finish stacking a portion of fudge on the plate for Gunther. He popped the last one into his mouth and turned to us with a grin.

"Couldn't resist."

That seemed to be a theme lately.

Leaving the kitchen with the treats, Shepard led us down the hall and up a flight of stairs to a partially open door at the end of the hall. Shepard knocked lightly.

"You up for company?" he asked.

I didn't hear a reply, but he pushed open the door. Gunther was sitting on a made bed, looking down at his hands.

"Hi, Gunther," I said. "I brought you something sweet and chocolatey."

He looked up at the plate Shepard held and then at me. "Thanks, Everly."

The bites on his neck had healed to the point they were barely noticeable. And his coloring looked a lot better.

"We miss you at Blur. Think you'll be coming back soon?" I asked.

"Heard the dishes were piling up last night," he said, taking the plate and setting it on the bedside table.

"Yeah, the new washer's a little slow," I said.

He chuckled because the new washer had been Gunner with Shepard helping when he could.

"Yeah, you can't teach competence," Gunther said.

Shepard snorted as Gunther and I shared a small smile.

"He'll be back Wednesday," Shepard said. "Due to recent events, I'm closing Blur Mondays and Tuesdays until we get this infestation under control."

I inwardly winced at the loss of income.

"That makes sense," I said then glanced at Gunther. "You're not going out with them, are you?"

"I haven't been smothered with enough pack love to reassure everyone that I'm fit for hunting. The fudge will help me through it, though. Thanks."

I nodded and took that as our cue to leave.

"Interested in a tour?" Shepard asked when we were in the hallway again.

"Yes," Vena said, answering for us.

He led us through all three buildings, which were almost mirror images of one another. Some of the rooms had been converted to allow for larger families to live comfortably. Some were left as single units like Gunther's.

When Shepard opened a door that led to the back of the buildings, I was surprised by the manicured, park-like gardens lined with gravel paths. Bushes, flowers, vines, and trees bordered the meandering paths.

"This is beautiful," I said.

"Is this part of Rock Creek Park?" Vena asked.

"No. This is ours. The paths dead-end at a line of shrubs that separate us from the park. It deters lost park visitors from wandering onto our land."

Several seating areas were sprinkled throughout the extensive patio and out in the flower gardens. It was peaceful here, and there was enough room for everyone without feeling crowded.

My eyes paused on a woman walking near flowering bushes. With a silent groan, I realized it was Sierra. A man stood off to the side of her as she poked her hand into the bush and rustled it.

"How is she?" I asked Shepard.

"She's healthy but doesn't like being here."

"How long will you keep her?" Vena asked.

"That depends on her," Shepard said. "Right now, she's being uncooperative. Won't answer most of our questions, and she's evasive on the few she has answered."

"When has she ever been cooperative?" Vena asked.

She wasn't wrong.

"Sierra hasn't opened up about what happened or who she was working with," Shepard said. "Until she does, it's not safe for her to leave."

"When we found Miles, she couldn't name the vampire because he'd never given her a name," I said.

Shepard sighed and watched her continue to search the bushes lining the path ahead. "Yeah. There's a possibility she doesn't know. But she's also my only lead that might help us find Anchor."

Vena's attitude evaporated as she considered Sierra, and I knew we were both thinking the same thing. Since Sierra's vampire had sent her to Blur to gather information on the werewolves, it made sense that Sierra might know something useful. *If* we could get it out of her.

"Can we talk to her?" I asked.

Shepard looked hesitant for a moment, but he gave a nod. "Maybe she'd like to talk to you instead of me."

Vena and I walked over to Sierra while she was still poking around in the bushes.

"Master?" she whispered. "Are you there?"

I glanced back at Shepard and quietly asked, "Is she on medication?"

He shook his head no.

"I think the vampire took more than her blood," Vena said to me.

I gently elbowed Vena, not wanting Sierra to hear her. If

Sierra had been thralled and fed upon, she was a victim and should be treated like one. Still, I moved to the bush to see if there was something inside that would cause Sierra to think a vampire was in it. But there was nothing that I could see.

Was this then what being thralled meant? Desperately looking for the vampire who controlled you? I thought of what had been done to Gunther and hoped it hadn't been done to Sierra. How would it feel to want someone who tortured instead of loved? It would break my mind.

"Hi, Sierra," I said gently. "How are you?"

She glanced over and immediately glared when she saw Vena and me. "Why are you here?"

"We brought fudge as a get-well for Gunther. There is plenty in the kitchen if you want some."

"For Gunther?" Sierra scoffed. "He was let off easy."

"What do you mean?" I asked.

"Nothing." She walked to the next bush, peered into it, then walked to a cluster of flowers.

Vena shot me an annoyed look. I knew her well enough to understand Sierra was one more smart comment away from losing her soft approach. Vena was worried about Anchor and wanted answers now.

"Are you looking for something?" I asked, watching Sierra's continued search.

"Don't you have someone else to bother?"

"I just thought you might want a friend to talk to," I said.

She snorted. "Why would I ever be your friend, mutt-slut?"

"What is your problem?" Vena demanded, lurching forward a step. I stopped her with a hand on her shoulder.

"Interesting pet name coming from you," I said. "Is that

why your master wanted to kidnap people? Because he hates werewolves?"

She tilted her head at me. "Is that why the werewolves kidnapped me? Because they hate vampires?"

"You weren't kidnapped," I said at the same time Vena angrily said, "You drugged and kidnapped my brother. Don't act like you're the victim here."

"But she still is, Vena," I said. "She didn't ask to be bitten by a vampire."

Sierra laughed like I'd said the most hilarious thing in the world.

Vena narrowed her eyes at Sierra. Sierra grinned as she held up her hand, giving Vena the middle finger.

The man watching Sierra stepped in, and Sierra was escorted into the building. We rejoined Shepard.

"Is this how Sierra has been the whole time?" I asked.

"She has her moments where she is more aggressive than others."

"We read that humans who've been thralled or mentally enslaved by a vampire can return to normal after a while."

Shepard nodded. "The bond can fade, but it will depend on how long Sierra was under the vampire's influence."

"Can Anchor afford to wait for that?" Vena asked, her tone tinged with anger and fear.

"Or--" I stopped myself. It didn't matter if Cross could compel Sierra to talk. I couldn't tell Shepard about Cross. Even though part of me wanted Shepard to know how helpful Cross had been, I knew what would happen. Shepard would hunt Cross.

"Or?" Shepard prompted.

"The book Vena read mentioned a few ways to break a

vampire's thrall. Any chance that Sierra's master will come here looking for her?" I asked.

"If we kill her master, she'd be free of his thrall and probably willing to talk," Vena said.

"There is no we in this," Shepard said. "I want you two to promise to stay out of it."

It felt like his tone carried some extra weight when he met my gaze. The need to look away and nod my agreement rode me hard, and I struggled to maintain eye contact.

"Heard we have company," a familiar voice said.

The tension between Shepard and me broke when he looked at MC. I quietly let out a relieved breath and turned to look at MC as he joined us. His gaze flicked to Vena, and he winked at her.

"Looks like your tour stalled," he said to Vena. "I'd be happy to show you around so these two can finish their silent standoff."

"We weren't having a standoff," Shepard said.

MC ignored him and arched a brow at Vena. "Looked like a standoff to me. How about you?"

She crossed her arms. "Are you just here to cause trouble?"

"Not at all. You looked bored, and they looked like they wanted alone time."

"Would you mind giving me a few moments to speak with Everly privately, Vena?" Shepard asked.

Surprised by the request, I glanced at Shepard.

"It's starting to feel like your name stands for Mandatory Company," Vena said to MC. "I'm not a fan."

She turned on her heel and walked away from us. MC quickly followed her.

Did Shepard realize he hadn't endeared himself to Vena

just then? He needed to clue in on how much Vena was really starting to not like MC.

"She doesn't do clingy," I said for both Shepard's and MC's benefit.

I watched MC put a little distance between the two of them and knew he'd heard. When I looked at Shepard, he inclined his head in acknowledgment.

"I appreciate her cooperation and hope you'll be as willing."

"I've always cooperated with you, Shepard."

He studied me for a long moment. "Then can you tell me why parts of you smell like vampire?"

I blinked at Shepard as my mind raced.

"Define parts..."

"The scent is strongest on your finger and mouth, but I can smell his lingering scent in other places." His gaze swept over my front and I knew he wasn't eyeing my boobs as much as he was silently indicating where he could smell Cross.

Damn that complicated vampire. I'd told him he was going to cause me trouble.

"I am more than willing to tell you. However, considering what happened with Sierra and Miles, I think you're going to struggle with believing me when I tell you the truth."

"And why is that?"

"Because you believe there's no such thing as a good vampire."

Shepard's gaze softened, and in the next instant, I found myself wrapped in a warm hug.

"Oh, Everly," he said softly. "Did they get to you, too? Tell me who the vampire is, and I'll handle it."

I could hear his sincere worry for me and hugged him back.

"No one has done anything bad to me," I said. "And I promise, there were so many times that I thought bad things would happen. The shadow world isn't exactly all rainbows and kittens. But I found an ally."

He loosened his hold to grip my shoulders and look me in the eyes.

"Tell me what happened."

"We accidentally met a vampire. Well, met is maybe a misrepresentation of what happened. We stole from him."

The stunned disbelief in Shepard's expression would have been hilarious if I wasn't on the receiving end of it.

"However, he didn't go on a murderous rampage like we'd been led to believe he would. He was definitely annoyed but allowed us the opportunity to explain the misunderstanding. All without a single drop of blood spilled. I promise.

"Since then, we've been helping him a little, and he's been helping us a lot. Remember that little pickle Vena and I got in at Juicy? He saved us. He's the reason everyone there is dead. If he hadn't shown up when he did..." I let out a sigh. "It would have been bad. He's a friend, Shepard."

While I spoke, Shepard's tightly clenched jaw started to tic faster and faster.

"Please don't be mad," I added.

"Mad?" he said. "Everly, I'm not angry; I'm terrified. You stole from a vampire, and somehow, he has you believing he's a hero. Do you think he just happened to be there when you needed him? Juicy was a feeder nest unlike anything I've ever seen. That's why MC and his people are here. D.C. has an infestation. That the vampires took one of my own and did

119

what they did means they have no fear. The only reason they wouldn't fear us is because their numbers are out of control."

What he was saying made my stomach sink to my toes. Were there really that many of them? Here? In my hometown?

"And he's one of them, Everly," Shepard said, interrupting my thoughts. "He's not your hero or your friend. He's probably fed on you without you even realizing it. I want to take you to one of our females and have you checked for bite marks. Please."

"What? No. Shepard, I'm not going to strip down for some stranger because you don't believe me."

"Then strip for me."

"Whoa." I retreated a step, which he shadowed, maintaining contact.

"I think you're in danger, Everly. Please."

"I knew you wouldn't believe me," I said. "But Cross can help us. He can compel Sierra to talk. He already did–without biting her–when we were at her house."

"He was the vampire we chased," Shepard said, understanding.

"Yes."

He shook his head, looking down for a moment.

"None of that explains why you still smell like him," he said, lifting his gaze to meet mine again.

I blew out a breath. "I cut my finger making fudge. He licked it to heal it. That's all."

"And your lips."

I couldn't hold his gaze anymore. Like a coward, I looked to the side at the hedgerow.

"He kissed me," I mumbled.

"Do friends kiss?" Shepard asked.

I knew he had me there, and I wanted to swear. If I said yes, Shepard would think I was under Cross' influence; and if I said no, I'd be admitting Cross wasn't a friend like I'd claimed.

"Some friends do," I said finally.

"Really?" Shepard asked.

He captured my chin with one hand.

"Am I your friend, Everly?"

Before I could answer, his lips covered mine. Thoughts of why I shouldn't allow it fled at the gentle way he licked my bottom lip and coaxed me to respond.

Just as I gave in to the kiss, leaning into Shepard as he softly growled his response, a noise from the doorway startled me. As I stepped back, Shepard's fingers dragged over my skin. His hand remained lifted in the air between us, grasping nothing, and he looked like he was two seconds from closing the distance again.

I glanced at our audience.

Vena marched straight for me with MC following in her wake. Her gaze missed nothing. Especially not the delay between when I stepped away and when Shepard's hand returned to his side. But her expression was surprisingly closed off, leaving me to guess whether I'd get scolded or a pat on the back for kissing him.

When she reached me, she slipped her arm through mine and gave it a small tug.

"We have to go," she said. "Errands."

Errands? I gave her a questioning look, but the narrow-eyed gaze she sent back had me nodding.

"Right. Errands." I glanced at Shepard. "We'll see you at work."

"You're not leaving," he said.

"What? Why?" I asked.

"Everly, you just told me about a vampire who's been visiting you. Do you really think I'm going to let you two wander out of here with no protection? Vampires can't be trusted. Even with the smallest feeding, he can command you to his side at any time."

"Vampire?" MC questioned. He stared directly at Vena. "Let us help you."

Ignoring him, Vena leaned in and whispered, "Why did you tell him about Cross?"

"You know I can hear you, right?" Shepard folded his bulging arms over his chest as he eyed the two of us.

Vena sighed and met his gaze. "Listen, I'm sure we have the same opinion of vampires. The only good vampire is a dead vampire. But for whatever reason, Cross is different. It took me a while to trust him, but I do."

"How do we know you haven't been enslaved like Sierra?" Shepard said.

Vena frowned. "First of all, I haven't been fed on. Second, she's a lunatic who is trying to find her master in the bushes. That you would even put us in the same classification as Sierra is insulting. You know better than anyone what being enslaved looks like. Have we ever exhibited any of the signs?" She ticked her fingers as she said, "No obsessive behavior. No loss of appetite. No *unwarranted* explosive bouts of anger. No gaps in memory. And no unexplained absences."

She waited for Shepard's response.

He reached up and rubbed his jaw. Something he did when he was getting frustrated but trying to be reasonable.

"You said you trust me, Shepard," I said. "If you really do, then believe I have the sense in knowing who to trust, too. I don't hand it out like candy. He's earned it. Like you."

Vena grinned. "It's a trust circle. You trust Everly; Everly trusts Cross; and Cross trusts you to keep us safe. Now, are you going to be the one to break it?"

Shepard frowned at her.

"By trusting Everly, you believe that she knows what she's doing by trusting Cross," she said, pressing him.

Shepard muttered something under his breath. MC raised a brow at him but then smirked. *Did Shepard just swear at me?*

"I concede," Shepard finally said. "For now. But if you show one sign of being manipulated by him, I will find him and kill him. Do you understand?"

I quickly nodded. "I do. Enjoy the fudge."

"Let me walk you out," MC said.

"We know the way," Vena said with an edge to her tone.

"It's the least I can do for a guest," MC said, happily walking after us as Vena pulled me through the house and out the front door.

Once we were inside the car, she said, "Get me the hell out of here."

"What happened to make you so upset?" I asked once we reached the street and were headed away from Shepard's place.

"I'm so tired of Muscular Creep. No matter where I go or what I do, he's always around."

"Like in a stalker way or a friendly way?"

"Like a player simmering in the background and waiting for his opportunity. He's getting more aggressive in his flirting, and I barely refrained from decking him. Can't he take the hint that I don't like him? There will never be an opportunity for him."

"What happened to your infatuation with his muff mauler?"

She snorted a partial laugh, enjoying the pet name I'd been waiting to use.

"His pussy plunger–" I groaned and wrinkled my nose "– while glorious, isn't worth the entanglement. Moist Cornhole can take his mighty mallet back to California and leave me alone."

I stayed quiet for a moment and let Vena stew.

After a while, I asked, "Are you really mad at MC, or are you taking your frustrations out on him because you're worried about Anchor?"

She crossed her arms and looked out the window. "I suppose it might be worry," she muttered. "But that Monkey Cream still needs to back the hell off."

Normally, I didn't interfere with Vena's love life. She could handle any guy who came at her, but perhaps, with Anchor gone, MC's pursuit was more than she could handle. Pondering whether or not I should step in, my brain didn't immediately register the ping of an incoming text on my phone.

Vena picked it up to look at it.

"Who is it?" I asked.

She swore under her breath and began to read out loud.

"Let's trade information. Tell me about your fanged friend, and I'll tell you about your furry one."

CHAPTER NINE

"Who sent it?" I asked.

"Another unknown number. I am seriously regretting our trip to Sugar Mountain. Everything was fine before that."

To hear Vena say something like that struck a chord of fear in me.

"Hey, none of that. Regret doesn't change anything. Actions do. You taught me that. Now, you're going to text back, asking where and when and then we're going to text Cross and let him know someone's asking about him."

She was quiet as she typed the texts.

My phone buzzed again a minute later.

"Cross is headed to our house now," she said.

"Anything from–"

My phone buzzed.

"They want to meet at a club tonight at ten. Let me look where it is." She was quiet for a minute. "It's across the river. Twenty-five minutes from Blur and it's open until four am. I'll tell them we'll meet at two instead."

Part of what I'd loved about working at Blur was the earlier closing time. We were almost always out of there by one-thirty. Now that I knew what Shepard and his guys did, the hours made more sense.

"As long as Cross goes with us, it sounds like a plan," I said. "But you know ditching Doc is going to cause us problems, right? Especially after telling Shepard about Cross."

"Why did you change your mind about telling him?"

"Seeing Sierra like that and knowing how much you're worrying about Anchor. Not that I'm not worrying. I just didn't realize how much you liked him."

I glanced at her and saw her head tipped down toward the phone.

"I didn't know how much I liked him until he was gone," she said softly.

"We'll find him, and you can tell him," I said.

She lifted her head and gave me a sad, crooked smile. "Does that mean my V is ungrounded?"

"Only because you're exceptionally pathetic right now. But not when I'm in the house. You need to give me a heads up before you launch all your muchness at Anchor."

"Deal."

I pulled up in front of our house and caught movement in my rearview mirror. With a frown, I watched the truck park a block down, just on this side of the curve in our road.

Vena saw I was looking back and turned in her seat.

"Is that MC's truck?" she asked.

"Let it go," I said softly. "We have a few hours before our shift starts. You can watch some reruns of *The Other House* while I whip you up something sweet."

When we got out of the car, I noticed Doc's little electric number a block down in the other direction.

"Still want to let it go?" Vena asked.

"Yep. I dropped a bomb on Shepard, and he's freaking out. Do you know what he wanted to do?"

"What?"

"A strip search for bites."

Vena cackled so hard that she stumbled.

"Figured you'd enjoy that," I said.

"The man is devious. You still haven't said how you ended up lip-locked with him. It looked impressive, by the way."

I unlocked the door as I rolled my eyes at her.

"Don't ask."

She chuckled again and followed me inside. I didn't see Cross standing in the opening between the living room and the dining room until I'd tossed my purse on our couch.

His eyes were flickering between brown and black as he stared at me.

I stood there like an idiot for a moment. Vena cleared her throat and patted my back.

"Kissing brings nothing but trouble," she said. "That's probably why he has two of his guys following you."

Cross held up three fingers and nodded toward the back of the house.

Then he closed the distance between us and pulled me into his arms. The kiss he planted on me was absolutely toe-curling and would, without a doubt, cause Shepard to lose his mind when I went in to work later.

When Cross finally eased up and looked at me, I could barely remember my name.

"Am I the only hungry one here?" Vena called from the kitchen. "How about a sandwich?"

"Sounds good," I murmured, holding Cross' gaze. He still

hadn't said anything, and I wasn't entirely sure if the anger simmering in his gaze was due to the people surrounding my house or knowing Shepard and I had kissed.

Cross let out a long breath then leaned in to press a kiss to my forehead. Fingers entwined with mine, he led me to the kitchen, then took out his phone. He surprised me by sending a group text.

Cross: Is there any additional information you would care to share with me?

Me: I told Shepard you're a friend. He didn't believe me because he could smell that you'd kissed me. Then he kissed me based on my claim that friends can kiss.

Vena glanced at her phone and set down the mayo knife to add to the conversation.

Vena: He also offered to strip-search her before giving her the kiss that was panty-melting hot. Just in case you wanted details.

I shot Vena a dirty look.

Cross: I do not want details. Why did you tell Shepard about me?

Me: They have Sierra at their place. The vampires told her to kidnap Miles and get information about the werewolves. The fact that Gunther was kidnapped by vampires right after and that Anchor is still missing seems related, right? I was hoping you could talk to her again.

Cross: Did you think Shepard would give me permission to speak with her?

The look Cross gave me made me mad enough to drop my phone on the counter and walk away from him. He caught my wrist. Refusing to turn around, I tried tugging it free. He didn't loosen his hold. Instead, he moved to stand in front of me.

"Forgive me," he whispered. "But you have to know that wolves and vampires can never be friends, let alone work together. They are too stubborn for that."

"I agree Shepard is stubborn, but he also needs you to get through to Sierra so we can find Anchor."

"The only way that will happen is if Sierra is removed from their custody. Even if Shepard would grant me permission to talk to Sierra, I'm not stupid enough to walk into a wolf compound alone. I can deal with a couple of wolves, but not their entire pack."

I supposed it would be too much to ask them to break their long-lived hatred for each other for the greater good.

Cross' gaze whipped across the room at the front door.

"Text me later," he said.

He planted a kiss on my forehead and was down the hall and into my bedroom before I blinked.

The front door crashed open, and Doc and Tank rushed inside. Like a SWAT team, they searched the house and came up empty. Cross had escaped through my bedroom window again.

"He was here," Doc said. "I smell the vamp everywhere."

Tank stepped over to me, his nose twitching. "Everywhere. Including on Everly."

Doc came over, his nose wrinkling as his eyes scanned me, stopping at my mouth.

"If you start sniffing her butt, I'm calling Shepard," Vena said.

Doc frowned at her but took a step back. "Tell me what happened."

"I already told Shepard about Cross," I said. "He's a friend."

"A kissing friend?" Doc questioned.

"I think the kisses stopped being friendly a while ago. It's now a battle," Vena said. "Cross kissed her. Shepard kissed back. Now Cross again. Really, they should just cut out Ev as the middleman and kiss each other."

The men cringed as if Vena had nut-punched them.

"I'll have to tell Shepard," Doc said.

"About the kissing suggestion? I highly encourage it. While you're at it, tell him we also didn't agree to three wolves," Vena said. "I appreciate the security, but our neighbors are going to start calling cops with all the loitering vehicles out there."

Doc waved Tank out the door. He trailed after him as he brought his phone to his ear.

"Think Shepard will be over here soon?" Vena asked.

"I hope not."

"Why? He needs to cover up all traces of Cross. And judging from Cross' kiss, Shepard will have to put in some overtime."

I rolled my eyes. "Can we forget this and just watch *The Other House* reruns until our shift tonight?"

"I'm game for that." She slid a sandwich to me. "Sandwich O'Vena, madam."

It was ham and cheese. I took it gratefully along with a glass of water.

Sitting on the couch, I flipped on the TV and pulled up one of our favorite episodes of *The Other House*. As the opening credits rolled, Doc knocked on the door and let himself in.

"Do you mind if I hang out in here?" he asked. "Shepard wants Tank stationed outside."

Vena waved to the chair. "Have a seat. Do you want a Sandwich O'Vena?"

He raised a brow.

"It's ham and cheese," I said.

"Oh. Yes. Please."

"I'll make some for Tank, too." As Vena went to the kitchen, she said, "Pause it when the show starts. I don't want to miss anything."

When Vena was out of the room, Doc leaned toward me. "Are you sure you're okay?"

"I'm fine. I'm not bitten or thralled. There's no need to worry."

"You know we'll worry."

I paused the show at the opening scene. "Vena, it's on." I then glanced at Doc. "I can't stop you from worrying, but please trust me when I say that Cross is different."

Just like Shepard, Doc didn't believe me, but when Vena handed him a plate with three sandwiches stacked on it, he fell silent as he ate.

"We already know Donte is the wolf in this season," Vena said, settling in next to me. "I can't wait to know about the current season's wolf. I bet it's Chase."

"It's not him," Doc said. "It's--"

Vena launched at him, her hand pressed against his mouth as sandwiches flew into the air. Ham and cheese slicked with mayo dropped with a splat onto them and the couch.

Doc peeled ham from his cheek.

With a sigh, I paused the show again to get towels. When I restarted it, Doc wisely kept his mouth shut and ate the destroyed remnants of his sandwiches.

The next hour flew by without any Shepard appearance or text. I wasn't relieved since I knew I'd need to face him at work. The urge to go shower tugged at me, but I knew it wouldn't do any good. The damage had already been done. Doc had smelled Cross on me and reported it. No amount of washing would undo that. But wouldn't it be a little less of a slap to Shepard's nose if I didn't waltz into work smelling like fresh Cross?

"How many times are you going to sigh like that?" Vena asked. "You're distracting me from the goods."

The goods being the shirtless workout on the screen.

"Something wrong?" Doc asked.

"Yeah, something's wrong. You tattled on me, and I'm worried about what Shepard's going to say when I see him at Blur." Another sigh escaped me, and I slouched deeper into the couch.

"There-there," Vena said with mock sympathy. "Now that you've received some pity, shut it and pay attention. Donte's shirt is off."

I ended up skipping the second half and showering before work instead of drooling over Donte's abs with Vena. When I emerged with my hair styled and enough perfume to make a werewolf wheeze–Doc proven–I was a little calmer about facing Shepard.

Doc followed Vena and me into work, going so far as to linger by the lockers until we'd stowed our things.

"What in the heck do you think we're going to do? Run?" Vena asked with annoyance. "You know where we live, Doc. Besides, I'm here to collect my poor unloved bill-babies, not abandon them."

"Bill-babies?" Doc echoed.

"She means the money people leave on the tables," I said. "You know...tips."

"That's my girl," Vena said, slapping my ass. "Now, go make nice with the boss so we can both get paid."

Doc snorted and shook his head at her.

I rolled my eyes but did as she said and made my way to the meeting room. Surprisingly, Shepard didn't show his face until it was time to assign sections. And he didn't ask me to stay after either.

"Looks like the perfume worked," Vena mock whispered on the way down to our sections.

As soon as the doors opened and patrons started filling the tables, I forgot about being a participant in the Shepard-Cross kissing contest and focused on delivering drinks with a smile. The tip money rolled in like usual, and the hours on the clock ticked by unnoticed until the last call.

Vena's laugh rang out over the music as she served a group of fae. I glanced at them to make sure she was okay, but she had everything under control, keeping a careful distance even while delivering one of her signature flirty winks.

I turned to check my next table and caught sight of Jaws frowning at Vena from Anchor's usual spot. We needed to find him soon. He knew how not to judge the servers for their friendly smiles.

Shepard was at the bar when I came to collect my drink orders. He nodded to me as he set them on my tray. It felt normal. Normal was good. Why was I so nervous then? Could he smell my nervousness over the perfume? Was that why he was being nice?

I delivered the drinks and started to clean up as my tables emptied. Vena did the same and joined me at the bar to count out tips after the last patron left. Shepard was there, cleaning glasses, and smiled at Vena's happy squeal over a fifty she'd been given.

"What did you need to do for that?" Jaws asked from behind us.

Vena slowly turned, obviously hearing the same tone I had. I internally cringed and spun around to face Jaws.

"She learned how to be a people person," I said, keeping my tone cluelessly upbeat. "You should give it a try. It starts with a smile and a kind tone. It doesn't work well when she's hungry or tired though. Then she tries to draw blood. Are you thinking about being a cocktail concierge yourself?"

Jaws stared at me as I smiled at him. Behind us, Shepard chuckled. It wasn't filled with humor.

"I think you owe the ladies an apology, Jaws. They know how to do their jobs. Learn how to do yours. Am I clear?"

Jaws nodded once to Shepard, mumbled an apology to us and left.

"And on that note," Vena said, sliding the bartender split toward Shepard, "I think we should head out. Thanks for the tour this morning. See you again Wednesday. No closing your doors permanently."

"I won't," he said.

His gaze lingered on me as I quickly set my portion on the bar and followed her out.

Doc was already waiting by the back door. He didn't say anything as he got into his car. Neither did we. He did frown a little as Vena got in behind the wheel. I smiled and waved as I buckled just like normal, though.

As soon as she started out, she handed me her phone. I turned off the tracking. Then I did the same to mine. When she was almost to the highway, she coasted through a yellow and smirked as Doc stopped for it.

My phone buzzed.

Doc: Wait for me.

"Shepard is going to be so mad," I said as Vena sped up and took a turn that would lead us to After Curfew.

"It's always easier to apologize later than to ask 'Daddy' for permission to go," she said.

I rolled my eyes at her. "Did Cross confirm that he'll meet up there?"

She looked at me. "You just said to tell him someone was asking about him."

"I said as long as he's with us, I was okay with this meetup." My tone conveyed my frustration and disbelief.

"And I thought that's why he was coming to the house. To discuss how to time this. Not my fault the conversation was cut short."

She wasn't wrong, but it still annoyed me. I started typing up a text, but Vena stopped me.

"Everly, if you tell him now, he'll run straight there. What do you think will happen if the guy they're asking about shows up with us? They won't tell us what we need to know. You know that. The club is a public place. We're going during peak hours. We can get the information and text Cross on our way out."

"Blur is a public place, too," I said. "Remember how that almost wasn't safe?"

She sighed–a defeated sound. "You're right. Your call."

I hated it when she left stuff in my court. I couldn't blame her when things went horribly wrong then.

"Fine. We'll at least drive by," I said and watched the phone for the text or call I knew was going to come as soon as Doc rolled up to the house and discovered we were MIA.

It took less time than I anticipated. By the time we got to

the club, I had five missed calls and the same number of texts. But, at least, the club didn't look like a shady cover business like Juicy.

Feeling guilty for making everyone worry, I sent a reply text as Vena searched for a parking spot.

Me: We're running an errand. We'll head home soon.

Shepard: An errand at 1:30 a.m.?

I cursed under my breath as Vena zipped into a parking spot before anyone else could steal it.

"What?" Vena asked. "I parked fine."

"No. I told Shepard we are on an errand, and he's questioning it because of the time. We better hurry. It looked like a long line waiting to get in."

She grabbed my arm to stop me from getting out.

"Tell him we're going to the adult store, and ask if he has a preference on toys. It'll buy us time. And here." She dug into her meager cleavage and pulled out her knife. "Hide this for me. It looked like they were doing pat-downs to get in."

"Texting Shepard that we're going to an adult toy store is not helpful," I said, unbuttoning my top two buttons and tucking the closed blade between the girls.

"Oh, it could help a lot." She opened the door and stepped out.

My phone rang.

"It's Shepard," I said.

"Give him the adult store excuse, or he'll never leave you alone."

Me: Won't be able to hear you. Give me 20 minutes.

Hopefully, that would be enough to get him to stop hounding me. While I knew his reason for tracking me came out of safety, I should be allowed to go somewhere without him knowing every detail.

This was one of those times.

"We should have dressed up," Vena said, eyeing all the club girls in the long line. "I bet those bouncers only let in the pretty people."

"We were asked to come here," I said. "Let's see if we're on the list."

Vena skipped the line, which elicited angry responses from the people waiting.

"Maybe we should wait," I said.

"We don't have time."

She pulled me with her to the bouncer, who looked as big as some of the guys at Blur. He took one look at us and said, "Back of the line."

"We were told to meet people here," Vena said.

"Don't care. Back of the line."

"If you have a list, look at it," she said.

With an annoyed huff, the guy reached around him and grabbed a tablet. "Name."

"Everly and Vena."

He glanced up at us, really looking this time, and set the tablet aside.

"Arms up. Feet apart," he ordered.

He felt for weapons on both of us before grabbing the red rope barrier and letting us inside. "Go to the VIP lounge. Back of the house." On our way to the door, I heard him radio, "They're here. White shirts, black skirts."

The loud music that thumped through the speakers greeted us through the door, followed by a thick crowd that didn't give way. Vena had to push through, which was no easy task. This late, clubbers were already drunk and dancing. A man sloshed a drink, spilling it on my shoes.

"There has to be a better way," I yelled over the music.

If Vena heard me, she didn't stop to reply. We continued through to the dance floor, getting gyrated on by several men and a few women before we reached the other side. I smelled like sweat and alcohol.

We stopped at the roped entrance to the VIP lounge where another bouncer stood. He gave us a once-over. "Names."

"Vena and Everly," Vena said.

He let us through to a staircase that led to a loft. I hadn't been nervous before, due to the crowd, but as soon as my foot hit the first step, my stomach churned. We had no idea who was up there or what they wanted. We had one knife and no muscle. I felt like we were walking into Juicy all over again and we were going to die this time.

I grabbed Vena's hand. "This isn't a good idea."

CHAPTER TEN

"This place is full of humans," Vena said. "Look around. Not a fae or dwarf in sight. And the muscle isn't the furred variety. Plus, this is a weapon-free zone. We'll be okay."

Her words were calm and reassuring, but her sweaty hand as she pulled me up the stairs said something else.

At the top, we opened the door to a glassed-off room. Comfortable black leather couches lined the three walls, and groups of chairs took up the middle of the VIP lounge. The music was muffled, giving the people in the room a reprieve from the deafening speakers.

Most of them had turned to look at us when we'd entered. Vena confidently scanned the room.

Did she think our contact was just going to stand up and wave? I thought as my gaze swept the space.

At the back of the room, two men stuck out from the rest. They were hard not to notice.

Both wore black leather pants and unbuttoned black shirts, making their bodies blend together as they sat in an oversized chair under the dim lighting. The only difference between the two men that I could tell at this distance was that one had long dark hair and the other wore cat ears on his head and a diamond collar around his neck.

I tried not to gawk at their public display of horniness as the one with the cat ears lowered himself to rub his face on the other man's chest, his tongue coming out in flicks. His hand rubbed more than just chest as it dipped low into the shadows their bodies created. It was then I noticed the cat tail on the butt of his leather pants.

Before the cat-man could get too carried away, the long-haired man coaxed him back up to resume his attention elsewhere. The cat-man's grazing fingers followed his mouth up the other man's lean body.

The long-haired man watched us with eyes painted in black eyeliner and mascara spiking above and below his eye in theatrical goth style.

In a show of possessiveness, the cat-man curled onto the man's lap, wrapping his arm around his lover and threading his fingers through the man's hair. Cat-man tipped his head to whisper into his ear.

Goth-man gave a nod and then petted the cat, murmuring to him. Eventually, the cat relaxed enough to begin licking the man's neck.

The long-haired man gestured for us to join them.

"Is that him?" I asked Vena, hoping we could talk to someone who wasn't playing with a human cat.

"Won't know until we ask," she said.

She started forward. Resisting the urge to grab the back of her shirt, I followed closely.

The man being licked and kissed smirked at me when we reached them.

"Everly," he said. "It is a pleasure to finally meet you. You look delicious. My name is V--"

The cat-man bit him. While the bite drew blood, it didn't seem to faze V. However, it screamed jealousy. And when the cat-man turned his head to hiss at me, showing long fangs, it screamed vampire, too.

"Shit," Vena said, shoving her hands between my boobs. The knife was out and unsheathed a second later.

V inhaled deeply and chuckled. "You've saved us a truly concerning dilemma, Vena. Thank you."

"Fuck you and die," she said, holding her knife out.

He laughed outright. "You think you'll kill us with that paltry blade? You're adorable."

I grabbed Vena's arm and tugged it down.

"What was the dilemma?" I asked with false calm.

Humor danced in his eyes. "Oh, I like you."

"You might want to tone down your words of affection. Your cat doesn't appreciate them, and neither do I."

The cat stopped growling low at me and smiled. It was a hundred times creepier than the first tooth display. Probably because of the blood painting his mouth. He slowly licked it off.

"Pet," the cat said, "you were right. She is unique and interesting. I can see why she caught Cross' interest."

V, who was apparently nicknamed Pet, stroked a hand down the cat-man's back.

"You know I'm rarely wrong, Master."

The cat was the master, and V was the pet? Weird. I tried not to let their obvious role reversal break my brain.

"Before we can tell you anything about Cross, we need some kind of proof you know something about Anchor," I said.

The whole room started laughing, proving just how thoroughly screwed we were. While the rest of the club might be human, the VIP section wasn't looking that way.

"Anchor? The missing werewolf that your Master has been searching for?" V asked. We know nothing about him."

"Master?" I said at the same time Vena said, "Then why did you–"

Glass shattered behind us, flooding the space with loud music and shouting.

I spun around, but it was too slow compared to how quickly Cross moved. He caught me in his arms, his gaze black and full of rage as it swept the room.

"Leave or die," he growled at the onlookers.

Half the people in the room bolted through the broken glass doorway.

V moved Master off his lap and stood to clap. "Well done, Cross. An impressive display of power."

Cross left me and had V by his throat in an instant. His nails broke the skin, sending rivulets of blood down V's neck. V continued to grin at Cross.

My phone picked that moment to ring.

"If that's Shepard, answer the phone and tell him to send his pack," Cross said. "There's a vampire infestation here."

I scrambled to answer the call as several of the vampires hissed.

"Shepard, we're at After Curfew," I said in a rush. "It's another vampire nest. Cross says to send your pack."

Shepard swore in my ear. Someone yelled, and a hand closed over my shoulder.

My gasp barely left my lips before Cross was tearing the vampire away from me with an order to close my eyes. I did and held onto Vena as I shook in my sensible waitressing shoes.

Why hadn't I called Cross first? Why? I chanted the question in my head and tried not to hear the squelching sounds.

"Everly," Cross said, cupping my face. "Where are you hurt?"

"Hurt?" I echoed, opening my eyes.

He had a drop of blood on his cheek.

"You were hurt," he said. "That's how I knew where to find you."

"No," I said, shaking my head, unable to look away from that drop of blood. "I'm not hurt."

He inhaled slowly, and his gaze drifted to the front of my shirt. His head followed. With his face dipping to my cleavage, I finally saw the room. It was trashed hard, and there were three dead vampires on the floor. None of them were Pet or his Master.

Then I felt Cross' tongue on my skin. My eyes went wide, and I turned my head to look at Vena.

She grinned at me. "My bad. I think my knife scraped you on the way out."

I pushed Cross' head away from my cleavage, and he stumbled back a step like he was drunk. Vena grinned and picked up my phone, which I'd dropped. I saw my call with Shepard hadn't disconnected and cringed as I held it to my ear and watched Cross shake his head.

"Shepard, the vampires are gone, and we're fine. We're leaving now and heading straight home. I'll let you know when we get there."

I hung up without waiting for his reply.

"Yes," Cross said. "You're right. We should leave quickly."

He grabbed my hand and ushered me down the stairs. Vena was right behind me. The dance floor was empty now even though the music still played.

Outside was chaos. People were still running around, and some were recording in another direction and saying things like, "Did you see how fast they moved?" while we jogged to the car.

Cross helped me into the front seat then took the keys from Vena. We pulled away just as the sound of sirens rang out in the distance.

"Who was that guy?" I asked.

"His name is Vivian Di Rossi," Cross said.

"What did he mean by, 'You're choosing the wrong side'?" Vena asked from the back seat.

"Who said that?" I asked, realizing I'd missed something.

Cross sighed. "He meant that I was siding with the werewolves over my own kind. Why were you there, Everly?"

I looked out the window, unwilling to admit my stupidity had almost gotten me killed *again*.

"It was the meetup for that text I messaged you about. The one from someone saying they would exchange information on Anchor for information on you," Vena said. "We weren't going to tell them anything about you, though, Cross. I promise."

He gave a dry laugh.

"They already learned what they needed."

I turned my head to look at him.

"What did they need?"

"Proof of how important you are to me, Everly. And now they know."

"That's all they wanted to know?" Vena asked. "They said it was an exchange."

"Are you surprised?" Cross asked. "You're dealing with vampires."

"We didn't know they were vampires until we got there," I said.

"You should have told me you were going tonight," Cross said. "At the very least, I could have scouted the location for you." He didn't yell or look mad. Well, maybe just a little.

He reached over, taking my hand and bringing it to his lips. "What would have happened if I was too late? Had they been after your blood and not information, I wouldn't have gotten to you in time."

I glanced back at Vena, who shrank in her seat.

"But you got there in time," Vena said.

I felt the curl of Cross' lips as he kissed the back of my hand again.

"Why did I beat the wolves there?" he asked. "I thought they were tracking you."

"We turned off the tracking," I mumbled, hoping he wouldn't lecture me, too. I already knew I was going to get an earful from Shepard.

Cross' grip tightened on my hand but not enough to hurt, just enough to know that he was upset.

"I'm sorry," I said.

With a sigh, he gave my hand one last kiss and then released it. Pulling over to the side of the road before we reached the house, Cross looked at me. "Promise me that you'll inform me when you do things like this. I'm not here to stop you. I'm here to protect you. I can't do that if you don't tell me anything."

When I nodded, he glanced down at my cleavage. "Is the cut healed? You still have the faint scent of blood."

I glanced down and shifted my girls to get a better view. "Looks okay. Just a spot on my bra."

"Wasted," he muttered and then opened the car door. "Don't go anywhere alone. Stay with me or the pack. Never alone. Understand?"

I nodded again.

Cross leaned over, his hand wrapping around the back of my neck as he pulled me into a kiss that had Vena scolding. I only heard a little of it as Cross did his best to make me forget about the dead bodies in the club.

When he released me, he said, "Promise me you'll tell me your plans so I can help you."

I nodded once more, unable to do anything else but be Cross' bobblehead.

When he stood from the car, Vena slipped into the driver's seat and closed the door. Cross stepped out of the way so she could pull back onto the road.

My phone rang. "It's Shepard." I swiped to answer. "We'll be home in a second."

I quickly turned the tracking on both our phones to prove it.

As Vena turned the corner, we saw Shepard at our doorstep with the phone to his ear. He paced back and forth in front of the door, his fingers threading through his dark blonde hair.

When he saw our car, he stilled. A tingle of trepidation ran through me as our gazes met through the windshield.

"Want me to drive around the block?" Vena asked softly.

Shepard slowly shook his head, proving that he'd heard, and I swallowed hard.

"I don't think that will be a good idea."

She parked in front of the house, and Shepard was there to open my door.

"Thank you for making the right choice for a change," he said.

"Hey," Vena said.

He gave her a sharp look.

"If I were to start asking questions, would I discover that what happened tonight was because of your influence?" he asked.

I frowned, not liking the way he was talking to her. Or the way she looked down.

"I wish Anchor were here, too," he said softly, which stopped me from calling him out on his bullying behavior.

"That's why we went there," I said. "We had a lead on information regarding Anchor. Unfortunately, it didn't pan out."

He inhaled slowly, radiating barely contained rage.

"I can smell blood and vampire on you. I'm going to need more than 'it didn't pan out,' Everly."

"You're right. Let's go inside." I didn't wait for his approval before making a beeline for the lit-up house.

When I opened the door, Doc stood from his place on the couch. His gaze shifted from me to the person behind me. I didn't look to see if it was Shepard; I already knew it was.

"I think I'll make us all a nice cup of tea," I said, dumping my purse near the door.

Shepard caught my wrist and spun me around. Two

seconds later, I was backed into a wall with an up-close view of Shepard's rapidly rising and falling chest.

"No. You're going to start talking. Now."

"Hey," Vena said, sounding angry. "Everly didn't do anything to deserve–"

Shepard's attention snapped to Vena. "You're next."

"We get it," I said, struggling to control my rising temper. "We screwed up. We were *there*."

"Take your clothes off," he said.

"What?"

"This is too many times, Everly, that you've come back from a close call, smelling like the same vampire and offering half-baked excuses for why. Strip so I can see how bad it is?"

"It's none of your business how bad it is," I said, offended and angry.

Something flashed in Shepard's eyes. "Strip, or I'll end up tearing your uniform, Everly."

"I think there's a misunderstanding," Vena said. "Everly, he's not talking about your bloody bra. He still thinks you were bitten and under Cross' influence. And I'm happy to strip for you, Shepard, even though I don't smell like Cross. I'm not his flavor, apparently."

"Not helping, Vena," I said, holding Shepard's stare. "And she's right. I thought you were talking about my bra."

I unbuttoned another button to show him the very small blood stain on the center of my work pushup. His gaze locked on my cleavage as he inhaled.

"Doc, call Moreen. If Everly doesn't want to show me, she can show her."

I frowned. "I just showed you!"

"All of it."

"I'm not showing anyone all of it," I said, crossing my arms.

"It smells like you already did."

I seethed, my temper reaching a level typically reserved for Vena on one of her don't-fuck-with-me period days.

"I'm about two seconds from kneeing you and finding out if you yelp like a dog or whimper like a man, Shepard."

Some of the anger left his gaze, and his lips quirked slightly.

"Is that so?"

"I appreciate that you care about us. Truly, I do. We need that extra level of concern lately. And given what's happened with Sierra, I absolutely understand your fear that my brain's been tampered with. But if that's the case, monitor me just like you do Miles and Sierra. I'm betting neither one of them has been degraded with a strip search."

Shepard exhaled heavily and shifted his gaze to the right.

"Neither one of them means as much to me as you do, Everly."

"Then don't do something that will push me away."

"I'm trying not to." He backed up a step and ran his hand through his hair. "Okay. Fine. Starting now, you're under twenty-four-seven watch. No more separate cars. No more closed bedroom doors at night. Your guard is going to be within four feet of you at all times."

"Well, that's going to make going to the bathroom a little awkward," Vena mumbled, earning a warning look from Shepard.

"No problem," I said. "We can do that."

"And there will be six men watching the house at all times. I could smell the vampire's scent trail all over the place out there."

Vena's expression lost its lingering humor. "Are you kidding me right now? You're wasting that many people here? Because of Cross? We already told you he's fine. You should be using your manpower to search for Anchor."

"You should have thought of that before pulling tonight's stunt," Shepard said.

Their gazes locked. Both were too stubborn for their own good.

I headed to the kitchen. "Vena, you use the bathroom first."

Vena pivoted on her heel and marched to the bathroom.

Turning on the faucet, I filled the kettle and started heating it while I fished out the nighttime calming tea. Everyone was going to need a strong cup of it before bed.

I felt Shepard watching me from the kitchen entry but didn't look at him or talk to him as I went about my task. I hoped that meant he had enough sense to know when to back off.

"Everly, talk to me," Shepard said.

"I already agreed to become a virtual prisoner. What else do you want from me?"

"For you to not put yourself in danger. To not smell like vampire every time I see you."

"I agree to the first. And I hope you know I've never once purposely put myself in danger. The last few weeks have just been really unlucky for me.

"But I don't agree with your second request. Cross is the only vampire I talk to, and whether you like it or not, he's been helping me and your pack. He doesn't bite me or compel me. He was the one who rescued us tonight, and he also said to tell you about the infestation at the club, which has been two clubs that have been taken down because of him. And by doing so, he has ostracized himself from the vampires."

"Everly--"

"He picked his side by rescuing me and outing them, Shepard. Cross will probably be hunted now by his people. I don't want him being hunted by you, especially since he's been helping you. And he's told me repeatedly to trust you; that you will keep me safe. He doesn't have any prejudices against you like you have for him."

"Everly, you can't trust vampires. He probably has an ulterior motive for helping you."

"I am one comment away from shutting down this conversation and quitting Blur."

Shepard blinked and then raised his palms. "We'll table this discussion for the morning when we've all slept and have had time to reflect."

The kettle whistled, and I turned my back on him while I poured the water into mugs and dropped tea bags into them.

"Where is Doc?" I asked, handing one of the mugs to Shepard.

"He'll patrol outside."

"Who is inside?"

Shepard hesitantly blew steam from his cup. "Me."

I considered him for a moment. "I'm not stupid or ignorant. I choose to ignore what I don't want to deal with. Before now, it was the game you and Cross have been playing with me. Kissing me where the other one kissed me. Touching me so the other one knows and can smell their scent on me.

"Believe my warning, Shepard. I'm not going to be a chew toy between you and Cross. I'm taking my cup of tea and going to bed. I'll leave the door open, but I swear if you start checking me for bite marks while I'm sleeping, you will learn what fear is. Got it?"

He dipped his head in acknowledgment, and I carried Vena's cup to her room to set it on the nightstand. Just as I was leaving, she came out of the bathroom.

"It's all yours," she said.

"Thank you. I put tea on your nightstand."

"You're my favorite roommate." She leaned and whispered, "Who is my other roommate tonight?"

At my scowled expression, she gave a nod. "Want to bunk with me tonight?"

Ordinarily, I would have said no. I liked my bed, and Vena tended to spin like an alligator catching its prey. Only, the prey was her blanket, and I would be left to spoon her for warmth if I got cold. But after the deaths at the club and the argument with Shepard, I could use a little BFF time. I'd just make sure to wear my spring pajamas.

"You can tell Shepard he can use my bed if he wants to," I said and placed my cup on her nightstand as well. "I'll go shower."

Maybe once I didn't smell like Cross, Shepard's unhinged mind could reset.

I hurried through my shower, looking forward to drinking my tea and sleeping.

However, Shepard was waiting outside of the bathroom door, blocking my path to Vena's room.

CHAPTER ELEVEN

"You don't need to run from me, Everly," Shepard said with a hint of regret. "I'm worried about you. I don't want you to feel like a prisoner; I just want you to be safe. If sleeping with your door open when I'm here makes you that uncomfortable, then close it."

I could see the worry in his eyes and the sincerity. It was hard to stay mad in the face of either of them.

"I'm not running," I said. "And I do feel safe with someone sleeping on our sofa. But I agree with you that I've had a few too many run-ins lately and could use a little cuddle time. Vena doesn't mind."

Vena's door closed loudly.

I leaned out of the bathroom to frown at it.

"If she's not willing, I am," Shepard said softly.

My pulse skipped as I tipped my head to look up at him.

"Uh, I think I can manage on my own until she's in the mood," I said. "But thanks for the offer."

His eyes glinted as he nodded. "You know where to find me if you need me."

"Yep."

I watched him retreat to the living room and hurried to my room before he turned off the lights.

When I picked up my phone to scold Vena, I saw a text from Cross.

Cross: Sleeping?

Me: Not yet. Why?

Cross: I'm concerned and want to make sure you're all right after everything you witnessed this evening.

Me: I'm fine and well-guarded.

Cross: I noticed. Six wolves outside.

Me: Yeah, and Shepard inside.

Cross: Good. Then I know you'll be safe.

I snorted then froze and glanced at the open doorway. Hearing nothing, I looked back down at my phone.

Cross: Stay with Shepard and his people, and stop going places alone with Vena. Let me look for her missing wolf. I'll be in touch. Sleep well, Everly.

I smiled slightly at the message then set my phone aside and snuggled into my bed, feeling safe.

MORNING LIGHT relentlessly battered my eyelids. I groaned and rolled over.

"What is it with men watching her sleep?" Vena asked.

I bolted upright, looked at the spot next to me then at my open door where Shepard leaned against the jamb. He sipped coffee while Vena peered around him to roll her eyes at me. In the meaningful glance she gave me then Shepard, I could read her mind.

You missed the perfect opportunity to tap that, Everly. When the boss wants to give you a bonus, you grab your ankles and take it like a big girl.

I frowned at her. "Go away. I'm hearing your lecture in my head."

"Good. You deserve it."

She left, and Shepard arched a brow at me. "Who else has been watching you sleep?"

"Cross has on a few occasions. I don't know if sleeping fascinates him or..." I shook my head, and Shepard looked down at his cup.

"Or if you fascinate him?" Shepard asked. "I think we both know the answer to that."

After Cross' confession yesterday, I did, but I didn't want to say that to Shepard. I'd been honest enough already before my cup of coffee.

"Was everything quiet last night?" I asked, getting out of bed.

"For the most part. A phone started ringing before seven. I checked both of yours. It was Vena's parents asking if she had time to go over today." He pushed off the door frame. "I'll let you get dressed."

I grabbed my phone on the way to the bathroom to see if Vena had texted me. Instead I saw a text from Cross.

Cross: I understand.

Confused, I scrolled back a bit, and my mouth dropped open.

Cross: Keep me appraise of your plans for the day once you're awake.

Me: She claims you're not like the others. If that's true, leave her to me.

Cross: She's a smart, independent woman, capable of making her own choices, even when we strongly disagree with them. Rather than try to restrain who she is, find ways to keep her safe.

Me: That's what I'm trying to do. Your kind keeps trying to kill her. My kind protects her.

Cross: I am not my kind and am uninterested in hurting Everly or controlling her will. Also, one of your guards fell asleep last night. The one in the red truck. Be more diligent, or leave so I can protect her.

Me: Over my dead body.

Cross: I understand.

They had a pissing match using my phone? I shook my head and brushed my teeth.

After I finished, I found Vena in the kitchen. She shoved a bowl of dry cereal in front of Shepard. I snatched the bowl away and put it on the counter as I foraged the cupboards and refrigerator for something better. I wasn't sure if he deserved a better breakfast than dry cereal, but *I* did.

"Are your parents back from their archaeology trip?" I asked as I grabbed bread, eggs, cream cheese, and jam.

She peered around me at the counter. "Are you making French Toast roll ups?"

"Yes. Now, focus. What did your parents say?"

"They're back in town and want us to come over for dinner. We can pick up Miles on the way. I already let him know that his presence is going to be required and no fairies allowed."

"Where do your parents live?" Shepard asked.

Vena frowned at him. "Far away and not near any vampire infestations. Instead of worrying about us, find Anchor."

I placed my hand on her arm. She shook it off and left the kitchen.

"I only want to make sure the area is safe," Shepard said.

"I know. And I appreciate it, but you've been crossing a few lines. One of them was having an argument with Cross on my phone."

He muttered something then targeted me with his light grey eyes. "I was making a round through the house. When I stopped in your room to check your window because of the broken screen, a text came through. I wasn't looking to be nosey. I just thought you might get backlash from last night's incident. Then I saw it was from Cross and--" He glanced away and flexed his hand. "I need to talk to Doc. I'll be back."

I watched as he escaped through the front door and knew it was going to be another long day.

Focusing on what I loved, creating delicious foods, I cracked a couple of eggs and beat the hell out of them.

Vena returned to the kitchen a few minutes later. The contrite look on her face and the apologetic smile she gave me had me shaking my head at her.

"I get it. You're worried about Anchor. Don't forget that Shepard is, too. He's worried about us all. Try to be more understanding about where he's coming from when he goes in uber protector mode."

She sighed. "Yes, Mom."

Vena managed to play nice when Shepard reappeared and joined us for breakfast. She said she'd clean up, and Shepard offered to help. Leaving them to make peace, I went to my room to get ready for the day.

Having a day off was rare. If Vena didn't talk me into some weird outing like rock climbing or hiking, I typically spent time researching recipes and experimenting in the kitchen. With our guards, I wasn't sure I was up for creative time in the kitchen. So I settled in to stream a movie on my phone.

Twice, I felt Shepard peek in on me, but each time I paused the movie and looked up, he was gone.

Hunger and boredom drove me from my room around lunch. I knocked on Vena's door.

"I'll be holding your sandwich ransom in the kitchen," I said.

The door swung open before I reached the dining room.

"I negotiate with terrorists," she said. "What do you need to make me a club sandwich with extra bacon?"

I snorted. "Bacon, tomato, and sliced turkey. You're getting a grilled cheese."

She made sad sounds. "We should go to Miles early. I bet Mom already went shopping."

Vena liked food as much as any other person, which meant she wasn't asking to go to her mom's because she was hungry. She was bored, too.

"Sure," I said, already pulling out what we needed for a "fancy" grilled cheese.

Keeping with the tenuous peace we'd established, I made three sandwiches and handed Shepard his.

Vena cleaned up again while I grabbed my phone from my bedroom.

Me: We're heading to Vena's parents.

Cross: Alone?

Me: With Miles.

Vena stood by the door, waiting for me. I grabbed my purse from the table and noticed Shepard was already outside on the front lawn.

"I wonder if they brought me back any souvenirs," Vena said as she happily left the house and headed to the car.

I prayed there were no souvenirs. Any time her parents went on their archeology digs, they brought back things that should have never been unearthed. The shrunken heads from a few years ago still horrified me.

Shivering at the thought of the tiny shriveled heads, I rubbed my hands over my arms.

"Are you okay?" Shepard asked. "Perhaps you should stay home."

"I'm fine. I was just thinking about all the horrible souvenirs Vena has gotten over her lifetime."

"Horrible?" Vena squawked. "Do you think the statue was horrible?"

"It was a fertility statue given to a sixteen-year-old who liked to tease boys. Yes, it was horrible."

"What about the stone tablet?" she demanded.

"You mean the stone tablet that had a curse written on it?"

Vena tapped her finger to her chin as she thought. "What about the sixteenth-century bowl?"

I sighed. "That was an Asian bong, and it had penises engraved on it. Not a good gift for their fourteen-year-old daughter."

"I don't know. It came in handy as a change jar."

Shepard cleared his throat. "We should get going."

"We?" Vena asked. "There is no we. It's only Everly and me."

"Until I find the vampires from last night, I'm staying with you. That's not negotiable. You already agreed to it."

Vena crossed her arms. "My family's house is out in the middle of nowhere. We don't have to worry about vampires."

"You don't think they can track you there?" Shepard asked with a laugh.

Vena pressed her lips together. We were likely thinking the same thing. Cross hadn't had any problems tracking me either. While I didn't believe any vampire there last night had gotten a taste of my blood, the truth was that I *had* bled. Did we want to take that chance? Not just with me but with her family too.

"I'll let you go with us on one condition," Vena said.

"What is it?"

"Tell me what you're doing to find Anchor, and promise to keep me in the loop at each step."

"That's pack business, Vena," he said gently.

She grinned. "According to you, we're like family. And family means pack. If it didn't, why else would you have seven people here watching over us? Or are you saying Everly isn't a part of your pack anymore and doesn't need to follow your orders?"

And that was why it didn't pay to argue with Vena. She knew how to twist a person's words. Great when it was used on my behalf. Kinda sucked on the rare occasion she used it against me.

Shepard narrowed his eyes at Vena. "I stand by what I said."

"Good. Then you can tell me how you're going to find Anchor on the way to get Miles." She opened the backseat door. "Please make yourself comfortable."

He glanced at the backseat and then at us. "We'll take my SUV."

"No. We're taking my car so my parents don't think something's going on," Vena said with a smirk. "What's wrong? Don't want to be seen in my car?"

He scratched his jaw. "We'll take your car, but I'll drive."

She smirked again. "Neither of us will want to answer the questions my parents will ask if they see you driving the car they bought their precious daughter. Besides, you don't know where we're going."

He glowered at her before proceeding to wedge himself into the backseat. Vena closed the door with a chuckle and practically skipped to the driver's door.

"Can you text Miles that we're on our way?" she asked me as we pulled away from the curb.

"On it."

"Are you in a hurry?" Shepard asked.

"Yes, for you to start telling me what you're doing to find Anchor."

I twisted in my seat to look back at Shepard. His gaze held mine for a moment before shifting to Vena's in the mirror.

"Everything," Shepard said. "I am doing everything in my power to find Anchor. I know you're worried about him, but please don't do reckless things to find him on your own. Anchor would never forgive himself if you were hurt attempting to locate him."

"Ouch. You go right for the guilt knife," she muttered.

My phone buzzed. I looked down at it expecting a message from Miles.

Cross: Is there a reason Shepard is going to Vena's parents with you?

Me: Yeah, he doesn't trust Vena farther than he could throw her.

Cross: Understandable.

The phone disappeared from my hands, and I twisted to

scowl back at Shepard as he tapped out a message on my phone.

"If you want to talk to him that badly, take his number and use your own phone. I don't appreciate you using mine."

Shepard glanced up at me as he continued typing.

"I'll take his number, but I doubt he'd answer me."

"You might be surprised," I said.

"Yeah, you're both stalkery and overly interested in where Everly is and who she's with. Lots of bro bonding potential there," Vena said.

I shot her a look.

She shrugged. "This is why I don't go for aggressive men. Fun to look at and maybe great in bed, but they try to take over your life. Might want to reconsider swimming in that pool."

Shepard handed me my phone. "I apologize, Everly. I've done as you suggested and have his number now."

I took my phone and looked at the messages.

Me: Everly thinks she can trust you. If you've compelled her to believe that, I promise you'll regret ever looking at her. If, on the off chance, you truly are different, I'm giving you a chance to prove it. Meet with me in person. I'll text you from my phone since she's upset that I'm using her phone.

My gaze flew to Shepard's. "No. No way are you meeting him in person."

"What?" Vena asked, glancing at me. "What's going on?"

"Nothing to worry about," Shepard said.

"Shepard wants to meet Cross in person," I said.

Vena snorted. "Cross isn't that dumb."

Shepard's phone buzzed. He looked down at it and scowled.

I snatched his phone out of his hands, well aware that he let me.

Bloodsucker: *laughing emoji* I'm not stupid enough to agree to meet with you in person. Your kind likes to multiply and chase. Plus, Everly would be very disappointed in me if I bruised any of you.

"I'm not sure I agree with him," I said, tossing Shepard's phone back to him as Vena pulled up in front of Miles' apartment.

The front door opened, and Miles jogged out with his research satchel over his shoulder and a grin on his face.

"You made good time," he said as he got in.

He glanced at Shepard.

"Miles, that's Shepard," I said. "You met him briefly when we rescued you."

Miles held out a hand to Shepard. "I really appreciate all you've done for me."

Shepard shook his hand and smiled. "You're welcome."

They chatted a bit as Vena headed for her parents'. I snuck a glance at my phone and considered sending Cross an apology text. Not wanting to start anything up with Shepard again, however, I slipped my phone into my purse and sat back to listen to Miles gently probe Shepard for werewolf information.

As Miles went into research mode, my attention drifted away. Too wrung out to care about pack life, hierarchy, and population, I leaned my head back and watched out the window.

Finally, Vena pulled down the familiar long stretch of road that led to the Hunter house. Trees shaded the car from the afternoon sun, giving my eyes a reprieve from the glare I'd been squinting against.

I glanced back to find Shepard had visibly relaxed. A near smile was on his face as he looked out at the untouched nature. I realized in that instant that D.C. might be his home, but Shepard was more comfortable away from the city. And perhaps away from the burden of responsibilities. Out here, he only had to worry about Vena, Miles, and me.

Vena parked in the driveway and hopped out as the front door of the house opened and her parents hurried out.

Dana and Garner Hunter were lean and fit from their physical work at dig sites. If I had to labor under the scorching sun, I'd be burnt to a lobster red, but they were tan as if they had spent a week at the beach instead of whatever desert they'd been combing.

Mrs. Hunter rushed to hug Vena and then Miles. Mr. Hunter gave me a quick hug before Mrs. Hunter bumped him out of the way and wrapped her arms around me, squeezing me until I gasped.

"Honey, let her go before she pops," Mr. Hunter said.

"I'm just so happy to see everyone," she said as she released me and turned her gaze on Shepard. "Did we get a new son?"

"Mom, this is Shepard," Vena said. "He's Everly's...friend." Vena smirked at me. "Shepard, these are my parents, Dana and Garner Hunter."

Mrs. Hunter arched a brow at me then eyed Shepard.

"Nice to meet you, Mr. and Mrs. Hunter," Shepard said.

Mrs. Hunter's eyes lit, and she grinned at me. "Where did you meet? I want to hear all the details. Any plans to get married yet? You know my rules on marriage."

Vena nodded. "If you don't think you could live in a remote

corner of the globe with only him as a companion for the next year, you'd better keep your ring finger free. Dead men are better than the wrong men."

"Dead men as in mummies," I clarified to Shepard.

Mrs. Hunter smiled at Vena. "I knew one of my lectures would stick. I'm glad it's that one."

"I think you'll need to tell it to Everly again, just so it sinks in," Vena said with a wink aimed at me.

"No need. Shepard and I are only friends," I said.

Mrs. Hunter waved off my protest. "You don't have to be embarrassed with me. It's good that you found a partner." She took Shepard's arm and led him to the house. "I have a few warnings I'd like to give you. Do you know, by marrying Everly, you'll have Vena as a lifelong squatter?"

"Mom! You're saying that like I'm a leech!" Vena hurried to follow.

"I have plenty of room at my house," Shepard said with a grin aimed at me.

Mr. Hunter clapped a hand on Miles' shoulder and steered him to the house. "What have you been researching lately?"

I shook my head and followed everyone inside.

Before I made it to the door, I heard a cracking noise like the snap of a branch. Scanning the tree line, I didn't see anyone or any animals.

Not brave enough to stay and find out where the noise came from, I ran into the house and nearly knocked Miles' bag off his shoulder when I bumped into him.

CHAPTER TWELVE

VENA'S PARENTS LED US TO THE LIVING ROOM AS THEY ASKED their kids what they'd been up to. Neither Vena nor Miles mentioned vampires or werewolves. Both stuck with the mundane happenings like finally dragging me to the Shadow Market and how I'd jumped at every little thing.

While they laughed, I could tell that Shepard was less amused even though he smiled. So, I redirected the conversation to focus on Mrs. and Mr. Hunter's last dig. They readily grasped the topic and produced the prerequisite souvenirs. The mummified finger they gave Vena was supposed to bring good luck and had me internally gagging.

Thankfully, my phone buzzed with a message, saving me from having to share fake appreciation for it.

Cross: How well do you trust Shepard?

Me: That's a weird question coming from the guy who told me that I was safe in Shepard's company.

Cross: Do you trust him to leave your virtue intact?

I almost laughed out loud as I read his message again. Virtue? Did he think I was still a virgin?

Smothering my humor, I glanced at Vena. She was still focused on her finger. Shepard wasn't, though. He was watching me closely with a trace of concern in his expression. I shook my head to indicate everything was fine and slipped my phone into my pocket to answer later.

"Do you think what you've found will pay out?" Miles asked his dad.

"It will, but I'm not sure it'll pay as much as we'd hoped. The dwarves who were interested in the mining maps sounded hedgy when we contacted them. You know how this game works. Now, we wait to see and hope there are multiple interested parties to drive up the price."

Miles nodded and Mrs. Hunter caught my eye.

"Would you and Vena mind giving me a hand in the kitchen?"

"Sure," I said, standing. Vena made a face and sighed loudly but followed.

As soon as we were in the kitchen, which Mrs. Hunter seemed to think was out of Shepard's hearing range, she turned on me with a grin.

"He is gorgeous, Everly. You definitely have an eye for men. Any chance you can help Vena?"

"Mom," Vena said, drawing it out as she sat at the island.

"What? Your taste in men is horrible. You always go for the flirts. Find one that will stick with you."

"What happened to a dead man being better?" Vena asked.

"They're better than the wrong man, but the right one is the goal," her mom said. "Having a partner alongside you out in the field is worth more than a thousand dwarf mines. And you've always loved a good hunt. This time, try for a man."

Her mom moved to the fridge, and Vena made a help-me-out-here face at me. I pulled my phone from my pocket and slid it toward her as I accepted a fresh bunch of snap peas from Mrs. Hunter.

"Vena's not mature enough for serious yet," I said. "But she's getting there. She can make my coffee just the way I like it now, do her own laundry, and even makes her bed."

"I'm done with both of you," Vena grumbled as she typed on my phone.

I laughed with Mrs. Hunter before reassuring her.

"Vena's not purposely going after Mr. Wrong. Mr. Right has just been a little slow in showing up. I have a feeling that'll change soon though."

"Oh?" her mom asked, giving me her full attention.

Vena gave me a warning look as she set my phone on the counter.

"Yep. She finally said yes to working at Blur. It's filled with men just like Shepard. Give her some time. I'm sure someone she likes will show up."

Her mom was grinning from ear to ear at the promise of a partner in Vena's life. Vena shook her head at me behind her mom's back but got to work peeling and chopping carrots as ordered.

After Mrs. Hunter had dinner in the oven and the table set, we returned to the living room. Vena and I were sipping wine with her mom while Mr. Hunter and Shepard enjoyed a beer from Zimbabwe. Miles had excused himself a while ago, and I could hear the occasional creak in the ceiling above to indicate he was moving around on the second floor.

"So what do you do for a living?" Mrs. Hunter asked Shepard.

"I run a nightclub in D.C."

"Oh? A business owner?" She elbowed Vena like she should pay attention.

"Mom, if you're that interested in marrying me off, why don't you just arrange a marriage," Vena said moodily.

Mrs. Hunter gave her a 'don't tempt me' look before focusing on Shepard again.

"The club you run wouldn't be Blur, would it?" she asked.

"The very same," he said with a smile.

"Good. We've been meaning to stop there since Everly started. We'll make time soon."

"I'd be delighted to have you," Shepard said. "Let Vena know when you'll be there so I can have the staff watch for you."

Mrs. Hunter's smile grew. "If Vena knows ahead of time, she'll plan not to be there."

"Everly and Vena agreed to work every night we're open during summer, so I don't think that'll be an issue." He turned his gaze to Vena. "You won't leave me in a bind by calling in at the last minute, will you?"

She slumped a little in her chair. "No."

My phone buzzed in my pocket, and I slipped it out to look at the message a moment before someone knocked on the front door.

Cross: MC is here. Also, you should stop allowing others to use your phone.

I looked at the previous message that Vena had sent on my behalf.

Me: Someone sweet-talked Everly out of her virtue a few years back. But that's not really any of your business, is it? Who she lets play on her playground is her decision, not yours. And she seems to like Shepard a lot.

I lifted my gaze to glare at Vena.

She smirked at me.

"Vena!" her mom called. "There's someone here for you."

Vena raised a confused brow at me before heading to the door, but Shepard cut her off.

"Stay here," he said. "I got this."

Vena's brow rose a fraction more before she settled next to me. "What is going on?"

I turned my phone so she could read the text from Cross. Vena bolted to her feet. I grabbed her hand before she could leave and tugged her back down to the seat next to me.

"There might be an important reason he's here."

"What reason?"

"I don't know." I glanced at Mr. Hunter to find him already nose-deep in a thick book. Whispering, I said, "It could be about the vampires or Anchor. Let Shepard find out. MC will be gone soon."

"He better be. I don't need Missing Common sense showing up at my house to harass me."

As soon as those words left her lips, Mrs. Hunter arrived in the living room with her arm threaded through MC's.

"We have another person joining us for dinner," she said with a grin. "Won't this be fun?"

With the way both Shepard and Vena were glaring at MC, it definitely would not be fun.

"I'm going to go check on dinner," Vena said, standing.

Mrs. Hunter smiled politely but shook her head. She didn't want her daughter to turn the food into ash.

"Fine. Then, I'll go see what Miles is up to." Vena marched out of the room.

MC watched her go but didn't look too fazed by her angry

departure. Either he wasn't a man who took hints or he was as dumb as a troll because he merely smiled at Mrs. Hunter and took a seat across from Mr. Hunter.

"Tell me all about yourself," Mrs. Hunter said to MC as she sat down. "Blur sure has some handsome men working there."

While she interrogated, I motioned for Shepard to follow me to the kitchen.

"Why is MC here?" I asked as soon as the door was closed.

"He wanted to tell me what his pack found at the club."

"He could have called you to tell you. If he's here to harass Vena--"

Shepard pulled me toward him in a loose hug as he rubbed my back in a soothing motion. While part of me hated that he was placating me, another part liked it. A lot. At my core, I was a hugger. So, I soaked up all the comfort that Shepard was trying to give me.

"I was about to tell him to leave," he said softly, "but Mrs. Hunter was too fast and invited him to dinner. I'll get rid of him as soon as it's done."

"But--"

"And I'll make sure he sits at the other end of the table away from Vena." Shepard pulled back just enough to peek down at me. "Okay?"

I grudgingly nodded. "It's not that I don't like MC, but he's being too assertively persistent with Vena. She'll snap if he keeps going."

"I'll talk to him about it."

Turning from Shepard, I checked the timer on the oven. It would still be a while before dinner could be served.

"I'll let Vena know about MC," I said. "Keep him away."

"I will."

Shepard followed me out of the kitchen and then headed to the living room while I went upstairs.

I found Vena in Miles' room. She leaned against the wall and watched as he rummaged through his closet.

"What is he doing?"

Vena shrugged. "He said he's looking for old research that he wants Dad's opinion on."

"Is that wise?" I whispered.

"Not sure, but we'll find out soon enough." She glanced at me. "Why is Maximum Chaffing here?"

I fought not to laugh at her agitated creativity. If I did, she'd take it as a green light to get even more creative.

"He wanted to give Shepard an update and will stay for dinner," I said.

Vena snorted. "He could have called."

"That's what I said. Shepard promised to make sure MC is seated at the opposite end of the table and he'll leave as soon as dinner is over." I wrapped my arm around Vena and gently squeezed. "He'll be gone soon enough."

"Found it!" Miles said, pulling out a box. Tucking it under his arm, he closed the closet door and glanced at us. "Is this a party, or can I go downstairs?"

Vena and I stepped out of his way, and he bounded out of the room.

"We should go, too," I said.

"You better stay next to me at all times. I won't be held accountable for my actions if you run off with Shepard."

"I'm not running off with anyone." I turned her toward the stairs. "Besides, dinner smells amazing. Neither of us will want to miss it."

She frowned. "I'm not even hungry anymore."

"Pretend."

As we walked down the main stairs, a thought struck me. How had Cross known MC was here?

I slowed and pulled out my phone.

Me: Are you at Vena's parents' house?

Cross: I'm feeling slighted that I don't get dinner as well.

Me: Do you really want to have dinner with two wolves?

Cross: I'd rather sleep for another 300 years.

I smiled and was about to tuck my phone into my pocket when I ran face-first into Shepard's chest at the bottom of the stairs.

His arm wrapped around me to steady me as he plucked the phone from my fingers.

"He's quite contrary, isn't he?" Shepard asked, reading the text while holding me. "He wants me to keep you safe but would rather be apart from you for three hundred years than dine with me."

"Like you're any better?" I said in a whisper. "You say vampires and werewolves can't be friends, yet here you are, having text conversations and desperate to meet him in person."

Shepard released me and gave me a flat look.

"I wouldn't have any interest in Cross if he'd leave you alone."

"Liar," I said with a smirk. "You keep stealing my phone. And I know you scrolled back to look at my message history. You didn't get to where you are by being stupid. I know you know that Cross is different. Stop being so stubborn about it."

"Being different doesn't mean he's safe," Shepard said, handing my phone back. "Don't let your guard down, Everly."

"I won't. It takes a lot to earn my trust."

He nodded and tucked my arm into the crook of his elbow. "I came out here to tell you we've moved to the dining room."

I let him escort me there and saw everyone else was already seated and waiting. Mrs. Hunter sat at one end and Mr. Hunter at the other. Vena sat to her Mom's right with Miles between her and MC. I headed for the seat across from Vena.

Mrs. Hunter beamed at us as Shepard held out my chair for me. "You two look so good together." Her gaze shifted to Miles. "You should switch seats with MC so he can sit next to your sister."

Vena's hand went under the table as Miles and MC started to rise. Miles immediately sat and smiled at his mom.

"I haven't seen you and dad in weeks. If I sit here, I get to talk to both of you."

Mrs. Hunter awwed and put a hand over her heart. I didn't buy his bullcrap, though. Knowing Vena, she had her knife poking into his side.

I glanced at Shepard, who'd taken the seat next to me, and caught his slight head shake at MC.

Mr. Hunter passed MC the first dish, and conversation started back up with ease, sticking to the safe topic of their dig and current research.

"It's disappointing that we didn't find the maps we were looking for, but you know how rare it is to come across maps today. It seems like everything's already been discovered," Mr. Hunter said.

"Maybe it's time to start looking into what Grandma and Grandpa had been researching," Miles said.

My gaze flew to him then to Mr. and Mrs. Hunter. The pair shared a look and glanced at the guests before smiling slightly and shaking their heads.

"A good researcher knows when to call something a dead end. My parents taught me that early on," Mr. Hunter said.

"True," Miles said. "But I don't think it's a dead end. I found a map that I think links to the book Grandpa was working on."

Something thumped under the table. Although neither Vena nor Miles moved, I was pretty sure she'd just kicked him.

"Do you remember what was in that book? Something about stones, right?" Miles asked, undeterred.

Mr. Hunter leaned back in his chair and considered the table for a long moment before looking at Miles with an easygoing smile.

"It's been a decade since I looked at it. And honestly, I've done so much research on other projects between then and now that I don't really recall. Let's go to the study after dinner and see what we can come up with."

Miles nodded and continued eating. Vena looked like she wanted to murder him. MC and Shepard were sharing a look, not oblivious to the current underlying tension.

"Anyone up for billiards after dinner?" I asked, desperate for a change in topic.

"That sounds like a lovely idea," Mrs. Hunter said. "We can save research for another day when we don't have guests."

Miles frowned at me, but I ignored him. Didn't the idiot realize I was saving his life?

Vena and I helped Mrs. Hunter clear the table while the rest went to set up the first billiards game.

When we were in the kitchen alone, Vena turned to me.

"What the hell is Miles thinking?" she whispered.

"He's probably bored," I said. "Look at how it felt having Shepard in our house for just a few hours this morning."

She sighed and rolled her eyes, and I knew she was already

mentally forgiving Miles for bringing up the taboo subject of her grandparents.

We loaded the dishwasher and finished cleaning before joining the rest. The guys were playing teams against each other, and the Hunters weren't faring well. However, once we were in the room, MC's attention shifted to Vena, and he kept missing shots.

Every phone in the room rang with a weather alert before the game ended.

My eyes went to the prematurely darkening sky as Vena read the message.

"That storm front came in fast," Mr. Hunter said.

"There's no way you kids will make it back before the storm hits," Mrs. Hunter said. "You're staying the night. Don't even think about leaving." Her gaze shifted to Shepard and MC. "There's plenty of room for both of you as well. I hope you'll stay, too."

"Wouldn't dream of leaving," MC said with a smile.

Vena's hand shot to her hidden knife. I quickly steered her from the room.

"We'll check on the pajama situation," I called over my shoulder.

"We have plenty of things you can wear, dear," Mrs. Hunter said. "Don't worry about it."

"You know Vena is picky," I said with a forced laugh.

My best friend didn't struggle as I dragged her by the arm up to her parent's walk-in closet.

"Find pajamas," I said as a rumble of thunder vibrated the walls.

She glared at me. "All I needed was two seconds."

"I know you're mad, and you can vent as much as you want

to me. Just remember that MC is helping the D.C. pack. Once they find Anchor and take care of the vampires, MC will be back in L.A. and out of your life. This is only temporary."

She grumbled and pulled out a full-length flannel nightgown with birds and flowers on it. The ruffles on the wrists and hem made me cringe.

"This is yours since you want to try to use wisdom with me," she said.

"It's summer and too hot for a flannel nightgown," I said.

"My parents keep the house cold."

"I think you should wear it to cool off MC." I grinned as she realized I was right.

Pulling out a second hideous nightgown, she smiled back. "We'll be twins. I think the only guy who would be turned on by this full-cover monstrosity is Cross."

"No guy would be turned on by this."

Vena shrugged. "Girls in his day wore stuff like this. All these ruffles could be what gets him going. Should we test out my theory?"

"No. He wouldn't dare come into the house with two wolves. And–"

"And?"

"I'd never want anyone to see me in that."

"Including Shepard?"

I sighed, knowing what she was doing. Verbally cornering me into admitting I liked both of them wasn't going to help the situation, though. So I pulled off my clothes, deciding it wasn't worth my time or energy to get worked up about a nightgown. If this caused Shepard and Cross to tap the brakes, then maybe that was a good thing. Right now, I felt like the rope in a tug-of-war game anyway.

Once the heavy bird-and-flower material dropped to my feet, I spun in a circle for Vena's approval. She snickered and put on her nightgown as well.

Linking arms, we headed downstairs to find Shepard sinking the eight ball and ending the game.

Eyes swiveled over to us at our entrance.

"Um, dear," Mrs. Hunter said with a wince coating her voice. "It's summer. Those are much too warm. I'm sure I can find you something better than my mother's old nightgowns. Where did you even find those? I swear I tossed them years ago."

"They were in your closet," Vena said. "And I think they're perfect."

I wasn't sure the gown was doing what she'd hoped, though. If MC's expression said anything, it was that he'd have no problem ripping it off Vena.

"I know," Mrs. Hunter said. "You can wear one of Miles' t-shirts."

MC glanced at Miles, likely sizing him up. The way the shifter grinned told me he was already envisioning how much of Vena's ass would be exposed.

"Nope," Vena said. "With the storm and these old windows, it's going to be a cold night."

Mrs. Hunter scoffed. "We had the windows replaced five years ago. Hardly old."

Mr. Hunter placed a hand on Mrs. Hunter's shoulder. "Let Vena wear what she wants. It's no use talking her out of something when she has her mind set. Plus, I quite like that she's wearing the nightgowns."

Likely, that was because Mr. Hunter knew Vena never had a sense of modesty.

"Oh, all right," Mrs. Hunter huffed. "Let's get everyone settled for the night." She looked at me and the two other guests. "We only have one guest room. Everly, why don't you and Shepard share? MC can stay with Vena."

Shepard choked on a cough.

"I think it's best if I stay with Vena," I said. "Shepard and MC can stay together in the guest room."

MC shook his head. "I have no problem with Mrs. Hunter's suggestion."

"I do," Shepard said. "I think Everly's plan is best."

I smiled at him.

The thunder rumbled the house, and the lights flickered then went out.

"I'll get everyone an emergency flashlight from the hall closet," Mr. Hunter said. "I think we'll need to retire early for the night."

CHAPTER THIRTEEN

VENA FELL BACK ONTO HER BED AND RUBBED HER HANDS OVER her face.

"At least we don't have to sleep in the closet this time," I said, trying to console her and make a joke. It didn't work.

She bounded off the bed and started pacing the room again.

"If it weren't raining, I'd go for a run," she said.

"Wouldn't recommend it. There's a Massive Canine who might think you're playing fetch."

She finally cracked a smile.

"Better?" I asked.

"A little. I just hate the way my mom thinks that being with the "right" guy will help me settle down. The right guy wouldn't ask me to settle down. He wouldn't try to stop me from hunting. He'd have my back, you know?"

I sat down on the edge of the bed and watched her move.

"Where's this coming from all of a sudden? Because she suggested MC share a room with you? You know that was more to poke at your dad for supporting your choice of sleepwear."

"Don't kid yourself. She saw a man willing to drive from D.C. for his boss. Do you know what that is in her book? Responsible. Down to Earth. Safe. I should tell her he's a werewolf."

I rolled my eyes at her. "Should we raid the pantry for some rage snacks?"

"I'm not leaving this room." She gave me sad eyes and handed me a flashlight. "But a snack might help."

Shaking my head at how well I knew her, I motioned I'd go and silently slipped from her room. Across the wide hallway, the door to Shepard and MC's room was still closed. Hoping that meant Shepard would keep MC contained for the night, I went downstairs.

While walking the hallway, a flash of lightning illuminated everything briefly. I counted to eleven before the boom of thunder rattled the nearby windows. After it faded, I used my flashlight to guide me.

Just outside the kitchen, a soft glow from Mr. Hunter's study shone into the hallway. I poked my head in and saw him scribbling notes at his desk. Leaving him to his work, I slipped into the kitchen and hunted in the cupboards for a bag of chips.

The sound of the rain lashing the windows had my attention drifting to the windows, though, and I stared at the dark panes for a moment.

Cross wouldn't still be out there, would he?

Setting the chips on the counter, I moved to the back door and cupped my face against the glass to look out. In the next flash of lightning, I saw him standing under the trees in the backyard. He wasn't hunched or trying to hide from the deluge. He just stood there like it was a sunny day with a light breeze and stared back at me.

When I turned the lock, his lips curved at the corners. He was insane. Or just really didn't care about the elements at all. He had fallen asleep on a stone slab after all.

Sheltered by the awning, I stepped out into the driving wind. It tugged at my nightgown as I quietly closed the door behind me and crooked a finger at Cross.

He closed the distance between us in a blink. Water dripped down his face and off his perfect nose.

"You shouldn't be out here, Everly," he said as his warm gaze swept over me, flickering with black.

"I was about to say the same thing to you. Not sure if you noticed, but it's raining."

His grin widened.

"The rain doesn't bother me. But I do look forward to having a home of my own so we can have these conversations somewhere more suitable." As he said it, he trailed a wet fingertip down my cheek, jaw, then neck.

I shivered lightly.

"Please don't stay out in the rain."

"Are you inviting me in?"

The words were barely out of his mouth when his gaze jerked to the door behind me. He snarled quietly and vanished. The door burst open, and Shepard blurred past me.

"Dammit, Shepard," I said.

Knowing yelling or telling him to stop wouldn't do any good, I went back inside and resisted the urge to lock the door on his ass.

Instead, I tucked the bag of chips under one arm, grabbed

a bottle of wine with my free hand and headed to the hallway. Miles' voice drifted out from Mr. Hunter's study.

"...want to hear it, but it's related. I know it is. I saw Grandpa's book before Vena hid it somewhere again. The book has information about some valuable stones, and the map I found has–"

"Miles, that's enough," Mr. Hunter said sternly.

Cringing, I hurried past and tiptoed my way up the back staircase. Everything was quiet as I made my way to Vena's room until I opened the door to slip inside.

The harshly whispered threats Vena was delivering to a very unintimidated MC immediately stopped. She retreated a step, taking a deep breath as she glared at the floor.

MC reached out like he was going to touch her. The big idiot obviously didn't like his fingers.

"You should leave," I said softly.

He dropped his hand to his side, nodded, and looked at Vena.

"Think about what I said."

Then he left.

"I really hope that whole bottle is mine," she said.

I held it out to her. "What happened?"

"Massive Creep decided to march his ass in here and try to kiss me. After I punched the Moronic Cunt in the mouth, he had the balls to tell me I needed to let go of Anchor. That he was a better wolf. That *he* wouldn't try to hold me back from anything I wanted to do. As if Anchor ever did. Major Callous. Mega Cold-blooded. Muff Cream."

She tipped the bottle back and started gulping.

I quickly closed the door, knowing he must have heard her. Hopefully, he would get the hint that Vena's heart was already taken and her brutal words would be enough for him to back down. But I had my doubts. After all, he hadn't backed down from Shepard. Not really.

Escorting Vena as she continued to tip the bottle to her lips, I settled her onto the bed and set the flashlight on the nightstand so it faced up to the ceiling, bathing the room in a glow.

She muttered under her breath between each gulp of wine, and I knew I had to get her mind off MC, or she'd be hungover and in an even worse mood tomorrow.

"When I was in the kitchen, I peeked out the window and saw Cross standing in the rain."

Mid bottle tip, her eyes rounded, and she coughed, spraying some of the wine on her nightgown.

"He's here? Out in this weather?" She brushed off the wine with her hand, which made me cringe. "He's going to get struck by lightning if he stays out there by the trees."

"He wasn't there for long. Shepard ran out of the house and chased after him. I'm not sure where either of them are now."

Vena sighed. "Hopefully, Cross went home."

"Vena, he has no home. We were supposed to help him find one. I feel really guilty. All this time, he's been without a roof over his head while I've been sleeping soundly in my bed."

She patted my arm. "He's resourceful. And we'll find him a place soon."

Voices in the hallway drew our attention. We tiptoed to the door and opened it enough to peek out.

"Oh, you poor thing!" Mrs. Hunter said as she looked at Shepard, who was drenched. "How did you get so wet?"

He ran fingers through his hair, slicking it back from his face. Water rolled down his neck and onto his shirt, which clung to him like a second skin.

"I checked the car," he said. "I thought I left the window open."

"Let me get you a towel." Vena's mom hurried to the bathroom.

Shepard's hard gaze shot over to Vena and me. We both squeaked and jerked back into the room. Vena shut the door and grinned at me.

"You're in trouble." She hopped back into bed. "But I have a feeling there's a get-out-of-jail-free card, and he's about to make it easier by stripping off those wet clothes."

I shushed her. "He can probably hear you."

"Good."

I shoved the bottle of wine at her. "Drink so you and your mouth fall asleep soon."

Her expression immediately turned contrite.

"Aw, Ev. I'm sorry for poking too hard. You know I just want to see you happy. I don't care who you are with as long as they treat you like a queen." She grinned again. "And if you end up with Shepard, you would be queen...of his pack."

This time, I took the bottle away from Vena. "Obviously, I was wrong. Wine is the opposite of what you need."

She hugged my waist and then turned to lay her head on my lap and stared up at me as I sipped the wine instead.

"I will keep my nose out of it for tonight," she said.

"Tonight only?"

"I'm your best friend, roommate, and sister from another mister. How can I keep my nose out of your business for long?"

She was right. And normally, I didn't mind. But the

Shepard and Cross feud was getting out of hand. They needed a truce and fast before one of them died. How, though?

I sighed, knowing I wouldn't solve the issue tonight because I was too tired to think straight. Yet, there was something else that wouldn't allow me to sleep.

"Hey, Vena," I said softly, not wanting anyone to hear.

"Yeah," she said as if she'd already begun drifting off.

"I heard Miles and your father talking."

"What are they researching this time?"

"I think Miles wants to get back into your grandparents' research, but your dad shot him down pretty fast."

Vena nodded and then moved over to cuddle with her pillow. "My parents will never allow it. Miles will just have to look for something else to research."

I dipped down into the blanket and reached over to turn off the flashlight.

Vena was right. Her parents would curb Miles' research. All I had to worry about was a wolf and a vampire.

THE STROKING, feather-light touch on my hair woke me slowly. I didn't know why Vena was petting me, but I liked it. She was earning herself a club sandwich for sure today.

Smiling slightly, I opened my eyes. It wasn't Vena staring back at me, though.

From inches away, Cross' gaze swept over my face, lingering on my lips. My pulse skipped a beat. His eyes flickered black briefly before settling on their warm brown.

"Do you two normally sleep like this?" he asked softly.

I realized Vena had an arm over my waist and a leg over my legs while Cross lay in front of me.

"Yes, which is why I don't sleep next to her often. I'm either her body pillow, or she steals all the covers."

Cross chuckled and continued running his fingers over my hair.

"Not that I mind, but why are you here?" I asked.

He flashed a wide smile at me.

"The wolf's showering. I wanted to make sure you smell like me when you see him."

"Why do you keep antagonizing him?"

Cross' humor faded. "Because he will always have what I want. A life."

His confession made me profoundly sad for him.

I ran my fingers along his jaw, seeing his pain and loneliness. He wasn't a monster. He was an outcast because no one ever tried to understand him.

"You have a life, Cross. A really long one. Some people would give anything to have what you do, but very few of those people would be worthy of it like you are." Leaning in, I kissed his cheek. "Don't waste time on envying what someone else has. Embrace what you have."

He wrapped his arms around me and pulled me flush to his body. The move stole me from Vena, and she made small upset sounds.

Cross' lips skimmed my ear and that place just below it. My breathing hitched.

"You tempt me, Everly."

His tongue flicked my skin, and I was two seconds from making out with a guy right next to my sleeping best friend when he jerked away from me with a wide grin.

I barely felt his lips brush mine before he disappeared out of Vena's open window.

Her bedroom door banged against the wall. Vena popped up behind me, and we both stared at the wet, glistening expanse of Shepard's exposed torso as he bolted across the room. Water dripped from the ends of his hair, creating rivulets that ran over his shoulders, across his chiseled pecs, and bumped down every ridged ab until they hit the edge of the towel loosely wrapped around his waist.

"I forgive you for every mistake you've made so far, Shepard," Vena said. "Ditch the towel, and I'll forgive future ones, too."

He was out the window after Cross before she finished talking.

"Damn, that was a fine sight," she said, lying back down. "I'd give anything to see him in just his pretty necklace."

"There was a necklace?" I asked with a smirk.

We both laughed until someone cleared their throat in the doorway.

"Vena," MC said. "Can I speak with you for a moment?"

"Hell no." She pulled the blankets over her head.

With a sigh, I got out of bed and motioned for MC to follow me. Once I shut the door, I faced him.

"You're getting some friendly advice whether you want it or not," I said.

"I want it. What will it take to win her over?"

"Not acting like an obsessed stalker. Vena doesn't like the aggressive types. And you've been screaming aggression for days, MC. You need to back off and realize now is not the time. She likes Anchor."

"Anchor's not here, though, is he? I am."

I couldn't believe my ears. "And that's why she doesn't like you. You're putting your own thoughts and feelings before hers. She's worried about Anchor, and until he's back, I doubt she'll have a single romantic thought."

MC frowned, and I heard a small rumble.

"Growl all you want. It's the way things are. Can you imagine how you would feel if I decided I wanted you and started persistently pursuing you? Showing up at your house uninvited...telling you that I'm a better choice than Vena?"

"You reek of vampire. Wolves don't date blood bitches." He curled his lip at me.

I grinned. "I'll be sure to let Shepard know how you really feel about me."

Turning my back on him, I slipped inside Vena's room and checked the time. It was just after seven. Typically, it would be way too early for me to want to wake up. However, I loved Vena, and for her, I could make a sacrifice.

"Get up. Get dressed. If we move fast, we can be out of here before Shepard gets back from his run, which means MC will need to stay behind to give him a ride."

Vena bolted out of the bed. Her nightgown went sailing.

We were ready to go five minutes later.

"What about Miles?" I asked. "Should we leave him to get a ride with MC and Shepard?"

"Yep," she said, flinging the door open.

MC was standing in the hallway.

"Vena, I–"

"Good morning," her mom called, coming around the corner. "I thought I heard you two moving around up here. Are you hungry, MC? I was making some waffles."

"Yes, thank you, Mrs. Hunter," he said.

"Everly and I are going to have to pass on breakfast and head back early. MC, would you mind taking Miles back?"

Vena met his gaze, and I could see his conflict. He wanted to give her anything to make her happy, but by agreeing, she'd also be running from him. I felt a smidge of pity for him.

"Thanks," she said, patting his chest and walking by him with a smile on her face. She kissed her mom's cheek and kept going. I hurried after her down the stairs.

"Vena," her mom called as she followed.

Vena reached the front door and flung it open. She stopped in her tracks. I froze, too, seeing around her.

"Oh my," Mrs. Hunter breathed, proving she saw the same thing we were.

Vena's wish to see Shepard in nothing but a necklace had come true.

I'd known Shepard was fit and rippled with muscles, but seeing all of him spotlighted under the morning sun was more than my brain could handle. I averted my gaze. Even staring at the ground, the image of his golden, damp skin glistening in the light as he cupped two hands over his baby batter baster filled my mind.

Vena nudged me. "Toss him something so he stops hiding his panty pleaser."

"This is not the time," I said, even though I wanted a naughty nuggets sighting, too.

MC stepped around us and smirked as Shepard did his best to conserve a sliver of modesty in front of Vena's gawking mother.

"MC, get me a towel," Shepard said.

With a sigh, MC went back inside. Mr. Hunter and Miles

showed up not long after, and I suspected MC had something to do with it based on Shepard's scowl.

Shit. Why was I looking again?

"Do I want to know why you're standing in front of my home without any clothes?" Mr. Hunter asked.

"I doubt you do," Shepard said. "But I would be grateful if you could take Vena and Everly inside until MC finds me something to wear."

"And I'd be grateful if you come inside before the neighbors call the police."

Mr. Hunter nudged Vena and me back and motioned for Shepard.

As he walked past us, Vena and I both blatantly looked at Shepard's backside. It was beautiful, marred only by a red welt on his right cheek.

"Do you think Anchor is built like that?" Vena whispered.

"I don't want to know," I said.

"I do. And I'm going to find out as soon as we find him." She frowned, and I wrapped my arm around her just as MC returned with a pair of shorts.

Shepard excused himself to change–taking MC with him– and Vena turned toward the door. I caught her arm.

"We should wait for Shepard," I said.

She gave me a what-the-hell look.

"I know what I said. But now I'm saying wait. He was just naked in front of your mom. We can't leave him."

When it looked like Vena would dig in her heels, I added, "Do you really want to leave MC here to ask your parents all about you?"

She stomped her foot in a show of annoyance but gave a nod. "Fine."

Vena's mom coaxed us into staying for breakfast while we waited. We grudgingly went to the dining room since the kitchen table wouldn't accommodate so many people and claimed our seats from the night before, with Vena sitting beside Miles.

Miles took the books out of the bag he'd packed and began flipping through the pages. Since Mr. Hunter was reading the book he'd brought, Vena and I waited in silence while Mrs. Hunter finished breakfast in the kitchen.

Vena kept looking at her watch. Ten minutes. Then twenty passed. I knew she was wondering what was taking her mom so long, but I was starting to worry about Shepard. How long had it taken me to look Miles in the eyes after he'd burst into the bathroom to rescue me from a fairy all those years ago? At least a month.

I was about to text Shepard when he and MC arrived. Neither seemed to be in a good mood. Shepard glanced at Mr. Hunter before his gaze swept over me as he took his seat. I saw the way his nose twitched and knew he smelled Cross.

Mr. Hunter set his book aside and leaned back in his chair.

"I've played some pranks in my day. A few of them have resulted in the same undress as you were this morning. But, there's a time and place, boys. Make sure you're in a more secluded place next time. And not in front of my daughter. Or my wife."

"Yes, sir," Shepard said quickly.

"We understand," MC said a beat later. "It won't ever happen again."

I glanced at Vena. She studied her fingernails, avoiding MC as he leaned forward around Miles to look at her.

"Vena, if you have a moment, I'd like to apologize. Can we–"

"I'll go help my mom." Vena nearly sprinted from her chair.

"I can help," MC said as he rose from the chair.

"Stay!" Vena snapped.

He slowly sunk back onto the chair. Shepard and I both scowled at him.

Thankfully, Vena and her mom had breakfast on the table in ten minutes. Mrs. Hunter was her usual conversational self, asking Shepard and MC all sorts of questions. I could feel Vena's anger escalating. Tense, I barely ate anything.

As soon as Mr. Hunter finished, I picked up my plate. Vena took my cue and quickly grabbed her father's plate to take to the kitchen with me.

"You've got this," I said quietly. "Just a few more minutes, and we'll be on the road. And when we get home, we can take a morning nap. Doesn't that sound nice?"

She made a face at me.

"You just don't want me stabbing anyone."

"Exactly."

When we returned to the dining room, Shepard and MC were helping Mr. and Mrs. Hunter clear the rest of the table.

"We'll help with dishes next time, Mom," Vena said. "Love you both, but we need to go." She nudged Miles, who was still engrossed in his book, hard. "Get up, Miles, or walk home."

"Chill, Vena. What's the hurry?" Even as he complained, he closed his book and stood.

Everyone made their way to the door, and Vena and Miles said their goodbyes while Shepard and MC stepped outside. MC headed toward his truck. I didn't miss the scowl he shot

Shepard when he saw he wasn't joining MC and instead leaned against Vena's car.

I gave Mrs. Hunter a quick hug, promised to keep her updated on Vena's love life, then hurried after my friend.

Vena hopped into the car and started the engine before Miles could get in.

"I will leave you here," she warned.

He rolled his eyes but sat in the backseat with Shepard while I got into the front seat before she threatened to ditch me as well.

No one spoke on the way back to D.C. I caught Shepard watching me a few times, though. Once we dropped off Miles, the reprieve was at an end.

"Are we going to talk about why Cross was at the Hunters' or, better yet, why he was in your bed this morning?" Shepard asked.

He didn't sound angry exactly, but there was something in his tone that made me feel like I was in trouble. Yet, I knew I'd done nothing wrong.

"Technically, he was in my bed," Vena said. "And I don't know why we need to talk about who I invite into my bed. I'm an adult with full mental capacity to make my own decisions even if you disagree with them. Same for Everly. Right, Ev?"

I tipped my head back and closed my eyes. "I'm not doing this."

"Doing what?" Shepard asked.

"Choosing a side. I don't want to choose. And if the people in my life keep pushing, I'm going to lose my patience. No one will be happy with the result of that. So, let's just relax and enjoy the car ride home."

No one spoke, and I took that silence as agreement.

Doc was waiting outside the house when we pulled up in front of it, and Shepard was out of the car as soon as Vena parked. I watched Shepard say something to Doc.

"What has his panties in a twist?" Vena asked, reaching for her door.

"People get upset when faced with a truth they want to ignore."

"What truth?"

"That Cross isn't the evil monster Shepard wanted him to be."

We both got out of the car as MC's truck rumbled to a stop behind Vena's.

When he jumped out and Vena's head snapped in his direction, I quickly ushered her toward the house. Doc wrinkled his nose as we passed.

"I'm going to shower and nap," I said as he followed us inside. "No waking me."

"What if there's an emergency?" Vena asked.

"I don't care."

CHAPTER FOURTEEN

I DIDN'T LIKE CONFRONTATION OR ADVENTURE OR FAIRIES OR THE outdoors. I liked baking and relaxing, and I wasn't getting enough time in the kitchen to zen my stressed-out self. So, the next best thing was a nap. Vena knew even though she'd joked about an emergency. Naps were my reset. My escape.

However, this one wasn't as peacefully long as it should have been.

I heard my phone buzz several times as I slowly woke up and made mental bets with myself if it was Vena complaining about MC, Shepard complaining about Cross, or Cross complaining about Shepard. The chance that it was Cross seeing if I was alright was at the top of my mental pool.

Giving up on sleep, I checked.

Vena won. And she obviously hadn't spent the last hour napping like I had.

Vena: I'm going to bitch slap MC into next Tuesday if he comes back. Shepard might be next in line.

Vena: He doesn't have a plan, Ev. No clue where to even look for Anchor.

Vena: Hunting vamps is fine, but how long will it take to get one to talk? It's a waste of time when we already know who has the answer.

Vena: We're kidnapping Sierra today.

I couldn't believe what I was reading.

Me: You are officially insane. We are NOT kidnapping anyone.

Vena: So you're okay with what happened to Gunther happening to Anchor day after day after day just to what? Protect your moral standards.

Me: Don't make me question why we're still friends.

Vena: I'm not being mean. I'm pointing out the truth. What wouldn't you do if it were me, Ev? Why is Anchor any different?

I sat on the edge of my bed and considered her reply. When it came to Vena, there was very little I wouldn't do to save her.

Me: If we do this, we do it my way, not yours.

Vena: I will follow your lead. I promise.

Cross couldn't go to Sierra. At least, not while she was being watched by Shepard's people. And after the way Shepard flew out the window after Cross this morning, I knew it was pointless to ask Shepard if Cross could talk to her. That meant Vena's method was the only option. However, kidnapping Sierra from the compound wouldn't be easy. We'd need help.

MC would do anything to make himself look better in Vena's eyes, but I didn't trust him not to call in an IOU later. That only left one other person as an option.

I switched to the group chat with Vena and Cross.

Me: Vena and I have an idea about how to find Anchor. But it may cause Shepard to dislike you even more.

Cross: I snapped him with his own towel this morning and forced him to return to Vena's parents' home without any clothing. I doubt what you have in mind will be worse than that.

I stared at my phone with a growing smile, recalling that welt on Shepard's ass.

Vena: Cross, you are my new favorite person. I'm hitting the property search now and promise not to stop until I find you something.

Me: Vena and I want to liberate Sierra from Shepard's home so you can question her without interruption regarding her vampire connections. Are you willing?

Cross: When it comes to you, I'm always willing.

Vena's mad cackle echoed through my closed door.

Me: I have a plan on how to get her. We can't bring her to my house, though.

Cross: I know a place. Text me when you have her, and I will provide the address.

Me: Thank you.

Vena: Thank you! *heart emoji* *kiss emoji*

Doc knocked on my door.

"Everly?"

"Come in."

He poked his head in, and his gaze flicked to the phone in my hand.

"I'm glad you're awake. Do I want to know what's going on that she laughed like that?"

I crossed my arms and shook my head like I was disappointed.

"Probably not, but I'm going to tell you anyway because I don't believe in suffering alone. I'm not sure if Shepard explained what happened this morning, but he lost all of his clothes and had to walk into her parents' house completely naked. Vena saw everything."

Doc cringed a little.

"Yep, and she's not going to let it go. Her curiosity is piqued. And since she stayed put while I recharged, I agreed to take a field trip. Any guesses where?"

Doc shook his head slightly, and I could see the dread in his gaze.

"To where all the boy wolves live. Vena wants to know if you're all built like that. For the love of everything holy, Doc, we need to find Anchor soon. He distracted her."

Doc blinked at me.

"You're going there so Vena can..."

"Try to see another naked werewolf?" I finished for him. "Yeah, Shepard should have thought things through before he did what he did. Can you be ready to go in ten?"

Doc looked like I kicked him, and I grinned, not even trying to hide my amusement.

"We'll make it through today together," I said. "Hopefully, I can distract her with visiting Gunther if she veers out of control."

My plan was pretty brilliant if I thought so myself. At no point had I lied. Vena would totally snatch the opportunity to see a naked man if the situation presented itself.

Now, all I needed to do was convince Gunther to be our inside man by appealing to him just like Vena had appealed to me–through his potentially shared experience.

I sent a text to Vena and Cross with the plan, and Vena was ready at the door when it was time to go.

Doc let out an audible sigh as we piled into her car, and Vena took off at breakneck speed.

"They'll still be there even if you go the speed limit," Doc said.

"So, how many wolves stay at the house?" she asked, playing her part. "And are the showers communal, or are they private?"

Doc opened his mouth and then closed it. He then tugged his phone from his pocket and held it to his ear, giving me the just-a-minute sign with his finger.

Vena grinned from ear to ear.

By the time we arrived at the wolf lodge, Doc had been thoroughly harassed and was ready to bolt the moment he walked us inside.

"Let me know when you're ready to leave," he said. "Oh, if you're hungry, just go to the kitchen. It's close to lunchtime. If you want to say hi to Gunther again, he's been hanging out by the patio. There are guards out there that will watch over you."

When we both nodded innocently, suspicion crept into his gaze.

"That all sounds great. But who can I see naked first?" Vena asked.

Doc cleared his throat, mumbled something, then fled.

She chuckled and pulled me along the hallway and out to the patio. Gunther was right where Doc said he would be, and he was glaring at Sierra while she poked along the bushes. Only one guard stood on the patio to watch her.

"Hi, Gunther," I said, taking a seat next to him as if this was a real visit. "How are you doing?"

"I'm pretty much healed." The look in his eyes said it was only his body that had healed. His mind would take much longer.

I reached over to pat his arm, but he shied away from it.

"Uh, sorry," he said. "It's not you."

"No. I'm sorry. I shouldn't have tried to touch you."

He shook his head. "It's fine. I'm still a little jumpy from the...incident." He muttered a curse about vampires under his breath. While I would never wish what happened to him on anyone, his anger worked perfectly into our plans.

Pulling out my phone, I handed it to him.

"If you add yourself as a contact, I promise to bring you something sweet whenever you need it."

He looked from me to the phone, hesitated, then entered his info. As soon as he handed it back, I sent him a text.

Me: Revenge on the vampires would be pretty sweet, wouldn't it?

Gunther's pocket buzzed. He slipped out his phone and read it.

Gunther: How?

Me: This can't get back to Shepard. OK?

Gunther: Tell me.

Me: I need to get Sierra out of here. I have a way to get answers from her, but Shepard would never agree with my method. Can you help distract her guard while I get her out?

Gunther eyed Sierra. I knew no love was lost between the two of them, not after she'd drugged him and definitely not after learning she'd been working at Blur to collect information for the vampires.

Gunther: If you get busted, do you promise not to tell

Shepard of my involvement? I'm already on thin ice with him.

Me: I promise.

Gunther: Deal. How do you want me to help?

Me: Have a "medical emergency." I'll tell the guard I'll keep an eye on Sierra while he takes care of you.

Gunther nodded and pocketed his phone.

I quickly sent a text to Cross, asking for the address. He responded with the information almost immediately.

Vena, who'd been watching over my shoulder, went over to Sierra. I stood and slowly strolled toward them but paused halfway between Sierra and Gunther. When I glanced back at Gunther, he fell from his chair, shaking in convulsions.

"Gunther!" I yelled.

The guard saw Gunther on the ground and ran toward him. Clearly not medically trained, the guard scooped up the flailing wolf.

"Watch her," he said.

I nodded, not believing how well that had played out.

As soon as they disappeared into the building, Vena pounced on Sierra, and I hurried over to help.

"What are you doing?" Sierra demanded.

"Taking you to Master," I whispered.

She snorted. "I don't believe you."

"Why else would we get rid of the guard?" I asked. "You have one second to decide if you want to escape with us or not."

Even with her dislike of us, the promise of an escape was too good to turn down.

We ran as fast as we could around the building, ducking below windows and bolting to the car.

Vena barely waited for our doors to close before gunning the car down the driveway. I hurried to fasten my seatbelt and grabbed our phones to turn off the tracking.

"We're okay," I said once we were on the main road and hidden in traffic. "They won't be able to follow us now. Just in case, though, don't go straight there."

My phone buzzed in my hand almost immediately.

Shepard: I know what you did. Why did you take her, and where are you going? She's dangerous, Everly.

"He's not wrong," Sierra said, reading over my shoulder. "Where *are* we going?"

"Since you were taken, Juicy, your master's feeding den, was ransacked by Shepard and his people. They've been hunting down the vampires hard since then. Your master met with us at After Curfew a few days ago, but that's under watch now too. So we're headed to his new place," I said.

"I don't believe you. Pull over."

Vena kept driving as I twisted in my seat. "Tall, lean, dark hair, and a fetish for biting his boyfriend. Master likes wearing cat ears and calls his boyfriend 'Pet.'"

Sierra gave me a sulky look. "He doesn't have a boyfriend." Yet, her pouty tone and how she leaned back into the seat and crossed her arms indicated she knew he did.

No one said anything else for the next thirty minutes until we reached the office building that had obviously been vacant for a while.

"Nice place," Vena said, getting out.

My phone rang yet again. I ignored it and kept walking.

Sierra followed us into the lobby without a peep of resistance. I wasn't expecting Cross's sudden appearance in front of us. His gaze caught Sierra's and held.

"Give me your wrist, Sierra."

She lifted her arm even as she swore at Cross.

My continuously-ringing phone gave me a reason to look away as Cross bit her wrist.

"The faster we get the answers, the better," I said. "Shepard's going to have a mental break if we stay quiet for much longer."

"So don't stay quiet," Cross said. "Show him what we're doing."

"Show him?" Vena asked. "Are you sure you want that? He already hates you."

"What I'm doing is breaking Sierra's enslavement bond like you asked. And Shepard needs to understand that I hold no loyalty to my own kind so he stops chasing me and starts protecting you better. You slipped away from him too easily again."

"If you want him to like you, you might not want to say that within his hearing," I said as I dialed Shepard for a video call.

His face immediately filled my screen. He radiated worry and anger.

"Where are you, Everly?" he said with surprising calm.

"I'm with Sierra, Vena, and Cross." I tapped the screen to change the view, showing the other three.

Vena caught my nod.

"It's your turn, Cross," Vena said. "Tell Sierra to answer all of my questions. Thoroughly and with no lies."

"She will," he said.

"You told us that your old master wanted you to get information on the werewolves at Blur. Why?" Vena asked.

"He never said. He told me what to do, and I obeyed."

"What information did you give him?"

"Who was working and when. How many employees Shepard had on the payroll. Who seemed to be the leader. He wanted evidence of who led. Said he would have a ring that would indicate his status. I never saw a ring on any of them except Gunther one time. Gunther said it was a wedding band."

Shepard frowned as he watched and listened.

"Is that why they took Gunther?" Vena asked.

"Do you think I know? I was already in that shit commune the wolves call home."

"What about Miles? Why did your master tell you to take him?"

"He never said. He told me what to do, and I obeyed."

Annoyance flashed in Vena's expression.

"Tell me everything, Sierra," Cross said softly.

Her lips parted, and any hint of petulance faded from her face, replaced by subjugation. "When he was at my house, I overheard him asking Miles about a book and rings. He saw me and sent me away before I heard anything else."

"What about Anchor? What did your master want with him?"

"Anchor? He's just a wolf. My old master's only interest in them was how many there were."

"Tell us more about your old master," Cross said.

"He can shapeshift into a cat."

My mouth fell open at that revelation.

"That's how he moves during the day," she continued. "The wolves think he's just a vampire's pet cat. He's old. Older than his boyfriend. He likes sharing human men and women with him."

Shepard swore.

"What does he look like when he's a cat?" Cross asked.

"All black."

"Is there anything else you haven't told me?"

"No."

"Good," Cross said. "You will be more cooperative and less confrontational with the werewolves and your coworkers in the future. Now, sleep until Shepard tells you to wake. Do you understand?"

Sierra nodded, lay down, and fell asleep right on the dusty entry tiles.

Cross looked at Vena.

"She truly knows nothing about Anchor. I'm sorry."

Vena nodded in acceptance as Cross' gaze shifted to mine. I saw the tenderness there and recalled how he'd woken me up a few hours ago.

"Where are you?" Shepard asked, reminding me of the trouble I was in.

"We're at the abandoned office building that your men checked last night," Cross said. "Have your men fetch Sierra. I will spend some time with Everly before I return her."

The slow smile Cross gave me as he plucked the phone from my fingers turned my insides to mush. As Shepard swore, Cross tossed the device to Vena. He reeled me into his embrace. His fingers stroked over my back, warming my skin through the thin barrier of my shirt.

"I've done as you've asked. Now will you grant me a favor?" He dipped his head closer to my mouth. "Have lunch with me, Everly. Please."

I heard Shepard's curse cut off mid-way.

Cross chuckled and glanced at Vena. "Well done."

She grinned and lowered the phone. "I don't know why

you like poking the wolf so much, but I have to admit it is pretty fun."

Realizing she'd let Shepard see Cross and me at the end, I swatted Cross' chest and scowled at her. "What you both just did is not okay. We're supposed to find ways to help Shepard trust Cross."

"Oh, you are," Cross said. "He listened. It's a start."

I sighed in annoyance. "I'll take a rain check on lunch and do you a bigger favor by running damage control with Shepard."

Cross nodded and kissed my forehead. "Call me if you need anything."

As soon as he was gone, I turned on my tracking and called Shepard.

"There's no need to waste time and resources. I declined lunch, and Cross is gone. Vena and I will load up Sierra and bring her back to the compound. My tracking is back on."

I hung up the phone before he could answer, not ready to hear whatever he had to say. Vena and I had betrayed his trust by taking Sierra and again by showing him how affected I was by Cross. While who I liked was absolutely my business, it was wrong to flaunt my connection with a vampire when Shepard was doing everything in his power to keep the hundreds of thousands of people in the greater D.C. area safe from them.

"Let's go," I said then glanced at Sierra. "We should have had Cross carry her to the car before he left."

Vena nodded. "Especially since he said only Shepard can wake her."

Scanning the area, Vena walked across the room and over to a large dusty box. She flattened it and brought it over.

"Roll her onto it," Vena said.

"Easier said than done," I groaned at the dead weight.

Between the two of us, we rolled Sierra onto the box and dragged it to the car. It took some time though.

"What now?" I asked.

Vena eyed the backseat. "We get her upper body in; then I'll go to the other side. I'll pull, you push."

"Even if we manage this, someone is going to call the cops on us. It looks like we're moving a dead body."

"Then let's hurry."

Groaning and grunting, we stuffed Sierra into the car and were on the road to Shepard's place.

"Ready to go toe to toe with Shepard when we get back, or should we dump Sierra at the door and run?" Vena asked as she drove.

"We only got out of there with Sierra due to the element of surprise. With him waiting for us, we won't get Sierra out of the car before he sees us."

I had been half right. Shepard was standing in front of the door and watching as Vena parked.

Before I could help Vena with Sierra, he had me cornered against the car. He was not happy. Behind the fury in his gaze, I saw his fear.

"You broke Sierra out of my house and met with a vampire," he said, a low growl coming out with every word.

"You weren't getting anywhere with Sierra," I said. "And when will you finally admit Cross isn't like the other vampires? He can be trusted."

"I'll trust him when he's dead."

"If you can't trust Cross, then trust me."

He shook his head slightly. "You stole Sierra from my

house after repeatedly refusing to prove you're not under Cross' thrall. Do you really think I should keep trusting you?"

"Yes. That's exactly what you're supposed to do."

Regardless of how right he was, the stubborn set of his jaw pushed me over the edge. We'd had the same argument too many times. If he wasn't going to cave, then I was. Anything for peace.

"I'm tired of this." I pushed him back, well aware that he let me. "You want me to prove it? Fine."

I yanked off my shirt and threw it at his face. He pulled it away, his gaze skimming over my bare shoulders and barely concealed heaving chest as I went for the button on my shorts.

Vena caught my hand. "Let's just take a minute to cool off. You don't need to give the whole place a show."

"Who cares? It's not like I ever plan on coming back here after," I snapped.

She glanced over her shoulder at Shepard. "Everyone thinks Everly is the nice one...until she's not."

She snatched the shirt back from Shepard and said, "If you're smart, drop it and get Sierra out of here."

He quietly obeyed Vena's order, and she slipped the shirt back over my head.

By the time Sierra had been passed off to another wolf, I was covered and seated in the car with Vena blocking Shepard from getting close.

"You both need to back off right now," she said to Shepard. "You are being bullheaded, and Ev is clearly hangry."

Shepard ran a hand through his dark blonde hair, tugging at the ends before sighing. "I'm sorry. Let me take you both to lunch to apologize."

Vena glanced at me. "How about it, Ev?"

I looked away, hating myself for being the unreasonable one at the moment. Because that was the truth of it.

If I suspected Vena of being secretly thralled, I would have stripped searched her already with zero guilt. Yet, Shepard was holding back from forcing the issue because he wanted to respect me. Because he liked me. I *knew* that. Yet, for all that I was calling him stubborn, I was being just as bad.

"I could eat," I said softly.

Shepard got into the backseat, and Vena hopped behind the wheel.

There was little conversation as Vena drove to a restaurant. I felt Shepard's pensive stare nearly the entire time. So when Shepard opened the door for me at the restaurant, I thanked him. Then I saw where we were.

I shot Vena a look, knowing she'd taken us to one of the most expensive restaurants in the city. She grinned at me and looped her arm through mine.

"Shepard insisted on lunch," she said. "Didn't you, Shepard?"

He gave a nod and followed us inside.

As soon as we were seated and I scanned the menu, all my anger vanished.

"They have bacon-wrapped dates stuffed with blue cheese." I groaned and barely stopped myself from drooling.

"Do you like those?" Shepard asked.

He'd taken the chair immediately to my right and Vena to my left, leaving the spot across from me open.

Before I could answer Shepard, Cross appeared out of nowhere and sat in the vacant seat. He smiled at Shepard's low, threatening growl.

"Now is not the time to misbehave, my friend," Cross said softly. "The humans are watching. Imagine the fear you'd spread if they became aware of a vampire who could walk in the sun."

CHAPTER FIFTEEN

SHEPARD'S GAZE DARTED AROUND THE RESTAURANT. I COULD imagine him silently counting the number of witnesses and debating the risk. After a moment, he sat back in his chair and folded his arms in a relaxed pose.

"What do you want?"

"We need to have a frank talk about these two," Cross said.

"Not sure I like you talking like we're not here," Vena said.

The waiter interrupted to take our drink order. Cross asked for the appetizer I'd mentioned, proving that he'd been listening. As soon as the waiter left, he faced Shepard again.

"The vampires are up to something," Cross said. "For decades, they'd been supplying fae with humans but suddenly stopped a few weeks ago, cutting ties instead. *Before* they kidnapped Gunther.

"Why would they alienate themselves from their only allies and then kick the hornet's nest, so to speak, when they had no safe home to fall back to? It doesn't make sense. So I've been asking around while I look for your other missing wolf.

"Rather than focusing on you and your men, who have

been hunting them at night, do you know what the vampires chose to do? They sent a message to these two to meet up at a club with the promise of information about Anchor in exchange for information about me."

Cross shifted in his chair, interlacing his fingers as he leaned his elbows on the armrests to give the server room to set down our drinks. Shepard's gaze flicked to Cross' hands then to his face. Something about Cross' pose didn't make Shepard happy. And whatever had his dander up caused Cross to frown in return.

Then Cross ordered for all of us. Even Shepard. For a change, Shepard didn't react.

Once the server left, Cross considered Shepard before continuing.

"I arrived at the club in time to protect Vena and Everly and heard one of the leaders admit they knew nothing of Anchor. But the damage had already been done."

"I'd hardly call figuring out you have a thing for Everly damage," Vena said. "They already knew that. Why else would they have sent a feeder doppelganger to our house?"

I kicked Vena under the table, and she flushed. "Well, Cross seems to be in a reveal-all mood anyway," she defended.

"They knew I was interested. They were testing how much I care," Cross said without looking away from Shepard. "They were watching your people closely before that, though. One of the vampires has the ability to shift into a black cat. His scent was all over the crime scene for one of your recently abused pack members. I believe the cat was seen leaving the hotel on surveillance footage as well. The same cat has already visited Everly's home."

"I am so glad you didn't let me feed it," I said, remembering the incident. "It was at Juicy and Blur, too."

Shepard scrubbed a hand over his face and sat up straighter. His gaze dipped to Cross' hands again. "So you believe your people are going to use Everly to get to you?"

"Not my people. Others of my kind. And if they can't use Everly, they'll use Vena to get to Everly to get to me."

Shepard looked at Cross' hands for a third time. Or, more specifically, his ring.

"Why do you keep looking at his ring?" Vena asked, noticing the same thing I had.

"It's how he's able to walk in the sun," Shepard said. "And the reason he's so determined to win you over, Everly. His people didn't find out how much you mean to him. They found out how much you mean to me. He's been using you to get to me."

Cross snarled softly and leaned toward Shepard. "You continue to delude yourself, my friend. Why would I need to get close to you? Are you in some way important to me? You are not. I wasn't yet awake when Sierra was told to gather information on the werewolves in your club. It seems someone knows of your importance and likely knows Everly's connection to you as well."

Shepard swore under his breath.

"What's going on? What aren't you saying?" I asked.

Neither answered, and Cross settled back in his chair.

"Talk or we walk," Vena said. "No tracking app. No phone calls."

Both Shepard and Cross looked equally not okay with that. Cross spoke first.

"Long ago, another of my kind was very interested in the

power my ring possessed. I left my homeland to escape her and slept, hidden for centuries before I was forced back into the world."

I felt a smidge of guilt for my part in that forcing.

"My ring cannot fall into the hands of any of my kind." Cross' gaze locked with Shepard's. "You know I speak the truth. Now ask yourself why my kind would cut ties with a supporter and try to find my weakness."

He tapped his ring.

"It's a powerplay," Cross said. "They know what you have, Shepard, and they'll be coming for it. And once they have what they want, they'll move on to bigger game."

"Shit," Vena breathed. "You have that kind of ring, too, don't you?"

Shepard's whole face twitched.

"We need to work together to stop them," Cross said.

Shepard barked a laugh. "Together? Not in this lifetime."

Cross placed a hand over his heart in mock injury. "I thought we had something special after I marked your backside."

Vena's laughter rang out through the restaurant as Shepard scowled hard.

"Less attention drawn, please," Cross said softly.

Vena calmed. "So the vampires want you both for the rings you have. Why? I mean, I get why they want Cross', but why yours, Shepard? What does it do?"

Shepard glanced away, and Cross tapped his ring on the table to draw his attention back. "We're being transparent here. You owe the girls that much."

"There could be people listening," Shepard said. "This is not the time or place for it."

"Smell the air, mutt. You know as well as I do there are no wolves or vampires here. They are all humans."

"If you call me mutt again, I'll rip out your fangs."

Cross smirked. "You're cute when you're mad. But before you have your way with me, answer the question."

Shepard growled but said, "It gives me a boost of power."

"And?" Cross pressed.

"They don't need to know that."

"Cross, just tell us," I said, getting annoyed.

"The ring helps him rule," Cross said.

The table jumped, shaking the glasses and silverware.

"Cute," Cross said to Shepard. "As much as I appreciate the love tap, I'm more interested in Everly than you."

"As in all the wolves?" I asked Shepard, ignoring Cross' attempt to provoke him. "Even the L.A. pack?"

Shepard gave a slight nod.

Vena frowned. "I don't understand. How does any of this explain what happened to Anchor? If he's not with the vampires, where is he?"

Both Shepard and Cross shook their heads.

Shepard's phone buzzed. He glanced at the message and then scowled.

"What's wrong?" I asked.

Cross leaned over and glanced at Shepard's phone. "It's a text from MC, asking if Shepard has eyes on the two of you."

Shepard angled his phone away from Cross and cast an annoyed glance at him.

"Tell MC to mind his own business," Vena said.

Shepard typed a quick message. "I told him to focus on patrol."

The server returned with the bacon-wrapped date appetizer that looked like art on a plate.

"I think all this clearing of the air deserves a celebration. Bring us your most expensive bottle of wine," Cross said.

When the server left, I glanced at the wine list to find the most expensive bottle didn't have a price on it. I cringed but told myself it wasn't like Cross didn't have a huge stash of money in my bank account.

Shepard narrowed his eyes at Cross. "What do you want from me?"

Cross leaned back as the server returned with the bottle of wine and four glasses. She showed the wine to Cross, who nodded. Uncorking it, she took a glass and poured a very small amount into it and then let Cross sample it. He nodded again, and she proceeded to pour two fingers of wine into each glass. She asked if we required anything else; then she left.

"Well?" Shepard asked Cross.

"The only thing I want is to keep Everly and Vena safe, which means we have to work together. What do you want from me to make that happen?"

"Stay away from them," Shepard said.

"Since I have saved them from death twice now, we both know that abandoning them is not in their best interest."

"Isn't it? You're the reason they're in danger. I'll take charge of their safety. You're no longer needed."

"Move past this already, Shepard," I said impatiently. "Whether he avoids us now or not, the damage is already done, isn't it? And, apparently, I would still be a target because of my association with *both* of you. Rather than telling Cross to go away, accept his help. He's already proven himself multiple times."

Shepard looked like he wanted to swear but didn't. Instead he considered Cross for several seconds.

"Fine. Let's work together. You can go places and gather information my people and I can't. And, since there's only one of you, doing that is the best use of your time.

"I'll have someone at Everly and Vena's house with them around the clock. But, to ensure I'm not wasting resources chasing after you, I'd like you to avoid going there."

"Can't you just tell everyone–"

"No, he can't," Cross said, gently interrupting me. "If his pack knew he was working with me, they would lose faith in him, and he would be immediately challenged."

I glanced at Shepard.

"Will everything I said to you in front of your house cause problems?"

Shepard's gaze softened. "No. We understand the power vampires can have over humans and don't fault the humans for it. We fault the vampires."

I looked at Cross. His gaze swept over my face. I saw a hint of frustration in his eyes and something else. Sadness?

"I will concede to temporarily not visiting their home," he said.

"Deal." Shepard looked more relaxed again.

Did they both think this would prevent Cross from seeing me in person altogether? If so, they were delusional. I had the man's money in my account. He had suits to pay for and still needed a home.

Thinking of everything I needed to do made me wish for the days when I spent the majority of my time either at home, creating recipes, or at Blur, working toward financing my dream. Yet, I couldn't regret waking Cross.

Seeing an opportunity to free up my time again, I leaned in.

"Hang on. If this is a negotiation, I have a stipulation, too. Cross will stay away from the house, but you have to help him get a birth certificate."

"Not possible," Shepard said.

"You have connections all over D.C.," I said. "You should have no problem getting paperwork for him."

"It's illegal."

"Fine. Then Cross can continue to use my bank account, and I'll help buy him a house under my name. One with a really nice kitchen so I can spend my Mondays and Tuesdays off there, working on my recipes."

"I approve your suggestion," Cross said, a smile tugging at his mouth.

Shepard's hurt gaze locked on me, and I struggled not to feel guilty. But if he was going to be stubborn, so was I.

Vena jumped in to help. "Giving Cross an identity wouldn't just help untangle Everly from Cross, Shepard. As a bonus, you'd be able to keep track of him. Where he's living. What he's investing in. If he travels."

Shepard glanced at all of us before saying, "I'll see what I can do."

"No. I want your promise," I said. "You want me free from Cross' influence? This is the way."

Shepard exhaled audibly. "Alright. I give you my word."

Vena browsed properties on her phone while I savored the appetizer under Cross' amused gaze. Shepard watched me, too. But his expression didn't hint at humor. He was worried.

I appreciated his concern. I needed it. While I knew I was

safe with Cross, D.C. was infested with vampires who weren't safe.

However, when I thought of the VIP section at After Curfew, where we'd met Pet and Master, and the number of vampires waiting for an opportunity to snatch me, the food curdled in my stomach.

When the main course finally arrived, I couldn't enjoy it. After a few bites, I set my fork aside and waved the server over to ask to take it home. I even declined dessert.

"Are you sure?" Vena asked, watching me.

"Very." It had been an excruciatingly long morning, and I just wanted to go home.

The server arrived with the bill, and Cross indicated Shepard would take it. Shepard smiled at the waitress, but I could see the storm brewing as he looked at it.

"Thanks for the meal," Cross said, standing. "I'll see you around."

He vanished behind the server's back. Shepard's mask almost cracked. Instead, he handed over his credit card with a smile and asked the server to box Cross' untouched meal as well.

"Was there something wrong with it?" she asked.

"No. Just him."

She nodded and left.

My phone buzzed with a message.

Vena: What? No goodbye kiss for Everly?

She'd sent it as a group text to Cross, Shepard, and myself.

Cross: I have no intention of ever saying farewell to Everly.

I kicked Vena under the table when she would have typed a reply. The server returned with Shepard's card and a receipt.

"Thank you for lunch, Shepard," I said.

"Yeah. Thanks," Vena echoed.

"You're both welcome. And you should have come to me sooner about freeing yourself from him, Everly. I'll work on the papers Cross will need so he can remove himself from your life permanently."

Rather than think about whether I wanted Cross gone for good, I gave Shepard a small smile and stood as he pulled out my chair.

"So, did we clear the air about being possessed by the evil Cross?" Vena asked once we were outside again.

"For now," he said.

"Great! Then we'll drop you off at your place and head home," Vena said. "I am so ready for a house to ourselves again."

Shepard and I both paused walking to look at her.

"It's like you weren't even listening to their conversation," I said.

"What? Some vampires want to get us. Great. That's a nighttime problem, not a daytime one. All our watchdogs can show up before sunset. Until then, I call the couch, and no people. Except for you, Everly. You don't count as people."

"Thanks, I think," I said, giving her a dry look.

"Did you forget that there are two vampires able to move around during the day?" Shepard asked. "Even if there weren't, whenever you two have even a second to yourselves, you do something dangerous. Get used to company, Vena. It's not going away until this vampire situation is resolved."

She tossed him the keys. "Fine. You drive. I need to digest."

While Shepard drove us to our house, she continued her search for a home for Cross.

I didn't say anything, but I wondered if Cross would even want to stay in the D.C. area if the wolves knew his name and his kind was after him. He'd said he'd run once because of the ring. If Shepard helped him establish his identity in the modern world, wouldn't it be smarter for Cross to hide again?

"You're very quiet, Everly," Shepard said.

"It's not me you need to worry about when things get quiet. It's Vena."

"That's true," Vena said from the backseat as he parked in front of our house.

"Would you mind giving Everly and me a moment?"

"We don't need a moment," I said. "I'm not angry or thralled or planning my next escape. I'm tired and wondering what wrench life is going to throw at us next."

His expression softened. "I'm sorry I haven't done a better job protecting you."

"You've done a great job, Shepard. I'm sorry I haven't done a better job avoiding trouble."

"Same," Vena said from the backseat.

Shepard nodded and reached for his door. I took that as a sign we were good and got out.

As the three of us walked to the house, I was already imagining changing into my cooking clothes and experimenting in the kitchen. I had my stuff tossed to the couch and was in my bedroom before either of them could say a word to me. Vena took it as an opportunity to warn Shepard, though. I could hear her through the closed door.

"You're pushing her too hard about the strip search. I get why, though. My sister from another mister is hot and doesn't know it. Makes all the guys want to see her naked."

I opened my mouth to tell her to cut it out.

"I'm not some creep looking for a show, Vena," Shepard said. "You saw how he was with her. You saw his eyes flash black with hunger. Do you really think he hasn't bitten her?"

"I *really* think he hasn't. But if you're worried, I'll strip for you to prove I'm not under any influence, and then, once you trust me, I'll ask her to strip for me. Does that work for you?"

Shepard said something I couldn't hear.

"That's what I thought. When you want to go down that path, let me know. Otherwise, stop treating her like she's done something wrong. She hasn't."

Finished changing, I opened the door and joined them.

"Actually, I have. I know I broke your trust with what we did today, Shepard, and I'm truly sorry. You were just being so stubborn about listening, and Anchor-"

I glanced at Vena.

She nodded sadly. "And Anchor's been gone five days already, and you're worried about me doing something even dumber than asking a vampire for help?"

I nodded.

Shepard rubbed a hand over his face, looked down at the floor for a moment, then met my gaze.

"I'll do better from now on with the listening. Okay?"

"Thank you." I went to the kitchen and took out my notebook from one of the cupboards.

"What are you up to?" he asked, watching me.

"Stress baking," Vena said from the living room. I heard the opening credits to The Other House and the rustle of paper. Likely she was settling in to read some kind of paranormal book while we both enjoyed the background noise from our favorite show.

"Are you stressed, Everly?" Shepard asked, leaning against the counter as he watched me move around.

"How can I not be? I woke a vampire–thankfully a nice one–, Miles was kidnapped, and Vena and I almost died in the process and seem to have started a war between werewolves and the vampires. Gunther was hurt because of it, and Anchor's missing. And I'm doing things I don't want to do in the name of trying to keep the people I care about safe."

He moved as quickly as Cross, blurring in front of me. It took a second to register I was in his arms with his jaw pressed against my temple.

"It's not your fault, Everly. The hatred between vampires and werewolves started centuries before either of us was born."

His hand smoothed down my back, and after a moment, I wrapped my arms around his waist to accept his comfort and his forgiveness.

"I'm still sorry for my part in everything that's happened," I said. "I'm not trying to frustrate anyone or make enemies. Especially the enemies. It's not in my nature to hate like that."

"Lies!" Vena yelled from the living room. "You hate fairies and the outdoors."

Grinning, Shepard pulled back from me. His eyes might not turn black like Cross' did, but I still saw the hunger in them.

"Do you like peanut butter?" I asked.

"I do."

"Then, how do you feel about the best buckeye brownie apology you have ever tasted?"

"Don't tease me," Vena called. "Get baking!"

The hunger didn't fade, but he released me and returned to

leaning against the counter to watch me bake. As I worked, we talked. It was at a level we hadn't before, and I got to know the elusive and extremely sexy alpha who owned Blur better.

After topping the ganache frosting with sea salt, I went to change so we could bring the brownies to the pack house. Vena and I owed Gunther a quiet thank you and Doc an apology for running off on him.

"If you're willing to stay for a bit, you can have dinner there, too," Shepard said as I opened the door for the three of us to leave.

I wasn't prepared for the blue demon to dart out of the bushes at us. I squealed and fell back into Vena. Her quick reflexes saved us both from planting on our asses.

However, it wasn't me the fairy was after this time.

It darted right for Shepard's face.

Shepard growled, the low sound sending all the warning signals. But the fairy didn't stop. It dipped at the last second and grabbed Shepard's shirt, dipping its arm inside.

"What the—"

The fairy fisted Shepard's necklace and pulled.

Shepard backhanded it out of the air. It hit the awning and fell to the grass.

"You better hope no one saw that," Vena said. "Those fines are serious."

"Get a container," Shepard said, stalking toward it.

"Are you insane? You want to trap it?" Vena asked.

"It was after my ring."

My eyes went wide, and I hurried into the house to grab a jar.

When I came out again, I heard Vena.

"--feeding into her paranoia that they are plotting against

humanity. They're bottom-feeders, Shepard. They just like shiny things, which is probably why it was going after your bling."

"The bling that was completely hidden inside my shirt?" he asked dryly.

I handed him the giant pickle jar that still smelled like vinegar and dill.

He placed it inside and closed the lid.

"It needs air holes," I said.

"The jar is big enough for a few hours of air," he said.

I snatched it from his hands and headed to the kitchen. I didn't like fairies, but I also didn't want it to suffocate.

Vena followed me and leaned close to peek at it when I set the jar on the counter.

"Do you think he killed it?" she asked, tapping the jar.

"No. It looks like it's breathing. Wait...I think this is Miles' fairy," I said. "It looks the same. Why did it come over here?"

"Do you see that? Around its neck?" Vena asked. "It looks like a string necklace. Maybe it just wanted a bigger version of its own necklace."

"And you think I'm the stubborn one?" Shepard said with some disbelief. "It didn't see my necklace, Vena. It shouldn't have known I was wearing a ring on the chain at all. It wasn't there when I was standing in nothing but the ring at your parents' house."

Understanding what Shepard *wasn't* saying, I winced at Vena. "We should talk to Miles and figure out what's going on."

"Miles wouldn't send a fairy to steal anything," she said firmly, proving she'd understood Shepard's implication that Miles had sent the fairy to steal the ring. "You know him better than that."

"Exactly. He wouldn't steal or have someone steal for him. That would be something out of character. Something someone else would have to make him do."

Vena frowned. "I'll call him."

"No," Shepard said. "It's better to go to his house. If he's expecting the fairy to return, we'll catch him off guard."

Vena looked close to tears, and Shepard gave her a compassionate look.

"You knew it was possible that he might be under a vampire's control, Vena. It's why we've been watching him."

"But we were just with him. Sierra turned into a mindless puppet. Miles wasn't like that."

"Hey," I said, wrapping an arm around Vena. "If Miles is thralled, it's not his fault. Let's just go return his fairy and have Cross meet us. He can tell if Miles is under a vampire's control."

She gave a hesitant nod.

"It will be okay," I said. "Even if he's linked with a vampire, we'll deal with it. Can you find something to make some holes in that lid?"

Pulling out my phone, I sent a quick group text as Vena took out her knife.

Me: Cross, can you meet us at Miles' apartment in 15?
Cross: Yes.

CHAPTER SIXTEEN

VENA POKED LITTLE HOLES IN THE LID FOR THE FAIRY AND handed me the jar. The fairy's chest moved with each breath, affirming Shepard hadn't killed it.

"Tank," Shepard said into the phone. "You're with Miles, right?" Shepard paused to listen. "Good. Stay there with him."

I watched Shepard run his hand through his hair as he turned away.

"Things are worse than we knew. I can't explain over the phone but am going to ask for your trust over the next hour. Whatever happens, don't make a move unless I say." He paused again, thanked Tank, then hung up.

"Showing up with Cross is going to cause you problems, isn't it?" I asked.

"I trust Tank to stay quiet once I explain things to him."

"Just Tank?" Vena asked.

"Any of my pack."

She nodded, and we headed out to Vena's car.

Between Vena's worry for Miles and my fear that the fairy would escape and I'd be trapped in the car with it, neither of us was fit to drive. I handed the keys to Shepard. At least, if the fairy escaped, he'd be less likely to run into a light pole.

Vena sat in the backseat. I placed the jar beside her and buckled the seatbelt around it. It opened its eyes briefly, and I hurried to the front.

No one spoke during the ride.

When we arrived, I didn't see Cross. But by the time I had the jar unbuckled and turned around, I found myself face-to-face with him.

His gaze swept over my face, and I saw his inhale.

"Thank you for coming. We think Miles might be thralled and after the thing you mentioned at lunch."

"Ah," Cross said, glancing at Shepard.

Shepard glowered at him. "Let's get this over with."

"Not until I get assurances that your wolves will behave," Cross said.

"Tank won't make any move against you unless I say so."

"What about the other one?"

"Other one?" Shepard asked.

"The one that has been following you."

Shepard's gaze scanned the area.

"He's parked a few blocks away," Cross said.

Shepard muttered something I couldn't hear, but it made Cross' grin spread into a smile.

"Having a problem controlling your litter?" Cross asked.

"Let's get this over with." When Shepard plucked the jar from my hold and took my hand to escort me to the apartment, I didn't miss the way Cross' eyes went dark.

Vena knocked on the door.

It swung open, and Tank looked from Shepard to Cross.

Without asking anything, he backed up and let us inside. Cross hesitated on the threshold.

Tank backed farther into the apartment, allowing Cross more room to enter. Cross closed the door behind himself.

Miles was at the kitchen table, rifling through papers.

"Hey, Miles," Vena said. "Are you missing something?"

He glanced up. His gaze caught on the jar with the fairy.

The fairy was now wide awake and banging his little fists on the glass.

"What did you do?" Miles demanded, his face turning red.

His gaze–filled with anger and accusation–shifted from the jar to me. Why *me*? Yet, I saw in his eyes that he wasn't the Miles I knew.

It hadn't been a coincidence that the fairy tried to steal the ring from Shepard.

Cross was in front of me an instant later, a shield between me and Miles.

"Calm yourself, Miles," Cross said smoothly. "No one here is your enemy."

He plucked the jar from Shepard's grasp.

"Can you tell me why this poor creature was at Everly's home?" Cross asked.

Vena tugged me out from behind Cross so I could see Miles' now-calm expression as he glanced at the fairy.

"I sent her to Everly's."

"Why?" Cross asked.

"Shepard said he'd spent the night there to keep Everly and Vena safe. I figured he'd spend the night at their place again."

"Why are you interested in where Shepard sleeps?"

"Shepard has the ring my master wants."

Vena made a choked sound and covered her mouth with her hand. I rubbed her arm to soothe her.

"So you sent the fairy to steal Shepard's ring?" Cross asked. "Why not steal it yourself?"

"I'm too slow to steal from a werewolf."

"So was the fairy," Shepard said, crossing his arms. "Why does your master want my ring?"

"Speak the truth," Cross said.

"I don't know. The master only told me to find a way to steal the rings."

"Rings?" Cross asked.

Miles nodded. "Master already knows about yours. He told me to ignore it and focus on Shepard's."

"What do you know about these rings?" Shepard asked.

"I know my master wants them."

Cross and Shepard shared a look. I barely noticed as a memory teased my mind.

"Is that why you were asking your dad about the rings last night?" I asked.

"Yes. I know there are four rings, not two. I know that my grandparents found a book that referenced them. The map I found connects the rings to the book." His gaze shifted to his sister. "Where did you hide the book and the map, Vena? I want to give them to my master. He needs them."

"Why does he need the rings?" Cross asked.

"I don't know. He didn't tell me."

"Is there anything else your master told you to do?"

"No."

"Go to the couch and sleep, Miles. You will hear nothing while you rest."

Miles nodded, went to the couch, and fell asleep.

Vena broke down and started crying. I wrapped her in my arms.

"Hey, it'll be okay."

"No, it won't. He's fucking thralled, Everly. We know what that means. That fucking cat will be able to find him for the rest of his life."

"Which is why we need to find and kill his master," Cross said. "He gave Miles this task because he thought Miles had a chance to steal the ring and bring it to him. This works in our favor."

Vena pulled back and wiped at her face. "What are you saying?"

"That we allow Miles to lead us to his master." He stuck his hand into the pocket of his tailored pants and withdrew a ring that looked almost exactly like the one Cross wore.

Shepard cursed under his breath.

Vena looked from the ring to Cross. Anger flickered in her eyes.

"You want to send Miles to that psychotic vampire with a decoy ring? Are you insane? You know what he did to Gunther."

"It's the fastest way to find the vampire responsible for your brother's condition and end it. Once he's gone, your brother will be free."

Vena looked at me. The fact that she was looking to me for a second option instead of just agreeing without any consideration for caution had me hugging her.

"We've done crazier things solo," I said. "This time, we won't be alone. I trust Cross and Shepard to keep Miles safe."

She looked at Cross. "Okay. What do you have in mind?"

Since Tank kept glancing at Shepard, I said, "I think Tank needs an explanation before we make any plans."

"So do I," Shepard said. "How could you possibly have a duplicate made that quickly? You saw the ring this morning."

"As precious as that ring is to you, you are not its first owner. Nor will you be its last. I was there when it was created and understand its purpose. Perhaps better than you, which is why I had this made before I sailed to these shores."

He tossed the ring to Shepard. "As for the plan, it's quite simple. You will allow the fairy to steal that ring. The fairy will give the ring to Miles. And we'll follow Miles to his master after he believes he snuck away from his watchdogs."

Vena shook her head. "That's it? Just follow him? There are so many ways that could go wrong."

"His plan is as loosely plotted as yours usually are," I reminded her. "Now you know how I feel every time you bring up a plan. It comes down to trust, Vena. I go along with you because I trust you without reservation. Has Cross earned that level of trust?"

She looked at Cross, steadily holding his gaze. "Have I told you how sorry I am that I ever took your ring?"

"I hold no grudge."

"You might not, but the regret I feel is real. None of this would have happened if I hadn't–"

Cross moved suddenly, grabbing her by the shoulders. Shepard tensed, and Tank growled softly, but neither moved to intercede.

"What you view as your biggest mistake I now view as one of the brightest moments in my very long life. I will do everything in my power to change the regret you feel into appreciation."

Cross shocked the hell out of me by hugging Vena.

Her gaze shifted to me briefly before she gave him an awkward pat. Thankfully, Cross wasn't the clingy type and released her quickly.

"As soon as we're ready, I can wake Miles," he said.

"Wait." Vena dashed to her brother's phone, unlocked it, and enabled his tracking.

"Shepard, you can track him this way now, too. Just in case. But you both have to promise to have eyes on him the whole time."

"I will follow him on foot once we reach our destination," Cross said. "But the wolves should stay back and use the tracking. If my kind smells them too soon, the master will run. Do you agree?"

I looked at Shepard. He nodded at the same time his phone dinged with a message. He glanced at it and began typing a reply. Vena peeked over at his phone and swiped the phone from his hands.

"Why did you tell MC to escort us home?" she demanded as she read the message. "I'm not going anywhere with MC. Ever."

Vena shoved his phone back at him.

"If you're sending my brother in as bait, I have a right to be there. Ev and I will follow at a distance. I promise we won't get in the way, and we won't attract notice."

Shepard pocketed his phone. "I suppose it will be safer to keep you where I can see you to ensure you don't pull one of your ill-planned stunts."

"I'm slightly offended, but I will take this as a mutual agreement."

"Are we ready then?" Cross asked.

"Ready," Vena said.

I wasn't. Not really. Every time we did something like that, things went wrong. But I kept those dark thoughts to myself.

Cross plucked the fairy from the jar and held it at eye level. "You will forget everything since leaving this house and sleep until you hear the door close."

It gave a nod and fell asleep in his hand. Cross set it on the table.

"We'll be outside waiting for you," he said with a nod to Shepard. "Make it believable."

Cross went to Miles. "You will wake up after you hear the door close. You will forget that Vena, Everly, and I were here. Shepard arrived to check on Tank."

The three of us left to move the car so Miles wouldn't spot it the moment he left the house. We'd just parked at the other end of the block when Shepard and Tank left the apartment and jogged over.

I rolled down my window and Shepard leaned down to look at Cross in the back seat.

"The fairy stole the ring when it thought I wasn't paying attention," Shepard said. "I told Miles I needed to borrow Tank for thirty minutes. He's going to move fast."

A large black truck pulled behind us. Shepard swore softly, and Vena groaned.

"Change of plans," Shepard said to MC as he opened his door. "Vena and Everly don't need an escort home. We have a lead we're following instead."

"A lead?" MC asked, getting out. "On Anchor?"

I watched MC inhale and look at Cross through the back window. I glanced at Shepard, hoping that he'd keep his word to work with Cross now that it was three wolves to one vampire.

MC reached the car and leaned down to look at Vena in the driver's seat, but his gaze swung to Cross in the back, and he swore. The hair on his arms rippled before Shepard blurred around the car to push MC away.

"Get back in your truck," Shepard said as he opened the back door. "Tank, go with MC. Follow at a distance. I'll ride with Everly and Vena."

"And a vamp?" MC growled. "What the fuck are you thinking? Is this how you–"

"Go," Shepard snapped. "That's an order!"

MC glared at him but moved away from the car.

Shepard slid into the backseat with Cross.

"Is letting MC come with us smart?" I asked.

"Tank will ensure he keeps his mouth shut until this is over."

"First, you buy me lunch, and now, you're protecting me," Cross said with a smirk. "Be careful, Shepard. I might start thinking you're developing an affection for me."

Shepard growled, and Cross grinned.

"I really hope one of your own kills you," Shepard said as he rolled down the window. "You're stinking up the car."

"I could say the same. It smells like wet dog in here."

I glanced at Vena, who rolled her eyes.

Before the pair could bicker more, the apartment door opened, and we saw Miles dart to his car. As old and rattley as Miles' car was, we would have no problem tailing him.

Once Miles pulled out onto the road, we followed at a discreet distance.

"Is he heading out of the city?" Vena asked when Miles took 66 west.

I took her phone from her and opened the tracking app so Vena could keep her distance as we drove.

The sun was dipping lower in the sky when he finally exited near Wellington, and I hoped the vampire nest was close.

Miles turned into the suburbs, and Vena lagged back even more. It took another twenty minutes for Miles to park in front of a typical suburban home. Vena pulled over a few blocks down.

"Stay here," Cross said, opening his door as Miles hurried inside the house.

"What are you going to do?" Shepard asked Cross before Vena could.

"I'll check the house. We still have a few hours of daylight, so Miles is safe from my kind. I can handle any feeders in there. Wait for my text."

Cross disappeared into the house as MC and Tank parked behind us. MC got out and jogged to our car, opening the door and taking Cross' spot.

"It reeks in here," MC said. "Where'd the bloodsucker go, and when can we kill him?"

I turned in my seat to give him a what-the-fuck stare.

My phone pinged with a message at the same time as Vena's and Shepard's did.

Cross: The house is empty. Miles sent a text to an unknown number that he was here with the ring. Someone replied that they would be here in an hour.

Vena was reading the same message I was.

"That's just before sunset. Is Miles' contact delaying or is it not a vampire?" she asked with a frown. "A feeder maybe?"

"You're communicating with a bloodsucker? Are you out of your mind?" MC asked, reading over Shepard's shoulder.

"I suggest you shut your mouth," Vena said, glaring at MC. "That vampire is currently keeping my brother safe."

Disbelief reflected in MC's expression before he masked it and nodded at Vena. I saw her fist clench out of the corner of my eye. Obviously, she understood he was just placating her.

"We'll look suspicious sitting here like this," Shepard said. "Vena, if you trust me with your car, I'll stay here with Tank. Go with MC, and move the truck a few blocks in the other direction. Stay alert, and report any movement."

MC grinned, and Vena opened her mouth to argue, but I caught her arm.

"It's a good plan," I said.

She got out of the car without slamming the door and handed the keys to Shepard.

"Don't make me regret this."

"I won't," he promised.

"It's okay, Vena," MC said soothingly. "You don't have to worry about anything. I won't let any vamp hurt you."

She gave him a flat stare. "I don't need your help. I have a knife and a wicked kick."

We jogged to MC's truck and quickly exchanged places with Tank–I hurried to take the middle seat. MC drove the truck around, so we were watching a few blocks from the other direction. We had a decent view of the house, which was too quiet. I hoped that meant all was well.

Vena's stomach growled, and I realized that we had missed

dinner. With the nervous energy coursing through me, a skipped meal was probably a good thing.

MC tried starting a conversation with Vena several times as the sun sank lower in the sky. Each time, she ignored him completely. I answered him a few times, but by the looks he gave me, he wasn't interested in talking to me at all. So I joined Vena in her phone-staring contest.

Vena: You're not idiots. You know this is a trap by now. It was a stall tactic. They're waiting for sunset. Get Miles out of there, or I'm coming to get him.

MC's phone buzzed, and I looked as he read the message.

Dickhead Alpha: Get them out of here.

"I strongly suggest you don't try that," I said.

"Try what?" Vena asked.

"Taking us home," I said.

Her gaze shifted to MC, and I knew he saw the deadly dare there when he exhaled heavily.

"What are my choices?" he muttered. "Hope to get on your good side by staying here and watching you get hurt. Or acknowledge you already hate me, start this truck, and ensure the person I'd kill for won't get hurt."

I didn't see Vena's reaction to those words; I was too busy staring at MC with my mouth hanging open.

"That's a bit over the top," Vena said softly, proving the words had shocked her, too.

"You're unlike any woman I've ever met, and I'd give anything to get to know you just a little better. I know now's not the right time, but I want you to understand why I'm going to end up doing something you're not going to like tonight."

"It doesn't make sense to leave when we know it's a trap," I said. "At least, if we stay here, you can be their backup if things go wrong."

MC watched Vena, waiting for her to say something.

"If you start this truck and drive away, I'll just bail, scrape myself up in the process, and draw every vampire in the area here instead of to the house where Miles is waiting. Your call," she said.

MC leaned his head back against the seat and closed his eyes.

"I'm content being the backup," he said.

Vena and I watched the sun slowly set. It was a pretty sunset, but we could hardly appreciate it as we kept our eyes glued to our phones.

As the last tinge of pink and orange in the sky faded away, the door of a house three driveways down flew open, and several people ran out. Their speed gave them away.

MC swore softly and sent a text warning Shepard that vampires were incoming.

"What if there are other houses?" Vena asked.

MC tapped the steering wheel then started the engine. He didn't call attention to us but calmly drove down the road like a normal human would. Vena's car sat empty several blocks from the house where we'd left Cross and Miles.

Vena's hand gripped mine as MC continued forward. The house was completely dark with the front door open. Other homes on the block were lit up, and a dog was barking like crazy nearby.

MC parked in front.

"Stay here," MC said, getting out.

As Vena had pointed out, she wasn't one for listening. She

opened her door and was out a beat later. Something dark darted out of the house. It ran straight for Vena.

I opened my mouth to scream. A second later, MC was in front of her. He grabbed the vampire by the throat, his savage claws digging deep.

Another vampire went after Vena while MC was distracted. MC shoved the dead vampire away and turned toward Vena, seeing the vampire closing in. I could barely focus on them. Their speed blurred in my vision. Vena was caught as they clashed.

MC protected her, keeping himself between her and the vampire until he raked his claws across its throat. He moved again, blocking her from the vampire's spraying blood.

From the safety of the truck, I watched her lean her forehead against MC's back. She had to be shaking like I was. Maybe not as badly, but still. That had been way too close.

The vampire dropped to the ground a moment later, and MC turned to grip Vena's arms.

"Are you okay?" he asked.

"I'm fine," she said, glancing up at him. "Thank--"

MC swooped down for a kiss, wrapping both arms around her and bringing her flush with him.

My mouth dropped open.

For a frozen moment, Vena did nothing. MC took that as a sign to deepen the kiss. She pressed her hands against his arms. If she was pushing him, it wasn't doing a damn thing.

He growled low and cupped the back of her head.

I saw tongue and panicked. What if she bit it off?

I scrambled out of the truck.

"MC, stop!" I tugged at his arm. He didn't notice my presence or Vena's struggles. "Shepard!"

Just as I was about to kick in the back of MC's knees, Shepard ran straight at MC, grabbed him by the back of the neck and yanked him away. Vena stumbled as MC fell. I hurried to brace her.

When she straightened, she wiped her mouth with the back of her hand and reached to get her knife, but I stopped her. With the way Shepard was glaring at MC, she didn't need her knife.

Shepard and MC stood toe to toe, both looking ready to murder.

"I told you to leave and protect them! Is this what you call protection?"

MC pointed to the two dead vampires. "I did my job, unlike you! We kill vampires. Or have you forgotten? This is why you have an infestation beyond anything that I've ever had in L.A."

Shepard's jaw ticced as he glared at MC.

"Watch yourself. We're dealing with it, and you are here as my backup. If you can't fall in line and obey orders, pack up and get the hell out."

Cross, Tank, and Miles emerged from the house.

As soon as MC spotted Cross, a snarl ripped from him.

"Do your people know what you're doing?" MC asked. "Do they know who you're in bed with? You're weak, Shepard. You better be careful, or you won't be alpha for long."

Shepard's eyes narrowed on MC as he retreated to his truck. "Tank, go with him."

Tank jogged after MC and sat in the passenger seat before MC could lock the door. After a mutual glare, MC started the truck and pulled out onto the road.

Once they were gone, we all took a collective breath.

That's when I noticed the blood-stained clothes on Shepard, Cross, and Miles.

CHAPTER SEVENTEEN

"Is everyone okay?" I asked.

"We're fine," Shepard said. "We took care of the vampires that showed up, but the master wasn't among them. I'm afraid Miles is still under his control for now."

At Vena's frantic expression, Shepard added, "I'll bring Miles to my house. I want you two to stay there, too."

"While I agree that Miles should go to your house," Cross said, "I think a hotel suite with catering and a spa would be more suitable for Everly and Vena."

"Everly's not going to a hotel with you," Shepard snapped.

"Everly is an adult who can make her own decisions," Vena said, sticking up for me. "And a hotel sounds nice. Everly's had a rough few weeks."

I knew it had nothing to do with me and everything to do with Vena wanting a massage, and I fought not to shake my head at her.

"Between seeing her best friend get pampered with her at the hotel's spa under my care or watching her get mauled by the mutts you can't control, which do you think she would choose?" Cross asked.

Shepard's arm shot to Cross' throat, but Cross sidestepped and swatted Shepard's butt in the same spot as the welt had been.

"Come now. Let's not quarrel in front of the ladies," Cross said.

"Now we're ladies?" Vena asked me. "Thought we were hookers."

Shepard growled at Cross before stepping closer to me. "Everly, we both know it's smarter to keep Vena close to her brother so she doesn't talk you into something you might regret."

"Vena's right here," Vena said, scowling at Shepard.

I felt like I was watching a weird comedy routine. And I didn't hate it. Even though Shepard sounded annoyed, he was still talking to Cross, and I could see how much Cross was enjoying the interaction.

"As tempting as some spa time sounds, I think Shepard is right and we should stick with Miles. Considering how Miles is acting, the safest place for him is with Shepard's people. But that will only work if MC stays away from Vena so she doesn't try to stab him."

The humor left Cross' expression as he looked at Shepard.

"Do you swear your people will accept their presence?" Cross asked. "Don't pretend you didn't notice how your lackey looks at Everly. He is as dismissive of her due to her association with me as he is dismissive of you."

"I'll deal with MC," Shepard said, pulling out his phone and calling MC on speaker.

"What now?" MC answered.

"I need you to find somewhere else to stay tonight."

"Already arranged."

Shepard scowled at the phone. "I told you to go home, and you're going somewhere else?"

"Home is California. My temporary home is mine to decide."

"I expect you to follow orders MC, not twist my words to suit your mood."

"What does it matter? You wanted me gone anyway. But I am curious why I'm good enough to order around but suddenly not good enough to stay in your home.

"My guess is that, after tonight's latest failed attempt to get the vampire population under control, you want the girls tucked into your bed where you can rut over them. Vena deserves better. Consider this my official challenge for alpha. I'm over your bullshit orders."

Shepard's chuckle surprised me.

"You think I'm kidding?" MC asked over the speaker. "Our laws are clear. If you're challenged, you must respect the challenge or forfeit your right to lead."

"It's your funeral," Shepard said. "Tomorrow night after Blur closes. I'll text you the location."

"I'll be waiting for it."

The call ended, and I met Shepard's gaze.

"We can just stay with Cross," I said.

"That won't undo the challenge. Once it's made, it needs to be honored," Shepard said. He looked at Cross. "Are you willing to help keep an eye on things here tomorrow since all of my people will be preoccupied with the challenge?"

"Let me know where to be, and I'll be there," Cross said.

Since leaving the vampire house, Miles had stood woodenly at Cross' side.

"Is he okay?" I asked.

"Yes. I've compelled him so he wouldn't attempt to do anything that'll put him in any further danger. He won't remember this conversation either." Cross looked around the dark street. "Perhaps we shouldn't linger any longer, though."

We piled into the car. Rather than making all the guys squeeze into the back, Vena and I let Shepard and Cross have the front, and we sandwiched Miles into the backseat between us.

"Where should I drop you off?" Shepard asked Cross when we neared the exit.

"As soon as you exit the highway. I'll go to Everly's house and watch for movement there."

Shepard nodded. "I'll let my guys know."

"Don't bother. They haven't spotted me yet," Cross said with a smirk.

When Shepard stopped the car, Cross got out and opened my door.

"No reason to sit crowded in the back," he said, offering his hand.

The moment my fingers touched his, he pulled me into his arms. I tipped my head back to look up at his, and the sexy smile he flashed melted my insides.

"Until tomorrow," he said a moment before he brushed his lips against mine.

Shepard swore. Vena laughed. I struggled to maintain rational thought.

Then his lips were gone, and he gently guided me into the front seat and buckled me in.

Shepard's knuckles were white on the steering wheel as he pulled away from the curb. He managed not to say anything for a full minute. When he did speak, it wasn't what I'd expected.

"Are you okay, Everly?"

"Okay?" I echoed, looking at Shepard.

He glanced at me, his gaze sweeping my face.

"You didn't exactly have a say in whether or not you wanted that kiss."

I faced forward and looked out the windshield, trying to decide how to answer. While I hadn't instigated it or asked for it, I hadn't hated it. Cross was handsome, considerate, witty, and if it were Vena compiling his list of attributes, well-endowed both physically and financially.

"Sometimes a girl likes not being asked," Vena said from the backseat. "A take charge kind of moment can be hot. But the keyword is a moment. Guys who are all take charge and never stop to listen to how the woman feels is a big turn-off."

I could feel Shepard glance at me again.

"Are you really worried about how I feel about that kiss, or are you maybe looking for another reason to not like Cross?" I asked.

Shepard gave a slight shake of his head but never answered the question.

After a couple of minutes of strained silence, I asked, "Can we stop at home so Vena and I can pack for the night?"

"No need," Shepard said. "I'll provide everything you need."

I heard a smothered giggle from the backseat, and I knew I'd hear about this from Vena later.

Shepard didn't say anything else until we reached his home.

He pulled to the front door and escorted us inside. A middle-aged woman met him in the entryway. She had dark hair pulled into a low, functional ponytail, and she had a soft, motherly look to her. She took in the state of Shepard's clothes and then glanced at us.

"Lisa, this is Everly, Vena, and Miles. They're going to stay the night."

"Don't worry about a thing, Shepard. I'll take care of them," she said. "Why don't you clean up? Looks like you've been hunting vampires again."

"Put the girls in the suite, and bring them something to eat," he said before she shooed him away. As he walked off, he added, "Use the same protocol for Miles as we've used with Sierra."

After he left, Lisa gave us a once over. "What did he get into this time?" she mumbled to herself. "Come along. I'll get you squared away and fed in no time."

Vena looked at the woman like she did at me anytime I mentioned food. It was pure love. Any hesitation about staying here was gone.

We followed her upstairs to the suite Shepard had mentioned. The room was broken into two sections with a living area and a small kitchenette.

She directed us to the first door off the living room. "You'll find everything you need to shower and clean up in the bathroom. I'll have someone bring you clothing and dinner straight away."

I stepped through the door to find a large room furnished with a king-size bed and a small sitting area. A private patio looked out over the wooded park. To the back of the room was a master bathroom with a bathtub big enough to drown away stress.

Miles went to sit, but Lisa hurried him back to the door. "Let's get you to your room to clean up as well."

"He can stay here," Vena said. "I'll look after him."

"Don't worry about a thing," Lisa said. "Get yourself situated, and you can visit him later."

"Is that okay, Miles?" Vena asked.

Miles nodded emotionlessly and walked out after the woman. Vena frowned as she watched him leave.

"Go shower," I said. "Miles will be fine. You know they took good care of Sierra even though she was mean to everyone."

"I suppose. I just hate that he's like this. We have to find the master, or Miles will be--"

I turned her toward the bathroom. "Go. Get cleaned up first so we can eat. Then we'll think of a plan."

She nodded and closed herself inside.

Before Vena finished her shower, a younger woman delivered two sets of pajamas and a change of clothes for us. She also let me know dinner was on the way.

Placing the clothes on the bed, I listened at the bathroom door. Normally, Vena showered quickly.

I knocked when I didn't hear anything. "Vena, are you okay?"

"No!"

I opened the door to find her standing in front of the sink. She was wrapped in a towel and furiously scrubbing her teeth and tongue with a toothbrush.

"I can't get the feeling of his tongue out of my mouth!"

I had to turn away not to gag. The amount of foam coming out of her mouth was enough to wash a car.

"Pajamas are on the bed. Let me know when I can shower."

"When all the feeling in my mouth dies."

It was another two minutes before she emerged.

"Better?" I asked.

She shook her head. "Maybe after dinner. Or maybe once I find Anchor and can kiss him."

Since I didn't want her to wallow in doubt, I picked up pajamas and handed them to her. "Change and go watch TV. Dinner should be here soon."

In the bathroom, I stripped down to my bra and underwear and attempted to turn on the shower. It should have been easy. However, there was a smart panel that regulated temperature and water flow. It even had options for music or nature sounds. The only thing I couldn't find was how to turn the water on.

"I should be smart enough to work this stupid thing," I muttered to myself as I poked the screen. The lights changed from a blue-white to a yellow-white and then to pink. I poked at it again.

Water gushed from one of the side showerheads and doused me with icy water. I squealed in surprise and yelled for Vena. She wasn't the one to burst in, though.

Wearing nothing but a damp towel around his waist, Shepard moved me to the side and tapped on the screen. The water turned off, and the pink lighting went away.

"Are you okay?" he asked.

His wet hair fell around his head in a sexy, wild disarray. My gaze skimmed over his cheeks and strong jaw, catching briefly on his lips before landing on the clean, broad expanse of his chest.

A ring nestled between the valley of his chiseled, smooth pecs. It looked like Cross' twin, but with a blue gem instead of a red one.

Without thinking, I reached up to turn it. My fingers brushed Shepard's skin. He caught my hand in a loose hold, and I looked up at him.

"I wasn't trying to take it," I said.

"I know. But if you don't want me to kiss you again, you should refrain from touching me," he said gently.

"Oh." I didn't know what else to say while holding his intense gaze. Should I tell him that I hadn't minded our kiss? That I wasn't sure where I stood between him and Cross? Was I some prize in the middle, or was it something else?

My gaze shifted to my hand in his and the way his finger was lightly feathering back and forth over mine. Shepard or Cross? Cross or Shepard? They were both appealing and drew me in.

I glanced up again, studying Shepard's bright grey eyes.

He made a small growling sound and cursed. Then his lips were on mine. Not hot and demanding but soft, sweet, and asking. I tipped my head back and welcomed him in. He pulled me closer with his free hand pressed against the small of my back and deepened the kiss. My pulse started to race at the first caress of his tongue against mine.

I had to be crazy. What was I doing? I didn't want to be a part of their tug-of-war game. Yet, the way I felt in Shepard's arms seemed so real.

He tore his mouth from mine and nibbled his way down my neck.

"Everly," he whispered reverently. He set my hand on his chest, and I felt his racing heartbeat beneath my palm. "Do you have any idea what you mean to me?"

It was a huge red flag question. One that Vena would run from. Not me. Not usually. Why, then, did it feel like he'd blasted me with cold shower water? Maybe because he was a wolf. And wolves mated forever. I wasn't ready to give forever. Not right now.

I stepped back from him, breathing hard and wide-eyed.

"I'm sorry. I didn't mean for that to happen," I hurried to say. "It's been a bit stressful lately, and I'm not thinking straight."

His gaze swept over my face, without judgment but with a large amount of desire that made me want to step right back into his arms.

"I'm not a quick and easy type of girl," I said. "I'm not a prude, but I don't mess around. Not with my feelings or anyone else's."

"I know that, Everly. That's why I like you." He leaned in and pressed a kiss to my forehead. "I apologize for taking what you weren't willing to give. It won't happen again."

"I, uh–I wasn't unwilling, Shepard," I said, not wanting him to think he'd behaved like MC. "I just don't–" I blew out a breath. "You and Cross already have a lot of animosity. I don't want to be the reason for it to grow."

Shepard studied me and gave me a soft smile. "I understand. Thank you for clarifying."

He turned away, and feeling torn and sad, I watched him leave.

I liked Shepard. A lot. But when I thought of doing more with Shepard, I worried what Cross would think. And the same thing for doing more with Cross. Kissing both of them was enjoyable. So was their attention. But I refused to mislead either of them or become a pawn in their game.

Sighing, I stepped to the side, hit the button Shepard had used, then adjusted the temperature.

While I scrubbed both vampire and wolf scents from my skin, I considered the Shepard versus Cross problem. As I'd said, I wasn't easy. Neither was I the type to string two guys along. Yet, the thought of having a serious talk with Shepard and Cross about their intentions had me wrinkling my nose.

The shower didn't wash away my confusion or give me any answers. All it did was make me smell like Shepard's soap.

Dressed in my pajamas with the towel wrapped around my head, I emerged from the bathroom to find Vena in her pajamas, sitting on the floor in front of the TV with a plate in her hands. It was loaded with mashed potatoes covered with a stew-like gravy.

Mouth full, she gave me a tight-lipped smile and a thumbs up.

"Yours is here," Shepard said, drawing my attention to where he stood, dressed in a loose pair of shorts. When he took a step toward me, I saw *it* move obscenely under the soft fabric. My gaze flew to his, and he cocked his head as he closed the distance between us.

"Are you okay? You look flushed."

"Yep. Fine. Thanks for the food."

He frowned slightly. "About what happened..."

"What happened?" Vena asked, having swallowed in a large gulp. "What did I miss?"

"Nothing," I said before cringing and glancing at Shepard.

"That doesn't look like nothing," Vena said. "That looks like guilt. Did Shepard scrub your back while he was in there?"

"No. No scrubbing," I said, taking the plate.

"Oh. Interesting. Everly's blushing," she said with a laugh. "So there was some kind of Shepard action. Did you drop the soap?"

I shot Vena a warning look.

"Shutting up and eating," she said.

I sat on the floor beside her, purposely not looking at Shepard as I took my first bite.

Tomorrow couldn't come soon enough.

Someone knocked on the suite's door, and Shepard went to answer it. I only caught a few words of the hushed conversation–MC...Challenge...Pack support–and I realized the next day would bring its own set of challenges for all of us.

WAKING in a new place was disorientating. The bed felt way too comfortable, and the room was much darker than at home. Turning my head, I looked over to find Vena sprawled next to me on the king bed, taking up most of the mattress. I hadn't noticed with all the bedding and pillows.

Swimming to the edge of the bed, I stood with a stretch. The clock on the nightstand read eight. I was tempted to sleep more since we had to work later but knew today was also the day of the challenge between MC and Shepard.

I wasn't sure what that entailed, but I knew the winner would take control of the D.C. pack. While Shepard was capable, that didn't mean MC wasn't just as capable. What would happen if MC took control?

I glanced at Vena and acknowledged it wasn't a prospect I wanted to think about.

After a quick trip to the bathroom, I peeked out to the common living space to find our clothes yesterday had been cleaned and left in neatly folded piles along with a note on the coffee table.

Let me know when you wake up. I'll have breakfast delivered. - Shepard

I texted him.

Me: Saw your note. I just woke up. Vena is still sleeping.

Shepard: I'll be there in a little while. Is there anything you need in the meantime?

Me: We're good. Thank you.

I glanced at the phone, wondering why the conversation sounded stunted. I realized that was the nature of texts, but at the same time, I wondered if I was thinking too much about the kiss with Shepard.

Taking my clothes, I headed to the bathroom and got ready for the day. By the time I returned to the living room, Shepard had returned.

"Did you sleep well?"

I nodded. "The bed is like sleeping on a cloud. Have you checked on Miles? How is he?"

"He's fine."

After a courtesy knock, the door opened and Lisa came inside, leading another woman pushing a food cart brimming with covered plates.

"How much do you think we'll eat?" I asked with a laugh.

Shepard glanced at me. "I have a big appetite."

Was it just me, or was he no longer talking about food?

If the other women noticed, they didn't let on. They were too busy removing the lids and placing everything on the four-seat kitchen table.

I took in the sight of eggs benedict, French toast, crepes, bacon, sausage, fresh fruit, and cinnamon rolls. Everything looked lovingly prepared with artistic garnishes.

"Do you have a professional chef?" I asked after they left.

"One of the wives is a chef. I hired her to take care of the food here."

"With so many people, I assume she doesn't work alone, right?"

He nodded. "There is a job for everyone who wants to contribute."

Vena shuffled out of the bedroom. "I smell bacon." Her nose led her straight to the platter. She stole two right away and said she'd be back. Shepard and I sat down. Vena returned in seconds. What amazed me more was that she was fully dressed.

"Did you sprint?" I asked her.

"If there's bacon, I have super speed." She sat at the table and piled most of the bacon onto her plate along with one slice of French toast, one cinnamon roll, and one ripe strawberry. "For balance," she said when I eyed the single strawberry.

I shook my head at her and looked at Shepard as he placed a cinnamon roll on my plate.

"What does today's challenge mean for you?" I asked. "When you were talking about it with Cross at the restaurant, it sounded bad."

"It depends on the reason I'm challenged. MC says he thinks I'm leading poorly, but I believe he's challenging me because I pulled him away from Vena."

"Thank you very much for that," Vena said.

Shepard smiled at her and nodded.

"So you're not worried then? Do you need help with anything?"

"Actually, I was hoping to talk to both of you about that," he said. "While I'd rather keep you both here until your shift at Blur, I don't think it would be fair for either of you."

"Why?" I asked.

"Coordinating tonight's challenge is going to take up every minute of my time after breakfast."

"I hope you squash MC," Vena said with bacon sticking out of her mouth.

"I will."

"I want front-row seats."

Shepard's gaze shifted to me. "You'll have them."

"So where are we going if you don't want us here?" I asked.

"I want you here, Everly. Never doubt that. But for now, I'd feel better if you were at your house. I'll send Doc with you."

"Nope. Keep your guys out finding vamps so Miles can be free. I assume you need them to help with the challenge, too. Cross can guard us," Vena said. "We'll tell him to meet us there after breakfast."

"Okay, but Miles should stay," Shepard said. "And I'm only sending the two of you home temporarily until the challenge is complete. Then you're back here with me."

The fact he didn't say no to Cross surprised me. Hadn't he said no to Cross being at the house in exchange for getting Cross his identification papers?

"Are you okay with Cross watching us?" I asked.

"No, but he's my best option at the moment."

"I'll send him a text," Vena said.

"I can do it," Shepard said.

"What time are you kicking us out?" Vena asked.

I nudged her with my foot.

"Hey," she said. "I'm not complaining. I just had the best night's sleep, a gourmet breakfast, and an interesting interaction with the special feature in the shower. This place is great. But it's also not home, and I'd rather avoid MC until it's time to watch Shepard hand him his ass."

Shepard already had his phone out. Mine and Vena's pinged at the same time with a notification.

Shepard: Cross, can you meet the girls at their house and stay with them until they leave for work?

Cross: I'll be there. Don't worry about them. Worry about making sure your mongrel doesn't go after Everly.

Shepard: I'm handling it. Worry about your vamps, not me.

Cross: Of course, I worry about you. You're the only mutt I like to play with. Try not to get killed.

CHAPTER EIGHTEEN

VENA PARKED IN HER USUAL SPOT IN FRONT OF OUR HOUSE AND cut the engine with a sigh.

"We should have never agreed to stay there."

"Why?" I asked, getting out.

"Now I know how the other half lives. How can I go back to our crappy shower?"

I smirked at her. "We can afford this place. We can't afford that one...unless you changed your mind about MC and want a sugar daddy?"

She shot me a look. "Nope. Definitely not. But if it was Anchor, maybe." She sighed again. "We're on day six without even a hint of a clue. What are the chances–"

"Stop right there, Vena Bree Hunter," I said firmly. "Positive thoughts for positive results."

"But what if–"

"Nope. Our inside man has been out all night. He'll come through." I unlocked the door and let myself in.

The man in question was sitting on the couch, a sexy smirk tugging at his lips as he watched us.

"*Am* I your man, Everly?"

Vena snorted and closed the door behind us.

"Nope, you aren't," Vena said. "You haven't come through on anything yet."

"Any news after last night's bust?" I asked, ignoring his question and her response.

"A few interesting things. Let me have your phone." He held out his hand, and I immediately offered it. Rather than taking the phone, he caught my wrist and tugged me to his side. He leaned in and inhaled.

"You smell like Shepard."

"Well, I did sleep at his house and use his shampoo."

"Hmm."

"I can't tell if you said that because you like that she smells like Shepard or because you don't."

He shot Vena a dry look then gave me some space and focused on my phone.

"I found something interesting. Not your wolf, Vena, but I think you may still appreciate it."

I watched him browse to a website and enter a password, which redirected him to the app store.

"What's 'The Howl'? I've never heard of that app before."

"It's a social chat app exclusively for werewolves," he said, installing it.

"Are you serious?" Vena asked, moving around the couch so she could watch over his shoulder.

"Very serious. There is a channel dedicated to their efforts to find Anchor. There's not much information, though. Just locations they've searched and a list of people they've questioned. There's also a channel about tonight's challenge that you might want to read."

He handed my phone back to me once he had me logged in then helped Vena install it on her phone.

"I think there's a werewolf book with the same name," Vena said. "We read it in high school when we were doing a paper on myths vs. realities, remember?"

"Yeah," I said absently, already browsing the channels. "The Howl by Melissa Haag. It had fairies in it too. You liked when they sparkled everywhere."

Vena laughed as I focused on the app. The chat topics were grouped into channels and had clearly labeled discussion threads. "Missing persons" was all about Anchor. They'd split up the city and were searching areas methodically and questioning everyone they thought might have a connection to him. Cross was right that they weren't really getting anywhere, though.

The channel labeled "Challenges" under "Pack News" caught my eye. As soon as I tapped it, I saw information about Shepard and MC's challenge and swore under my breath.

"MC is the alpha of the L.A. pack?" Vena questioned, obviously seeing the same thing I was.

All the tension with the L.A. pack and how MC got so mad at being ordered around made more sense.

"If MC wins, we're moving," Vena said.

"That won't help you," Cross said. "Shepard isn't just a local alpha. He's *the* Alpha. If MC wins, he'll have authority over all packs across the globe."

Vena dropped her phone on my shoulder then woodenly walked around to take a seat next to me on the arm of the couch.

"He can't win," she said on a shaky breath.

"No, he cannot," Cross agreed.

I turned to look at him, noting the hint of concern in his expression. "What happens if MC wins?"

"Nothing good. Shepard understands his responsibility. He keeps the peace between the wolves and the other races."

"Except the vampires," I said.

Cross shrugged slightly. "So long as the vampires continue to hunt and use humans as cattle, the same humans that the wolves mate with, there will be no peace between our kinds."

"But you're different," I said. "You don't use humans as cattle."

"I do not. And I believe that's why Shepard isn't breaking down that door in an attempt to kill me right now."

"Aw, look at you making a friend," Vena said somewhat bitterly.

"I haven't given up my search for your wolf," he said. "Though six days might feel like an eternity to you, it's barely measurable time. Trust that I will discover where your wolf is."

She sighed and nodded. I tossed her phone to her.

"Distract yourself with spending Cross' money. He needs a house. Now that you know how the other half lives, make it good."

She gave me a weak grin and lost herself in the search.

"Since you're team werewolf now–" I said to Cross.

"I never said that."

"–I think it's time we introduced you to *The Other House*."

I leaned forward to pick up the remote, and when I sat back again, his arm settled around my shoulders. Did I feel right about kissing Shepard and snuggling up against Cross?

A kernel of guilt started to grow before I stomped it down. I wasn't dating Shepard. And I wasn't dating Cross. One was my boss, and I was the temporary money-keeper of the other one.

Once my status changed in their lives, I'd worry about putting a label on whatever this was. Until then, I was free to do what I pleased.

It wasn't like I was trying to hide one from the other. I needed to get out of my head and just enjoy my unlabeled relationships with Cross and Shepard. There was no need to complicate things. It wasn't as if either were spouting words of love.

Smiling, I cuddled in further and turned on the television.

When the intro to *The Other House* came on, Cross watched for a bit and then asked, "Is there a purpose to this show? I've seen people watching this on their phones."

"Figuring out who the wolf is," Vena said. "And ogling the eye candy."

Cross resumed watching for a few minutes. "You don't know who the wolf is?" he asked. "I can smell him from here."

"You're not that good," Vena said, rolling her eyes. "And we already know who the wolf is. This is a rerun."

"I was being facetious. I already know who the wolf is just by watching the intro." Cross pointed to the screen. "And I saw snippets of this season. The wolf is–"

I went from cuddling his side to straddling him with a hand over his mouth.

Pretend-scowling, I looked him in the eye. "There's a rule about *The Other House*—you never, never cry wolf. You can speculate, but never name."

His eyes crinkled at the corners as he smiled under my hand.

"Should I leave you two alone?" Vena asked. "I'm sure there's a missing sock I can try to find."

Cross' smile slipped away as his hands settled on my hips. His eyes darkened.

Scrambling off Cross, I paused the TV. "Who needs a snack?"

"Pretty sure Cross does," Vena said with a wink.

Sending her a warning look, I went to the kitchen and fumbled through the cupboards and refrigerator until I realized we needed groceries. Not that it mattered. I wasn't actually hungry.

Instead, I took two glasses of water back to the couch and handed one to Cross.

Our phones dinged at the same time with a notification as I sat down next to him.

"Looks like the location for the challenge has been set," Cross said as he scrolled through his phone.

"Does it say anything else?" Vena asked.

I nodded as I read with him. "It says delegates from surrounding packs will arrive soon. Looks like New York, New Jersey, Philadelphia, and Virginia." I skimmed a little further. "They are warning wolves to keep the cubs at home."

Vena blew out a breath. "This is a bigger deal than Shepard is letting us believe, isn't it?"

I glanced up at Cross. "Shepard will be okay, right?"

"In a fair fight between Shepard and MC, who do you think will win?" he asked.

"Shepard," I said. I had no doubt about it. But the key word was "fair."

"Cross, how did you find out about 'The Howl' app?" Vena asked.

"A vampire I met mentioned it. I borrowed the login information from him."

As soon as Cross mentioned the vampires, a shadow settled on Vena's face, and I knew why. If the vampires were reading the discussion threads, they knew exactly where the werewolves were looking and how to avoid them.

"We need to tell Shepard," I said.

"I agree," Cross said. "However, I hesitate to tell him on the day of his challenge. I fear distracting him. The werewolves cannot afford to lose him as their leader."

Vena nodded. "I'm with Cross. We should wait."

"Fine. Once the challenge is over, we'll talk to Shepard then focus on finding Anchor and the master," I said.

Cross brushed his hand over my hair. The look he gave me while doing it set my pulse racing.

Vena stood and wedged herself between Cross and myself.

She smirked at me. "Consider me your roadblock. We should be able to get through the episode now without any *bumpy rides*."

Rolling my eyes, I scooted over so we all had room. I watched the TV, willing the nervous energy coursing through my body to settle. It wasn't all due to Cross. I was worried about Shepard's upcoming challenge, too.

We spent the rest of the day binging *The Other House* reruns, eating takeout, and being as lazy as possible.

I enjoyed seeing Cross in this different light. The uptight vampire that used to speak old English could now relax and even tease. It was as if he was rediscovering himself in this new world. And it was sexy as hell discovering Cross alongside him.

Unfortunately, our time came to an end as Vena and I got ready for our shift at Blur.

Cross walked us to my car.

"Will we see you later tonight?" I asked, remembering that

Shepard had asked Cross to keep an eye on things while the wolves were busy doing their furry fight club.

"Not if everything goes well," he said, leaning in to kiss my forehead. "Tell Shepard to watch his back."

Vena snorted. "You've been very interested in Shepard's backside lately."

Cross winked at her and opened my door for me.

"Text me if you need anything."

"Same," I said, getting in.

As soon as Vena pulled into the employee parking lot behind Blur, I knew it wasn't going to be a typical night.

"Why are there so many cars?" she asked.

I shook my head, not having an answer.

Gunther was once again in his usual spot in the kitchen. However, Jaws stood shoulder to shoulder with him, helping with the dishes.

"Hey, Gunther," I called, pausing by the door to the lockers.

Gunther glanced over his shoulder at me and nodded, looking more grumpy than usual. His gaze flicked to Jaws, who'd turned to look at me as well. Then he shook his head slightly.

"Everly. Vena," Jaws said with a curt nod at us.

"Didn't know you aspired to be a dishwasher, Jaws. Was that something you dreamed of becoming since you were little?" Vena asked.

I grabbed her arm and flashed him my signature sugary smile.

"Sorry, Jaws. Vena's late this month and raging hard. Best to avoid her."

I pulled her into the locker room and closed the door. She got my mean face until she looked suitably apologetic. I pantomimed that she'd better behave or else. The or else wasn't the typical thumb across the throat move. I pantomimed a blow job then a chopping motion. Her eyes went wide, and she stuck her bottom lip out, understanding the Vena-V ban and her future sex life depended on her good behavior.

"We're here to make money, not friends," she mumbled.

"Or enemies. Play nice. Final warning."

She made a face but nodded. On our way out, I saw the door to the main bar swing closed behind Jaws.

Vena and I clocked in and left the kitchen to head upstairs. The main bar had extra guys in it, too. Buzz and Boulder were behind the bar with Hollywood and Ink. I gave Buzz a curious glance, and he shook his head slightly just like Gunther had.

Weird.

At the bottom of the stairs, Gunner stood next to Riff. Shoulder to shoulder, the pair of them completely blocked the way up, but they moved for us.

"Are we caught up in a hurricane of what-the-fuck, or is it just me?" Vena asked under her breath.

Neither of us was surprised to see Detroit and LA behind the bar in VIP.

"Are we sure a challenge means what we think it means?" Vena asked. "Cuz it's starting to look like they might be dating."

I almost laughed at her snark. However, the sight of MC waiting in the meeting room with Shepard killed our humor.

"Ladies," MC said with a smile. "It's good to see you again. I apologize on Shepard's behalf that you were inconvenienced last night and had to leave your home because the vampire situation hasn't been properly dealt with yet. It will be soon."

"Yeah, looks like I'm going to be cock-blocked for the next month cuz your grandma didn't teach me to play this nice," Vena said to me.

I elbowed her and looked at Shepard.

He didn't look nearly as upset as I would have been.

"Did you get everything settled?" I asked.

"I did."

Pam walked into the room behind us, cutting off any wolf or vampire talk.

"Full house tonight," she commented. "Are we expecting more trouble?"

"MC's group is thinking of taking over a nightclub and wanted to shadow us to see what success looks like," Shepard said.

Vena covered her mouth and coughed.

MC looked like he wanted to murder Shepard for half a second then smiled at Pam.

"Knowledge is power," he said. "The more I know, the better situated I am to lead with success."

Pam nodded and stepped off to the side as the others slowly joined us. Shepard went through and assigned our sections, placing Vena and me on the lower floor.

We hurried out of the room and to our stations. I could tell she wanted to say something, so once I was set up, I sent her a text even though it was against the rules to have phones on the floor.

Me: What?

Vena: One nut punch.

Vena: No, wait. Two.

Vena: Nope. I want to use his pooch pouch like a speed

bag until he coughs his babymakers out. He's too stupid for offspring.

Me: Harsh.

She sent me a screenshot of a conversation on her phone.

Major Cunt: As soon as you're set, please come up to the meeting room. We need to talk.

Vena: I don't think we do. You've said too much already.

Major Cunt: That's what I'd like to talk about.

Vena: No thanks.

Major Cunt: Tonight's going to change everything. For both of us. I want to be gentle with you, Vena, but you're making it difficult.

Gentle with her?

I looked up at Vena and met her angry gaze.

My first instinct was to go to Shepard. But wouldn't that be throwing fuel on an already combustible situation? So, I subtly shook my head at her in warning and sent another text.

Me: He's not wrong about things changing. Once Shepard wins, MC won't be able to pull this crap. Hang in there. The night will go fast. You'll see.

When Army opened the doors, my tables filled within ten minutes. It was as if all our nervous energy pulled customers to Blur. I no longer had time to think about the upcoming challenge. The most I could do was control my breathing so I wouldn't hyperventilate as I ran back and forth with drink and food orders.

On every pass, I glanced over at Vena to make sure she was okay and that MC wasn't making a move on her. But even MC was pressed into work at the bar. That didn't keep him from glaring at every man who talked to Vena, though. It was a good thing she had no interest in MC because he would take the jealous boyfriend act to another level.

Close to nine, Shepard helped me run food to my section.

"Are you okay?" he asked.

"I might need to stress bake cupcakes for everyone tomorrow, but otherwise, I'm okay."

"Hang in there," he said. "When this is all over, I'll buy you everything you need to stress-bake anything you want."

"Shepard!"

We both glanced over to find Mr. and Mrs. Hunter weaving their way through the crowd. I wanted to groan, but Vena's parents were watching us.

"You have a busy place here," Mrs. Hunter said to Shepard.

"It's a little busier than usual," he said. "Let me see if I can find you a table."

Shepard took charge of the Hunters while I went to the bar to fill more drink orders. Behind the bar, I saw MC watching Shepard and the Hunters. He started to leave his post.

"Hang on," I said. "I need drinks."

"The other guys will help." MC walked around me and veered over to Vena's section where Shepard found a table for the Hunters.

With a silent curse, I followed, knowing Vena didn't want MC anywhere near her or her parents. I might have fewer tips after ignoring my tables, but I didn't care.

As soon as the Hunters were seated, MC swooped in. Mrs. Hunter turned a dazzling smile at him.

Vena had been serving a table and didn't see MC or her parents until she turned around. The look she gave him made my imaginary balls retreat in sympathy.

"Oh, Vena!" Mrs. Hunter gave a wave. "Come over here for a second."

Vena and I arrived at the table at the same time.

"I won't keep you girls long because I know you're busy, but look how adorable you both are in those uniforms. Am I right, boys?" Mrs. Hunter asked.

Shepard dutifully nodded while MC undressed Vena with his eyes.

"I'm so happy you all work here together," she continued. "I know my Vena can take care of herself, but it's good to see she has people to look after her as well."

"I'll always look after her, Mrs. Hunter," MC said.

Vena's foot lifted, but I'd anticipated it and twirled her around to the bar.

"We have to get our drink orders," I said and hurried her away.

MC glanced from Vena to her parents. He then smiled and made himself comfortable at the table. I sent a warning look to Shepard, but he left the table with MC still there.

Giving me a slight shake of the head like the other D.C. wolves had been doing since we arrived, Shepard indicated he wouldn't stop MC. It made sense. MC was being a pain in the ass, but he wasn't harming anyone.

Mrs. Hunter laughed at something MC had said.

"We'll switch sections," I said to Vena. "Let me just serve the drinks that were already ordered; then you can take over."

Within a few minutes, we were in our new stations. MC noticed the change and flagged me to the table.

"Why isn't Vena over here?"

"Her regulars just showed up," I said, which wasn't a total

lie. The friendly dwarves who were regulars at the club had just sat down after other customers had left. "They tip well."

"She doesn't have to worry about money. I'll take care of her."

Mrs. Hunter smiled. "I love that you are so willing, but Vena is an independent girl. She'll get her own money. And thankfully, it's here at the club instead of with her obsessive love of treasure hunting. I swear that girl will bring the end of civilization with one of her discoveries."

Mrs. Hunter was joking, but after the whole Cross wake-up fiasco, the vampire uproar, and now the alpha challenge, Vena might actually succeed at bringing about the end of civilization.

CHAPTER NINETEEN

"You're welcome any time," I heard Mrs. Hunter say to MC as I took the next table's order. "In fact, the five of you should come back this weekend. It's been a long time since I had a full house like that, and I enjoyed it. You did too, dear, right?"

I knew she was asking Mr. Hunter without looking at them. And even if he hadn't enjoyed a full house, he would nod and go along with his wife. How much longer were they going to stay? They'd been nursing their drinks for over an hour already.

"I'll make it happen," MC said. "I really enjoy spending time with Vena but haven't been able to pin her down. She just broke up with her previous boyfriend, so I'm trying to be patient."

Vena was going to kill MC. I might, too.

I smiled at my table, assured them I'd be right back with their order, and moved to the Hunters' table, unwilling to allow MC to manipulate Vena into a corner. A cornered Vena was an extremely dangerous Vena.

"Actually, MC, Anchor was never officially Vena's boyfriend, so there was no break-up." I looked at Mrs. Hunter. "He went out of town unexpectedly a few days ago and hasn't yet reached out to Vena. She's understandably upset, but I've never seen her as interested in a guy as she is with Anchor."

My gaze slipped to MC, who looked like he was struggling to keep his cool. I smiled politely.

"They're slammed behind the bar, and since you came all the way from California to help Shepard, maybe you can take some pity on the guys and fix my next order of drinks for me?"

He smiled back at me as he stood, but it didn't quite reach his eyes.

"Duty calls," he said to the Hunters. "I'll be back as soon as things settle. I enjoyed talking to you."

I walked away from the table with him.

"I don't know what you *think* you're doing, but what you aren't doing is endearing yourself to Vena. She doesn't like being pushed, cornered, or commanded. She's going to come out swinging, and all the muscles in the world aren't going to save you. Understand?"

He paused and looked down at me.

"How long is she going to wait for a guy who isn't coming back?"

"Who says he's not coming back?"

"It's been six days without any word."

"So? Do you think she can just turn off her feelings? Be more sympathetic and think with your big-boy brain instead of the one in your pants, or the one in your pants is going to get punched. She already said as much."

He lifted his gaze and looked at Vena across the room.

"She's the one, Everly. I can feel it."

"Well, she can't. Now, are you going to make my drinks or not?"

He turned away from me and went behind the bar with Shepard. I met Shepard's gaze, and he gave me a small nod. Was that approval for trying to talk some sense into MC or for not losing my shit and throat-punching him myself? As I waited for the drinks, I decided it was maybe a little of both.

My phone buzzed, and I discreetly checked it.

Cross: It's too quiet tonight. No vampires anywhere. I think they're planning something during the challenge. Cancel it.

I saw he'd sent it to the group and looked up at Shepard. He caught my glance and checked his phone. I watched him type his reply.

Shepard: Can't. If I do, I forfeit the right to leadership, and we both know that's not an option.

Cross: Then Everly and Vena need to stay with me.

Shepard: And if your kind's plan is to go after you while my people are distracted, then what? The challenge will be the safest place for them. They'll be surrounded by hundreds of us.

Vena: What about Miles? If the vampires are doing something, is he going to be safe?

Shepard: We moved him at lunch. He's with an old friend of mine who I trust implicitly. He'll keep Miles safe.

MC brought my drinks over. "Something going on that all three of you are looking at your phones?"

"No." I pocketed my phone and carried my order away without a backward glance.

Pasting on my best waitress smile, I hid my worry that

Cross was right about something bad happening tonight and served the drinks.

Mrs. Hunter waved me over as soon as I finished.

"Is it true?" she asked. "Is there someone Vena likes?"

It took me a moment to remember what I'd said.

"Yes, but don't say anything. You know how she gets. The harder you push, the more she'll go her own way. And Anchor is a nice guy who could be good for her."

Mrs. Hunter laughed softly. "Is that your way of telling me to stop meddling in her love life?"

I smiled but said nothing, which had Mr. Hunter chuckling as Mrs. Hunter sighed.

"Well, I'll leave things be for now, but I'm serious about the invitation this weekend. I missed you kids. Come back for another dinner, with or without a plus one. Your choice."

"We will," I said, knowing Vena wouldn't mind as long as MC wasn't along.

"And if you can send me a picture of the man who you think caught her eye–"

"I think it's time for us to go, dear," Mr. Hunter said, standing and offering her a hand.

She smiled sweetly at him, stood, then hugged me.

"Don't leave me curious for too long," she said in my ear. "You know I have a curious mind and a cupid's heart."

I nodded and waved them off as I started clearing their table. My phone buzzed again, but I knew better than to check it while on the floor, so I waited.

When I returned to the bar with my next drink order, I saw MC cut Shepard off to get to me. The twitch in Shepard's jaw worried me. I didn't particularly care for MC, but the way he was pushing Shepard before the challenge made me wonder what kind of beating Shepard was going to dish out and if MC would survive it.

"I'll get that for you, Everly," he said with a smile.

I nodded, wondering what his deal was, and slipped my phone out as he started on the first drink. Cross had sent a message just to me.

Cross: Stay close to Shepard, no matter what happens tonight.

Me: I will.

The warning added to the ball of worry building inside of me.

MC made my drinks quickly, only glancing at Vena as she approached Shepard with her drink order.

As soon as my drinks were on the tray, I turned away.

MC continued to snag my orders every time I approached the bar for the rest of the evening. I didn't mind, even though I started to suspect what he was trying to do. If he thought getting on my good side would help his cause, he was sadly mistaken. At least, it was keeping him away from Vena, who'd definitely reached her stabby limit though.

I had hoped we would get through the night without MC making another move, but at closing, he stopped Vena as she dropped off dirty glasses.

"I know you're probably anxious about tonight," he said. "Don't worry about anything. Everything will be okay." He was about to place his hand on her shoulder, but the look she gave him had him pulling back slightly.

"The only way everything will be okay is if you lose and go home. You're not wanted here, MC." She turned and walked away.

Fists clenched, MC stared at her retreating form for a moment. He caught my gaze, and his eyes narrowed slightly.

"I told you she'll come out swinging if you corner her," I said softly.

I was too far away to hear him, but I was pretty sure he said, "So will I."

He cast a hate-filled glare at Shepard, who was still behind the bar, then whistled low. He and his pack filed out of Blur.

Once they were gone, the tension eased. Shepard came over as I wiped down tables.

"I need to leave too. Doc and Gunther will give you a ride. I've already talked to Cross. He'll be my eyes in D.C. while we're gone. If there's a problem, he'll alert us."

"Shepard, I'm getting a bad feeling about this. MC looked at you as if he wanted to kill you."

Shepard took my hand and toyed with my fingers before he looked at me.

"Don't worry about me, Everly. No matter what he does, he will never win. Do you trust me?"

When I nodded, he smiled. "Then don't worry about anything." He placed a kiss on my forehead and then called his goodbyes as he left with Boulder and Tank.

I hurried to get my station clean and my tips counted and distributed. Vena was right there with me.

"Are you both ready?" Doc called as we closed our lockers.

"Ready," I said.

We headed out to Doc's electric car. Vena and I sat in the back, and Gunther sat up by Doc. When Doc pulled onto the freeway heading out of town, Vena asked, "Where exactly is the fight happening?"

We'd seen the address on The Howl, but we hadn't looked it up, assuming it would be somewhere nearby.

"At a farm," Doc said.

"Won't people see?" I asked.

"It's owned by a pack member," Doc said. "They have an old pole barn that has plenty of space for all of us."

"Do we have to be aware of anything?" I asked.

"Just stay by me, and you'll be fine."

That was easy enough to do, but Doc's rigid shoulders didn't calm my anxiety.

Vena was on her phone, texting Miles. I read over her shoulder for something to do.

Vena: Heard you were moved somewhere else.

Miles: Yeah. I'm with some old guy who likes to play chess. It's not the worst. Heard you're off to have some fun.

Vena: I'd like to deny it, but watching someone I don't like get his ass handed to him is definitely going to be the highlight of my week.

Miles: Glad you're not staying home and missing the excitement. Tell me about it later.

His texts were just like the old Miles I knew. I hoped that meant he wasn't too far gone like Sierra had been.

The rest of the ride was quiet. Even Vena was lost in her own thoughts as she looked out at the darkness that surrounded us. The farther we drove from the city, the darker the roads became until it was only the headlights of the car that navigated our way. Paved roads became gravel, and gravel became dirt.

Just when I thought we couldn't possibly go farther, Doc parked behind a row of cars alongside the road. Up ahead, there was a faint light coming from the farm.

"We'll have to walk the rest of the way," he said. "It's not far. Remember, stay with me. If we get separated, just call my name. I'll come to you. Got it?"

Vena and I nodded and got out of the car as more vehicles parked behind us. We followed the string of people who funneled toward the farm.

There was movement out in the darkness, away from the road.

"Doc, someone is out there," I said.

"They're placing wards to keep humans away."

As we walked, the faint light grew brighter until we came up to a security point. When it was our turn to cross through, we were patted down. They found my charm, but I was allowed to keep it. However, they took Vena's knife and said she could claim it after the event.

Doc escorted us to the giant pole barn. Light spilled from the open doors, making it easier to navigate. Even though the structure was enormous, the sounds of people talking over one another grated at my already frayed nerves.

Inside, we went to where the D.C. pack was congregating. Sierra was among them.

"Why's she here?" Vena asked.

"No one to keep an eye on her back home."

We moved closer to the center of the D.C. crowd, and Vena and I looked around as we waited for the challenge to begin.

The L.A. pack was on the other side of the open shed along with a lot of people I didn't recognize.

"Who are they?" I asked Doc.

"Delegates and neighboring packs."

The one thing that stood out to me was how much bigger

the D.C. pack was compared to the L.A. pack. That made me feel slightly better.

I scanned for any sign of Shepard, but I couldn't see him anywhere in the shed. Was he waiting to enter until everyone was here? Waiting was torture, and I couldn't imagine what he was going through, knowing that someone wanted to take his place and his ring.

The sudden hush was a relief until I realized Shepard and MC had both walked in.

As they moved, Shepard reached back, grabbed the neck of his t-shirt, and pulled it off in one fluid motion that had me forgetting my name.

The doors slammed shut behind them, bringing me back to my senses, and I saw MC had removed his shirt too. Barefoot and shirtless, they moved to the center of the dirt floor and faced each other.

"What are the rules?" I asked Doc softly.

"They fight until one concedes or dies."

I turned to look at him with wide eyes.

"Don't worry. There's a reason Shepard's the head alpha."

An older man with short white hair stepped into the middle between them and started speaking loud enough that even Vena and I could hear.

"We're here today because Marvin Cootner, known as MC—"

"Did he just say cooter?" Vena whispered with suppressed mirth.

The old guy shot her a look. She cleared her throat and quieted.

"—has challenged Shepard Ulv for rights to lead the D.C.

pack." The man looked at MC. "Did you challenge Shepard Ulv's leadership of your own free will?"

"I did," MC said clearly.

"The only rule is that there must be no interference." The man looked at MC again. "You do this alone. Do you understand?"

"Why aren't you saying the same things to him?" MC asked.

"Son, it's you I'm worried about."

Vena smirked, and I saw MC's gaze dart to her.

"I understand that I'm in this alone," he said angrily.

The man nodded.

"Then let the strongest alpha win," he said, stepping back.

It was like a silent gunshot had gone off.

Still in human form, MC lunged at Shepard with a roar. The two collided, and the impact toppled the pair. As they fell, Shepard rapidly hit MC in the ribs.

The deep sound of those solid blows had me cringing.

As quickly as they fell, they rolled and sprang apart. They studied each other, slowly circling, and I saw a flicker of something in MC's eyes. Like they'd turned gold just for a second.

Shepard smirked at him.

"Already showing your wolf? That didn't take much," Shepard taunted.

MC growled softly. "Shut up and fight."

This time, Shepard launched at MC. He moved so quickly that he blurred. But the sound of them slamming together was unmistakable. I cringed again and saw Shepard on top of MC. While MC hit Shepard's side, Shepard rained blows down on MC's face.

I saw blood and turned away to watch Vena instead.

She was smiling until she noticed me looking at her.

"You okay?" she asked softly.

A snarl drew my attention to the fight before I could answer.

Shepard had gotten off MC, and as MC did a kip up off the ground. Shepard glanced at me.

"I'm fine," I said softly, knowing he'd heard Vena's question.

His gaze immediately returned to MC. So did mine.

MC's yellow wolf eyes were unmistakable now. He snarled at Shepard and lunged for him again. He was a blur, but so was Shepard. I waited for the sound of their impact, but it never happened. When MC reached where Shepard should have been, he stopped and spun around just in time to greet Shepard's fist with his face.

Vena's hand caught mine as I winced at the sound of a crunch and the fresh wash of blood coming from MC's nose. She didn't say anything as we both watched.

MC brought his arms up, protecting his face. As he did, I saw hair start to sprout on his forearms. Not a heavy coat like a dog but still thick and a few inches long. With the hair came heavier muscles.

I glanced at Vena. She met my gaze, showing a little of her surprise too. In all of the episodes of *The Other House*, we'd never seen the werewolf shifting. We just knew he was the werewolf because of his sight, speed, and sense of smell.

"Concede before you're hurt," Shepard said.

"You've got that backward," MC snarled.

His hand whipped out, crazy fast, and his newly sprouted dark claws grazed Shepard's stomach. Red slashes appeared in their wake, and I gripped Vena's hand hard. Shepard grunted but didn't step back from MC. Instead, Shepard took advantage of the opening to drive his fist into MC's ribs again.

I heard the crack from where I stood and winced again.

"Shouldn't be much longer," Doc said softly beside me.

MC snarled and spun away from Shepard. More hair sprouted on MC's torso, and his muscles thickened under it. His nose stopped bleeding when it elongated with his mouth into more of a muzzle.

Did changing heal them?

In wolf form, MC still maintained his balance on two feet. He was a huge, muscular beast that didn't conform to the body shape of the wild wolves in the forest but kept his human structure for the most part. Only larger, furrier, and wolf facial features.

I glanced at Shepard, who still looked very human, including the bleeding gashes on his side.

Why wasn't he changing?

"You're going to need to do better than that," Shepard said as his gashes slowly started to close.

He dove for MC. I heard the hits but didn't see them happen...only the aftermath.

MC was left standing, panting and spitting out blood due to his newly broken wolf-nose. It did not look like he would be sniffing Vena any time soon.

"Say you're done," Shepard growled. "Time to end this."

"You're right, we do need to end this," MC said with a snarl.

He shadowed Shepard's movement, sidestepping to stay facing Shepard. As MC drew closer to us, Doc put out his arm and pressed Vena and me farther back.

I was grateful. The last thing I wanted was to accidentally get in the way of those two fighting.

My phone buzzed with a message. Not taking my eyes off the fight, I pulled it from my pocket.

"A good leader knows when it's time to step down," MC said. "You've fucked up D.C. enough. What's your pack going to think when they find out you're working with vampires?"

There was a gasp from the women present and growls from the rest.

"See?" MC said with his back almost to us. "They don't like it. Step down, and let me take care of the vampire problem since you can't."

My phone buzzed again, and I finally glanced down.

Cross: They're here.

Cross: Get to Shepard.

CHAPTER TWENTY

Vena gasped, and I thought it was because she'd seen the message from Cross.

Then a hand closed over my throat, and my world spun as MC lifted me off the ground and turned toward Shepard with me. I couldn't see Shepard, only MC's rage-twisted canine muzzle and Doc standing just behind him.

Doc moved as I dropped my phone and gripped the arm holding me up.

"No interference," the old man yelled to Doc

I hit the arm holding me and gasped for air. His claws slowly broke the skin, and I felt the trickle of blood that ran down my neck.

A low growl sounded through the D.C. pack.

"You need to deal with this on your own, Shepard," the old man said as a warning to everyone.

"Even though he's killing her?" Vena shouted.

"Choose, Shepard," MC said. "Everly or your ring?"

"Screw the rules!" Vena charged at MC, but before she

could attack, the shed door burst open, and a blur streaked through. Vena was knocked aside.

Suddenly freed from MC's grip, I staggered a step as he dropped to the ground, holding his muzzle.

Cross stood between us. His dark, vampire eyes flashed in fury. I waited for them to return to normal, but he was surrounded by men who began shifting into their wolf form at the mere sight of him.

Pants were shredded from their transformation, littering the floor with material.

Cross looked at Shepard. "They're coming!"

The words barely left his mouth before more vampires flooded into the room.

Groaning, MC rolled to the side as wolves clashed with vampires. Growls, screaming, and shouting echoed in the shed that was becoming smaller by the second as vampires continued to arrive.

"Get them to safety," Shepard said to Cross.

But there was nowhere to go. We were being pushed into a corner with no exit. It looked as though the other women were being cornered off as well.

Cross cut down any vampire that came near us and swatted any wolves who incorrectly assumed he was a threat.

"Get back to the fight," Cross shouted after he smacked a wolf in the snout.

Doc ran for us in his human form with Sierra in tow. He placed her in our corner.

"You're hurt," I said when I saw blood seeping from his shoulder.

"Already healing," he said.

"Then stay here until you're fully healed," Cross said. "I'll tag in. If the girls come to harm, I will kill you myself."

"Go," Doc snarled at Cross as he pulled off his shirt and shifted into a wolf.

Cross was gone in an instant. He left a path of dead vampires in his wake.

It was like playing whack-a-mole, though. More vampires kept coming. There had to be three vampires for every one wolf. More than I would have guessed.

The wolves fought fiercely as they tore into the vampires, but the sheer number threatened to overwhelm them. Wolves dropped to the ground along with vampires. The dirt floor soaked up blood by the gallons, but even it couldn't keep up, and soon, puddles formed.

Doc defended against two vampires who attacked our corner. His back was ripped to shreds by one vampire as he tore out the throat of another. He tossed the vampire to the ground and twisted, clawing through the other vampire's chest.

Sierra peered around Doc to stare into the chaos of the main space.

"What are you doing?" I pulled her back. "Stay close."

She looked at me. "I think I saw my old master."

Vena and I looked at each other. "Master?" we said at the same time.

"You mean the cat guy?" Vena asked, glomming onto Sierra. "Where is he?"

Sierra pointed to a black cat that was scaling the rafters.

"He's going to escape," Vena said.

I wasn't so sure he wanted to escape. The way he paused as

he looked down at the fight made me suspect he was waiting for something.

The cat moved a little farther and looked down again. My gaze followed his and landed on Shepard.

I realized his target was Shepard.

"Time to hunt a cat," Vena said, edging around Doc and the vampires he was fighting.

"We're not going out there," I said. "We'll get killed."

"But we have to–"

"Vena, stop. The wolves will take care of him."

"They didn't even notice him." Vena pointed to Shepard, who was fending off three vampires. "Do you really think Shepard can–"

We watched the cat on the rafter above transform into Master. He was completely naked except for the cat ears on his head.

Vena cursed. "He's going to jump on Shepard."

She pushed into the fray, and like the loyal idiot I was, I followed.

We're dead, I thought to myself as we dodged and weaved through pairs that fought too fast to track. I tried not to think about the warm liquid that splashed into my shoes and saturated my socks as we jumped over bodies.

Vena veered to the side as two vampires attacked a wolf.

"If we get to him, maybe we can stop this fight," she said.

Master looked at us then. A grin grew from ear to ear as he leaped down, his nakedness coming flush up against me.

"Just the little human I need," he said, the hard band of his arm tightening around my waist.

I heard the sizzle from my charm a second before the acrid burnt smell filled my nose. It didn't stop the master, though.

His head darted down to the puncture wounds on my throat from MC's claws.

"Shepard!" Vena yelled as I gasped.

The master's tongue licked the skin, and I felt his mouth open wide. I pushed at his chest in panic as Vena swore and tried beating him off me.

A wild snarl erupted next to me as the vampire was ripped away. I glimpsed him flying backward, a smirk on his face, before the view was blocked by the broad expanse of Shepard's back.

He stood in front of me, taller than before, with his back covered by golden fur. He swiped out his hand superfast at the master, who spun just out of reach in front of him.

"Do you think I fear you, Alpha King?" The vampire blurred and appeared next to a wolf fighting two vampires a few yards to the right.

As we watched, the master jumped on the wolf's back and tore into his neck with his teeth.

Shepard growled and lunged for him, knocking his cat ears from his head. The master danced away with a laugh. Rather than follow, Shepard retreated back to us and put out his arm like he was shielding us. I set my hand on his back, letting him know where I was as Vena crowded close to me, her back to my back. Not that it would do either of us any good. We didn't have claws or weapons.

I wished more than anything they'd allowed Vena to keep her knife.

Shepard tensed under my hand and disappeared a moment later. I saw him closing in on the master, who was attacking another wolf.

I grabbed Vena's hand and pulled her in the direction of our safety corner.

Wolves and vampires were fighting all around us. So many vampires.

They saw us. Several stopped helping their companions fight the wolves and turned toward us.

As the first one blurred toward me, I screamed one desperate word.

"Cross!"

The sound that filled the room wasn't like the wolf snarls and growls or the vampires' hisses. It was pure rage and savagery and scary enough that I wanted to close my eyes.

Cross appeared in front of me, his suit jacket ripped and glistening with blood in the overhead lights. He moved wickedly fast, breaking the oncoming vampire's neck then moving to the next in a blur. One by one, they toppled in a circle around us.

Cross looked over his shoulder at me, his eyes completely black with the veins visibly spidering around it.

"You're still bleeding," he said. "Get to Doc."

I nodded, grabbed Vena's hand, and towed her with me as we followed Cross and his body trail to the other women. More wolves were with Doc, protecting the women there. They growled at Cross. The sound he made back sent shivers running down my spine.

He turned toward me.

"Do not leave this circle again."

I nodded and watched him disappear into the chaos.

Vampires littered the ground. I saw wolves too, but not nearly as many.

Through the churning bodies, I saw Shepard, still fighting

the master. Another familiar vampire was fighting not far away. He wasn't facing a werewolf three-to-one but one on one. And the werewolf was losing.

Pet, or as Cross knew him, Vivian Di Rossi.

My gaze swung back to Shepard's fight with Master.

"Pet's here," I said to Vena. "If Cross can kill him–"

Master looked directly into my eyes from across the room. The lapse in focus cost him. Shepard's wicked claws raked down the vampire's front from left shoulder to right hip. The vampire hissed and scrambled back, blood trailing down his pale skin.

Shepard pressed the advantage, moving crazy fast. Another vampire was thrown back from the wolf he was fighting and collided with Shepard's back.

Shepard spun around, claws already slashing. That vampire didn't stand a chance. Blood sprayed, splattering Shepard front then back as he faced Master again.

The interruption had lasted a few seconds at most, but it was enough time for Master to disappear.

"Where did he go?" I asked Vena, knowing she was watching the same thing.

"Rafters," she said.

I looked up with her and saw Master walking along the rafters like he was a cat but still in human form. Naked human form.

"That's disturbing," I said.

His gaze was locked on us, and he was closing in fast.

I looked at Shepard, who'd started killing the closest vampires. Cross was close to the door, doing the same. The vampire numbers were finally thinning.

"Shepard! Cross! Look up!" I yelled, pointing where I wanted them to look.

Both glanced my way then up at Master.

Shepard yelled something I couldn't hear. Cross nodded and continued fighting.

Shepard leapt over the heads of half a dozen people. When he touched down, I saw the way his thick thigh muscles bunched as he crouched and jumped again. His claws sunk into Master's foot on the beam, and he pulled him down with him as he fell.

Shepard landed gracefully on another vampire, breaking its neck in the process, and grabbed Master by the throat before he could escape. Shepard's grip tightened as he punched his other hand into the master's chest.

Eyes wide and unable to look away, I stared at the horrific scene as the vampire's death cry filled the room.

Another tortured cry rang out. Pet cut down a wolf as he bellowed his fury and sorrow. Wolves charged at him, and he fled from the shed. As if his retreat signaled their loss, the remaining vampires abandoned their fight and tried to follow in his wake.

I breathed a sigh of relief, my gaze sweeping the gore-spattered room as the wolves fought harder to stop those who remained from escaping.

Chest heaving, Shepard tore his hand free of Master and met my gaze across the space. Concern in his golden eyes forced me to smile my reassurance that I was okay.

Behind Shepard, a wolf crept closer. His eyes were on Shepard. I opened my mouth to warm him, but the wolf lunged forward, and his jaws clamped onto Shepard's neck from behind.

I didn't understand what was happening until someone said, "No interference. The challenge stands."

I couldn't believe what I was hearing. More than half the wolves were still fighting vampires, and they wanted Shepard to continue with the challenge?

Shepard growled and flipped MC off of him. The wash of blood had me cringing as MC landed and sprang to his feet. Not fast enough, though. The back of Shepard's hand sent MC into the wall where he dazedly slid to the floor.

Shepard glared at him, but his attention was pulled to the retreating vampires.

Cross blurred through the room, finishing off any injured vampires. But as their numbers diminished, the wolves targeted the vampire doing the most damage.

"Cross," I whispered his name. His blackened gaze caught mine.

"Go. Please." He gave a slight nod and blurred out of the shed.

The wolves took care of the remaining vampires trying to flee behind Cross.

Many began shifting back into human form, their nakedness causing me to look away a few times, especially when Gunther walked over to Master and let his bladder loose, shaking every last drop on the dead vampire who had given him so much pain and suffering. He then turned and walked away.

A growl ripped through the shed, drawing my attention to MC as he launched at Shepard again. MC collided with him, knocking him to the ground and biting into Shepard's shoulder.

I wanted to castrate every wolf in the building except

Shepard for their ridiculous rules. They'd just fought vampires, had so many seriously injured or worse, and they were still okay with MC pulling his bullshit? I fisted my hands and watched Shepard throw MC off.

As MC skidded along the ground, drenching his fur in blood, Shepard landed on him.

Growls and snarls filled the room as the fight for dominance continued, each wolf already at their limit. The packs watched on the perimeter, giving them enough space. But with so many bodies and blood on the floor, I didn't understand how they didn't trip and fall.

MC cried out as Shepard threw him into the wall. Shepard was right there, not giving MC a chance to recover as he shifted into human form and grabbed MC by the neck. The choking noises MC made were music to my ears.

MC's fur retreated, and he shifted to human, frantically pulling at Shepard's unforgiving grip.

"I...concede," MC gasped.

"You attacked me from behind twice," Shepard said with a growl. "You no longer have the right to concede."

"Please," MC choked as Shepard squeezed again.

No wolf in the room made a move to save MC, not even his pack.

MC's wild eyes searched for a savior, but when he realized he was on his own, he pulled at Shepard's arm again. "I'll trade you," he said. "My life for Anchor's."

Shepard growled. "What do you mean?"

"I have him. I'll bring him to you."

Shepard shoved MC hard, knocking his head against the wall. "You have Anchor?"

With Shepard's pressure on him, MC could only nod.

"Why?" Shepard growled.

"Vena is mine," MC choked.

"Someone get me my knife," Vena seethed. "MC is about to stand for Mangled Castration."

"I conditionally accept the trade. Anchor's life for yours." Shepard shoved away from MC. "Doc and Army, watch MC until we have Anchor."

Shepard accepted a small stack of clothes from Lisa, and I studied the rafters as he tugged them on. When Vena nudged me, I saw he and a few other men standing close to him had shorts on. But there were still many men who didn't wear anything.

He moved around the room, checking each fallen wolf and speaking to his people. He had sympathy for those who were grieving, compassion for those who were injured, and patience with the ones who remained as he divided them into groups to help with cleanup, injured wolf removal, and vampire tracking.

"We need half our uninjured to hunt the vampires that fled. Follow their scent trails and stick to packs of three or more."

Half the number left the shed in a hurry.

"A bunch of naked men scouring the area," Vena said with a grin. "That should be interesting."

"Most of us keep extra clothes in our cars just in case," Gunner, who was closest to us and completely unfazed by his nakedness, said.

"Griz? Tank? Get the farm truck." Shepard looked at his people as they hurried out. "I wish we had more time to mourn those we lost. But this location is no longer safe. We need to bury our dead quietly. I need ten volunteers. The rest of the uninjured need to escort the injured and females home."

His people divided up as several of the women quietly cried over still bodies.

"Work fast," Shepard said softly. "I don't want to lose anyone else."

Shepard headed outside with Vena and me on his heels. He stopped just outside the shed in the moonlight where a group of men stood.

"What the hell was that?" one of the men asked. "Were you aware D.C. had an infestation?"

"The vampire problem was bigger than I thought," Shepard admitted. "We had no indication it had grown this big."

"What about MC's accusation that you're working with vampires?" the man asked.

"There is a lot you don't know," Shepard said. "And it will take more time and privacy to explain than what we have at the moment."

"If the vampires have grown this large in D.C., what other cities are infested?" another man asked.

"We need to speak about this," someone said.

"I agree, and we will," Shepard said. "Tomorrow at dawn. Spread the word. All delegates should attend. For now, go home and recover. My home is open to you for however long you need."

Once the men began moving away, Vena was on Shepard. "We're not going home, right? We're getting Anchor."

I could feel the weariness coming off Shepard in waves, but he nodded. "I don't suppose you'd wait at my house while I get him?"

She shook her head. "We can get him on the way back to your place, right?"

Shepard called for Doc to bring MC.

Part of me feared MC would go back on his word and fight Shepard yet again.

CHAPTER TWENTY-ONE

When MC and Doc appeared, Doc shoved MC toward Shepard's SUV.

"Attempt to leave this car on your own and I will break your neck," Shepard growled. "I'm out of patience."

"Understood," MC said.

Shepard handed Vena the keys. "Drive carefully."

Vena and I shared a look as they both got into the back seat. We joined the mass exodus of cars and followed them back to the main highway toward D.C. Vena gripped the wheel and took every opportunity to pass that she could.

I took out my phone and sent Cross a text.

Me: Thank you for being there tonight. Are you okay?

Cross: I'm fine. How's your neck?

I smirked at the question and was tempted to text back "delicious" but decided not to throw gas on a potential fire.

Me: Fine. It's not bleeding anymore, but I could use a shower.

Cross: My imagination is stirring.

Me: Focus on not being hunted by Shepard's guys, please. Stay safe.

Cross: You too. Where are you staying tonight?

Me: At Shepard's place.

Cross: Good.

"Is Cross having any problems with my men?" Shepard asked.

I glanced over my shoulder and found him watching me in the dim light from the dashboard. MC snorted in disgust next to him.

"He's not having any problem," I said. "He was worried Vena and I were going to try staying home. I assured him we were not."

"It would be best if you both stayed with me tonight," Shepard said.

"*With* you?" MC said.

"Not your concern," Vena shot back. "Never was and never will be. And I swear on Everly's grandma's life that I will repay every injury Anchor has, like for like."

After a moment of silence, MC said, "Vena, I never meant–"

"Shut it," Vena and Shepard said to MC at the same time.

"I really hate it when you swear on my grandma's life," I mumbled.

"She's *our* grandma, technically," Vena said. "You promised you would share."

I sighed, remembering the promise I'd made when her grandparents had disappeared. "Fine."

"Tell me where we're headed," Vena said with a glare at MC in the mirror once we reached the city.

He directed her to an upscale apartment building in the suburbs north of downtown.

Shepard and MC got out, both looking like they'd been in a wreck. A neighbor saw them when we stepped off the elevator. She clutched at her heart with a startled gasp.

"Realistic makeup for a party," Shepard said with a smile. "Sorry for the scare."

The woman gave an unsure laugh and hurried into her place.

MC used a code at his door and called out that he was back.

The man who was waiting in the living room wasn't familiar. His gaze jumped from MC to Vena to Shepard to me.

"Who won?" he asked, proving that he knew about the challenge.

"Not me," MC said and turned to Shepard. "He's in the room at the end of the hall."

"You think I trust you?" Shepard asked. "You go."

MC moved down the hall and undid at least seven bolts from a steel door. The second he turned the knob, a whole lot of Anchor came charging out and barreled into MC, taking him to the ground and punching him in the face.

"Anchor?" Vena said.

The big guy froze and looked up at Vena. He immediately stood and caught her as she flew at him.

She cried. It didn't happen often and usually signaled an impending full meltdown.

"I'm so sorry," she said through her tears. "It's all my fault. Are you okay?"

She pulled back enough to grab his face and turn his head

between her palms to inspect him. In all honesty, he looked perfectly fine. Not a single bruise or bump.

"We didn't kidnap him to hurt him, Vena," MC said from the floor. "I'm not the asshole you think I am. I just wanted to give you a chance to see me."

Shepard kicked him with his foot as a reminder to shut up as Anchor grinned at Vena.

"I'm fine. They fed me. I had a bathroom to use. A bed to sleep on. The only thing they did to hurt me was to keep me from you."

She made a choked sound and jumped up on him, wrapping her legs around his waist as she clung to him.

"Okay, spider monkey," I said, reaching out and tugging her down. "You're not thinking clearly and might have regrets tomorrow. Let go of Anchor. Now."

Vena reluctantly released him as Shepard faced MC.

"Leave D.C. tonight."

"The vampires–"

"Aren't your problem. They never were. They were mine. And I need people I can trust to help me deal with the issue. Leave and know that every pack will know your betrayal."

"My betrayal?" MC partially growled as he stood. "I did what any wolf would do when he senses his mate. No different from what you're trying to do with Everly. Do you think that absolves you from allowing a vampire to–"

Shepard backhanded MC so hard bloody spit flew. I turned to Vena, and she hugged me to her chest.

"We'll wait outside," she said.

"No need," Shepard said. "We're done here."

We left the apartment with MC holding his face. Vena kept

peeking back at Anchor as we walked to the car. She tried to sit in the backseat with him, but I steered her to the driver's seat.

"Focus on the road," I said.

She gave me a wounded puppy look but got in and started the car, adjusting the rear-view mirror to see Anchor. I leaned over and fixed it.

"I'm going to remember this," she said but left the mirror alone.

On the way to the pack house, Anchor asked, "What happened at the challenge, and why does everyone smell like vampire?"

"The vampires broke in during the fight," Shepard said. "There's an infestation beyond what any of us expected. It was three to one for a while. We're meeting at dawn tomorrow to discuss."

"Was anyone hurt?"

"Many. Most will recover."

But there were some who would not. That fact lingered in the air, causing everyone to remain quiet during the rest of the ride.

When Vena pulled in front of the large housing complex, we weren't the only arrivals. At least half the people getting out of their vehicles were still naked. Too many were limping or leaning on someone.

We got out and made our way inside.

Lisa, who was there with more clothes for anyone who needed them, handed Shepard a hot washcloth from a pile as she greeted us.

"I'm so glad to see you." She tugged Anchor into a quick hug. "Are you okay?"

He gave a nod. "No harm done, just cooped up. A jog on the trails tomorrow and I'll be back to normal."

She gave a nod. "The kitchen's running full steam for those who need food. Are you girls hungry?"

After all the bloodshed, neither of us wanted to eat, so we shook our heads.

"All right. I'll bring up some clean pajamas in a bit."

Vena and I followed Shepard to the suite with Vena keeping an eye on Anchor as he walked the halls with us.

Before we reached the suite, Anchor stopped at a door. "See you tomorrow."

Vena looked at him and then me. There was a plea in her gaze.

I shook my head. "Not a smart move tonight."

She gave him a sad little wave and walked the rest of the way to the suite. Vena went straight for the bathroom, leaving me alone with Shepard. He cleaned the blood off his face and neck. Only hints of MC's bite marks remained.

He tossed the washcloth into the kitchen sink and reached for me, bringing me in for a hug I really needed. His hand brushed against my hair in a soothing motion. I wrapped my arms around his waist.

"Are you okay?" he asked.

"I'm fine," I said. "Might have a nightmare or two."

He leaned back enough to gently grab my chin and tip my head so he could look at my neck.

"I'll be fine," I said again.

He nodded. "I'm sorry you had to go through that. It was just supposed to be a simple fight."

"It's not your fault."

"I should have known about the infestation. It's my job, and I failed."

Guilt hit me hard, and he saw it in my eyes.

"What?" he asked.

"It's not your fault," I said. "It's mine and Vena's and Cross'."

He frowned slightly at the mention of Cross.

"Why do you believe it's your fault?"

"Yesterday, Cross told us about your social app. He learned about it from some vampire he'd talked to. Cross showed us your thread about search efforts for Anchor. We were all focused on that and not the fact you'd posted the location to the challenge. I never thought they'd attack. None of us knew there were so many of them. We didn't tell you the app had been compromised because we didn't want to distract you right before the fight."

Shepard shook his head and leaned in to kiss my forehead.

"Whether they knew or not isn't the issue. Our very purpose is to hunt and kill vampires. It's not your fault there were so many in D.C. That's the real issue and one I'm going to need to answer for."

"Are you concerned about the meeting tomorrow morning with the delegates?"

"No. They have a right to air their grievances, and I'll have a plan of action ready."

I pulled away. "Does that mean you won't sleep tonight?"

"I'll sleep enough to heal, but I don't need a full night. You do, though." He turned me toward the bedroom. "Lisa will be here soon with clothes for you. I'll see you in the morning."

"I want to go to the meeting," I said as I glanced back at him.

He nodded. "You're welcome to come, but you'll need to stay silent. Wolf meetings with delegates involved don't recognize human opinions."

"I just want to be there."

He placed a kiss below my ear, and I fought not to shiver. "You always have a place next to me. Night, Everly."

I walked to the bedroom and looked back at him, but he was already gone, and his bedroom door snicked closed.

By the time Vena emerged from the shower, pajamas and clothes for tomorrow had arrived. As she dressed, I quickly showered. I wanted the blood off me, and I wanted to snuggle with a pillow and forget everything that had happened.

The wounds on my neck didn't seem too bad. If not for the fact there were four on one side and only a single one on the other, the holes would look more like vampire bites than claw punctures. Bruising was already starting to form around them. I dabbed a little antiseptic on them and left them alone.

When I slipped into bed, Vena wrapped around me like a koala.

"What are you doing?" I asked.

"You blocked me from Anchor, so you get to be my cuddle buddy."

"I'll allow it for tonight. Only because I'm afraid of having nightmares, but loosen your hold a little so I can breathe."

She relaxed her grip on me. "If I never see a vampire again, I'll be happy."

"Except one."

She nodded, tickling my nose with a stray hair. "Except one."

After falling asleep in Vena's arms, I only woke one time.

Her feet were twitching, and her toenails raked across my leg. I flipped her to her side of the bed and fell back asleep.

It was still dark when I felt her holding me again. This time, it wasn't her toes touching me but a finger stroking my cheek.

"Vena," I groaned. "Go back to your side."

"Vena is on her side," Cross said.

I stared through the darkness that had the barest hue of dawn creeping into the room.

"What are you doing here?" I asked. "Are you crazy?"

"It's almost time for the meeting," he said. "But I wanted to see you first."

"You've seen me. Now go before they pick up your scent."

"I will as soon as I take care of something."

"What?"

I felt a light wisp of breath along my neck and then the barest caress of his tongue as it traveled along the sore spots where MC had drawn blood. The tingle of Cross' healing touch flowed in more places than just my neck.

My hands lifted to his shoulders. He made a soft sound, and his lips closed on my skin, sucking gently. I couldn't control my erratic breathing or the way my leg hooked over his hip. His hand gripped my leg, pulling me closer so our hips touched.

His mouth left my neck and claimed mine. He made my pulse race with his kiss and the feel of his weight rolling toward me.

"First house rule: Not while we're in bed together," Vena grumbled. "Get your own room."

Cross tore his mouth from mine and glared at her with black eyes.

I cupped his cheeks to bring his attention back to me.

"You should go," I said gently.

His gaze swept over my face, and he dipped his head to kiss me softly.

"Soon."

That single word sent a shiver through me as he disappeared.

"How does it feel to be clam-jammed?" Vena said sleepily.

"Good," I said. "I would have regretted it just like you would have."

"That's all hypothetical until we test it."

I sat up and got out of bed.

"Where are you going?" she asked.

"I told Shepard I wanted to be there for the meeting. I want to know what he's going to do about the vampires."

"All the vampires or just one?" Vena asked.

"Just get out of bed and get ready. The sooner we know what's going on, the sooner we can go home."

"I don't want to go home," she said as she got out of bed.

"Lies. You don't want to leave Anchor, which I don't think will happen. If we go home, there will be fewer eyes to see what you do to him and fewer ears to hear it."

"You think he'll come back with us?" she asked, a hint of her uncertainty in her tone. "With me?"

I turned to her and took her by the shoulders.

"Vena, he never left. He was kidnapped. There's a difference."

She nodded, but I could see she didn't believe me.

"You'll see for yourself," I said, ditching my pajamas for the clothes Lisa had given us last night. As soon as my head cleared my shirt, I turned to Vena. She was wearing a pair of loose-fitting jeans that had her frowning.

"Come on."

She grabbed my arm before I made it to the door and tipped my face so she could see my neck.

"Fucking MC. The bruise on this one is heavy." She touched the spot right where Cross had kissed me. "It's still bleeding a little too. Let's get a Band-Aid."

I followed her to the bathroom and let her put a round smiley face Band-Aid on it.

"Who knew Shepard had a sense of humor?" she said with a laugh.

"Pretty sure these aren't for him."

We left the bathroom and found Shepard at the door. He watched me as we approached, and I saw his nostrils flare.

"He was here?" he asked.

"Yep," Vena said. "He seems to have a thing for waking Everly."

Shepard's jaw muscle ticced as he looked at me. I held up my hands in surrender. "I didn't invite him, and I told him he shouldn't be here as soon as I woke up and saw him."

Shepard let out a long breath and came to me. His fingers slid along the back of my neck up into my hair.

"Everly, it's not a question of whether you invited him but if you wanted him here."

"Wanted him here? A vampire in a place filled with werewolves who have the sole purpose of killing vampires? I don't hate him, Shepard."

"I know you don't. I'm just trying to figure out how much you like him."

"So am I," I said, knowing that wasn't the answer he wanted from me.

"And what about me?" he asked. "Do you know how much you like me?"

"Still trying to figure that out, too," I said.

"Everly's not stupid," Vena said from behind me. "She knows you and Cross are having a not-so-subtle pissing contest when it comes to winning her affection. If you were her, would you be ready to hand over your heart when you're not even sure if the person trying to win it is after it because they like you or because they're just trying to piss off the person they hate?"

I watched Shepard close his eyes for a moment. He nodded, released me, and looked at me again.

"I understand. For the record, I don't like you because Cross does. I've liked you since the moment you walked through Blur's doors and asked for a job. I just never thought you'd be open to a relationship with an otherworlder."

He glanced at the window. "We should hurry if you want to make the meeting."

Vena and I followed him out the door.

CHAPTER TWENTY-TWO

We arrived at a large cafeteria with food stationed on one end. About fifty men, and a few women, congregated at the many round tables as they waited for the meeting. After a long shift last night and the bloody battle after, I craved carbs, protein, and a ton of sugar. However, I noticed that no one was touching the food yet.

Lisa placed pastries on the food table next to a fruit salad, and my stomach growled.

"We'll eat after," Shepard said.

Had he heard my stomach? Probably.

Leading us to a four-top table closest to the food, he said, "Have a seat. This will be over soon."

I watched as he headed to the opposite side where a small platform was situated.

Anchor detached from a nearby group and joined us at the table. As soon as he sat, Vena scooted her chair over to be closer to him.

"Can I have everyone's attention?" Shepard asked. "I'd like

to get through this quickly so the delegates can eat and be on their way."

As he addressed the room, I saw him in a new light. The way his gaze swept the room and took in every detail...the clear and concise way he spoke and the strong posture...he had a bigger presence that he didn't project when at Blur. Shepard truly was the alpha king.

"There are a few things I'd like to address. Number one, The Howl app has been compromised by the vampires. It's how they knew when and where the challenge would be."

A murmur floated through the room.

"Until we can come up with a better system, hunting schedules will be posted in the cafeteria every morning. I expect everyone to watch for it. Hunting vampires has always been our number one priority, and that will not change. What happened last night will never happen again."

A man stood. "What about the rumor you're working with a vampire? Are you sure it's not the vampire who tipped off the others?"

I glanced over at Anchor and mouthed, "Delegate?"

He gave a nod.

"The vampire you are referring to was the one who discovered our app was compromised while searching for information regarding Anchor's disappearance. I didn't ask for his help. In truth, I didn't want it. He gave it regardless."

This time, the rumble was louder and disgruntled.

"Quiet," Shepard warned. "He is unlike the rest of his kind."

"They're all the same," the delegate said.

The look Shepard gave him silenced him.

"Are they?" Shepard questioned to the cafeteria at large. "Because I only saw one vampire killing his own kind last night. I am not so foolish as to believe that's reason enough to blindly trust him. However, it is a reason to listen to what he told me.

"The vampires are planning something, and it's bigger than their endless need for blood. And until we fully understand what they intend to do, we need an insider who can get us information.

"No matter your opinion on this, I want it all made clear right now that the vampire known as Cross is under my protection. If you have a problem with him, you come to me. He is not to be killed. If I find that anyone has made a move on him, I will consider it an act against the pack. You will not like the consequences. Am I understood?"

A general hum of grudging acceptance filled the room.

"Delegates, when you return to your cities today, find out how bad the infestations are. We recently discovered the vampires here have changed how they feed. Use your city resources to look for clubs where they are using the humans as feeders. Licensed businesses right in the middle of your territories."

Several of the men exchanged troubled glances.

"We need to work together to stop them before it gets worse. Keep communication open, but not on The Howl. I will give you updates on the D.C. infestation as they become available."

As Shepard stepped down from the platform, Doc stepped up. "You all fought hard last night. Time to feast and remember the fallen. Eat, rest, and then get ready to work. We'll be pulling long hours until we've cleaned our cities."

Shepard sat at our table as the people lined up for

breakfast. Gunther stopped near the table and crouched down to Shepard.

"Boss, can I have a word?"

"What is it?"

He glanced around. "I'd rather not say here."

"Meet me after breakfast."

He nodded and headed to the food line.

"Miles!" Vena called, jumping out of her seat. She raced for Miles as he walked into the room. "Are you okay? How do you feel?"

He smiled at her. "Much better now." He gave a nod to Shepard. "Thank you for helping me."

"That's why we're here," Shepard said.

I gave his arm a grateful squeeze as I claimed a chair from a neighboring table so Miles could join us at ours.

While Master was dead and Miles was free, things weren't all cakes and cookies. Pet, and who knew how many other vampires, were still out there. But I was willing to pretend everything was fine for a while. We'd earned the respite.

We waited until the line dwindled to get food. Shepard and Anchor heaped their plates full until I could no longer see the plate underneath.

Vena grabbed a stack of bacon and balanced it with fresh fruit. I went with fruit and a chocolate almond croissant. Whoever made it had mastered the croissant layers, and I itched to give my own recipe I'd been playing with another go.

As we ate, Shepard's attention was pulled away as the delegates left for home. He stood to say goodbye to each one, taking longer to return each time.

"I think it's time we went home, too," I said to Vena.

Vena glanced at Anchor, and I knew she was dying for alone time with him.

"Any problems with us leaving?" I asked Shepard when he stopped at the table.

He shook his head. "Anchor, would you mind camping on their couch for the next few days? You've earned some time off, but with the pack out hunting in full force, I don't have the wolf-power to spare."

"Gladly," Anchor said then glanced at me. "Are you okay with that?"

"Yep. As long as you don't mind if Cross shows up unannounced."

"I think I can handle it," he said.

"We'll need you to drop us off at Blur," I added. "My car is there. We hitched a ride with Doc last night."

"No problem. Let me pack a few things first."

"Then we're all set. Thanks for your hospitality, Shepard," I said, standing.

"Anytime."

I could see Gunther waiting by the door.

"We'll get our things from the room and go. See you tonight."

Shepard nodded, and we started out as Gunther approached him.

"I think it's my fault, Boss," Gunther said as we left.

Part of me wanted to linger, but we didn't. Anchor sighed and shook his head before we reached the end of the hall.

"What?" I asked.

"Gunther's blaming himself. The vamps took his phone when they had him. He thinks that's how they got on the app."

"That's not his fault."

"Exactly," Anchor said.

We collected our freshly laundered clothes from Shepard's suite. They were free of any lingering reminder of the blood bath yesterday. We left the pack house with Miles and Anchor a few minutes later. Shepard wasn't there to see us off.

"Want us to drop you at your place?" Vena asked Miles.

"Actually, I was hoping to talk to you. And maybe Anchor. I think Shepard will want to know this too, but I didn't want to bring it up in front of everyone."

"What is it?" Vena asked, looking worried. "Don't tell me you're still–"

"No, no. Nothing like that. I'm fully me again. Free thinking and everything. Which is a good thing. I think I pieced together why the master wanted those rings. And for the record, I'm not calling him Master. That's the only name he gave."

"Get to the point," Vena said impatiently. "What did he tell you?"

"I don't think they're looking for the rings but the stones in the back of that book you found, Vena. Stones, as in gemstones. And guess who else was looking into those stones? Our grandparents right before they disappeared. They were looking into the history of them, which is why they had that book."

"Why is this important?" Vena asked.

"Shepard said the vampires are up to something, right? They want those stones. I think that's why Master told me to steal Shepard's ring. I think that's one of the gemstones. We don't know why or what those stones were for. But I think between the book and the map that we might have the keys we need to find the answer."

"Did you tell the master about the book and map?" Vena asked.

"No. I didn't have any contact with him after you both freed me from that chair. Only a number to text if I got the ring. I wanted the book because I thought the book and map could help me figure out what the rings were for so I would understand how to get them for Master."

"Okay. Then I think they're safest where they're at for now. We'll make plans to spend some time at Mom and Dad's soon. Until then, what are the chances you'll stay out of trouble?" Vena asked.

Miles laughed. "Never thought I'd hear that from you."

"It does sound weird, doesn't it?" I said.

"I have no plans of causing trouble and really hope it doesn't find me again."

"You'll be fine at your house now," Anchor said. "Shepard said the vampire who controlled him is gone, and you're smart enough not to open the door for unfamiliar guests now. Plus, Shepard will have your house marked for watching at night. Same as Everly and Vena's."

Relieved we were under werewolf protection for the unforeseeable future, I waved goodbye as we dropped Miles off at his place. It didn't take long after that to pick up my car and head home.

I walked into our living room with a sigh of relief and glanced at Vena to see if she felt the same. She was busy staring at Anchor.

"So...house rules still apply," I said. "No making out while I'm home."

"Says the girl who got a hickey while I was sleeping next to her," Vena said.

"Hickey?" Anchor asked, glancing at my neck.

"They're marks from when MC grabbed me," I said, waving away his concern with a glare at Vena. "But I'm pretty sure I have a lot to do in the next week or so. Errands and whatnot. Hopefully, some bank accounts to set up and a house to buy."

Pretending to look at my phone calendar, I said, "Looks like I have an appointment tomorrow around lunchtime. And I'll have to get groceries, too."

She grinned. "I'll stay home if you don't mind."

"I don't. Now, I'm going to go take a nap."

I closed myself in my room and sent a text to Mrs. Hunter.

Me: Plan on company this weekend. You might even get to meet the guy who finally caught Vena's eye.

She sent back a screaming GIF that made me grin as I sent a quick group text.

Me: Shepard, I know you're crazy busy, and I don't want to add to your plate, but I just want to make sure you're still going to help Cross become a legal citizen.

Shepard: It's already in the works. He should have his birth certificate by the end of the day tomorrow. He'll need to get his picture taken for an ID, though. Will that work, or is it like the reflection myth?

Cross: I'm flattered you're interested in a picture of me. I promise my image will not disappear or disappoint. Would you like me clothed or unclothed?

I chuckled at Cross' banter, knowing Shepard was probably cursing up a storm. Or maybe not. I was pretty sure Cross was secretly growing on Shepard.

Shepard: Unclothed if it's on a framed canvas so I can hang it over my dartboard.

Cross: I was hoping it'd be over your bed.

I snickered.

Me: I think we should discuss this tomorrow over breakfast. There's a new recipe I want to test.

Vena: Anchor and I are in. We want to see the portrait when it's done too.

Cross: I will be there. With clothes on. (Sorry to disappoint, Shepard.)

Shepard: Just tell me when to be there.

We were a quirky bunch, but we worked well together.

I couldn't wait for tomorrow.

EPILOGUE

PET...

THE SCENTS OF BLOOD AND DEATH FROM BOTH VAMPIRE AND wolf alike permeated the air around the shed. I waited, hidden in the shadows of the roof, as the wolves filed out. Some leaned on others due to their injuries. Others carried the dead. Theirs and ours.

Rage coursed through me.

My brethren had been sure we could beat the wolves, finally get control of the city, and gain the one thing the master wanted–the alpha's ring. We'd had the element of surprise and the numbers to win. It would have worked if one of our own hadn't betrayed us and sided with the wolves.

We had failed miserably, and it had cost us...cost *me*.

The one solace I found as I waited was imagining the master's reaction when she learned her favored pet had sided with the mutts. It wouldn't be pretty. Likely, she would torture the messenger, something I had craved to experience at her hands in the past.

The pleasure I found in pain after being turned was incomparable to the feeble joy I'd once loved as a human. I craved it more than I craved my next meal. For a time, the master had sated my hunger. Now, only Adriel could do so.

My perfect, dangerous Adriel.

I watched a wolf carry him out draped over his shoulder. My lover's hair swayed with each step. Inhaling, I tried to find his scent in the pungent mix but couldn't. I yearned for even the smallest hint of the man who wasn't my master by hierarchy but of my body. He alone owned it. Used it.

Tracking the wolf, I watched him deposit Master's body in a trench the wolves had dug a distance away. My skin crawled as they began throwing dirt on Adriel.

I had no idea if he was alive or dead, but I would not leave him to be discarded like trash. So I bided my time until most of the stronger wolves were gone, chasing the last of my brothers from the bloody battle scene.

The remaining group of wolves finished respectfully removing the dead wolves and called to the others. They left the farm with only a few wolves patrolling for any of my kind foolish enough to return--or stay as I had.

Quietly and swiftly, I blurred to my poorly buried Master and removed him. His body was gruesomely torn, his heart damaged. But I found a glimmer of hope since it was still inside him.

Adriel had been given the gift of cat shifting, and with it came nine lives. He had told me that over his long years, he had used many of those lives, never revealing how many might remain. I hoped there was at least one left.

Gathering him into my arms, I raced away before the wolves could detect me.

Distant howls rang out around us occasionally as I ran faster than any wolf could. We were a long way from our hideaway.

After losing Juicy, our nest had to keep relocating due to the wolves hunting us. But Adriel and I had found an abandoned warehouse outside of D.C. just for the two of us. Reeking of old chemicals, the air burned my nose any time we stayed there. But due to the smell, the place was safe from the wolves. Not even the other vampires knew about it. Only Adriel and I stayed there with the occasional toy we invited to spend the night with us. And dead toys couldn't tell tales.

We had shared so many delicious toys.

When I reached one of the tributaries from Eastern Bay, I paused to wash away the blood from his naked torso and kissed his cold lips tenderly.

"Stay with me," I murmured, clutching him to me as I set out to find a human to drive us across Chesapeake Bay.

I broke into one of the coastal homes and found a portly man who reacted with anger instead of fear at finding me leaning over him in the middle of the night. Grinning, I quickly fed and compelled him to leave a hilarious note for his vacationing wife about rediscovering his sexuality to explain his absence when she eventually returned.

Safely hidden away in the trunk of the human's car, I bit my finger and painted Master's lips with my blood.

"Taste me, Master. Come back to your Pet."

While my heart had beaten several times since the attack, his had yet to stir.

"Who will make me bleed if not you?" I asked, stroking his face.

When the car finally stopped and the trunk opened, what little patience I possessed had come to an end.

"Open the bay door and park inside. Hide your car well and be ready to come to me when I call for you."

Leaving the human to obey, I carried Adriel inside, upstairs to the loft we'd taken as our personal nest. Adriel called it our play palace. It had electricity, plumbing, furniture, and a comfortable bed.

Anchoring his lithe and motionless body to mine, I eased him onto the bed then stood back to look at him in the soft lighting.

Fuck. How the hell did I fix him when he was so mutilated and blood-deficient?

Biting my wrist, I held it over the gaping wound in his chest and let the droplets slide along his pale skin right onto his still heart, hoping it would start the regeneration process. I didn't close my wound until a pool of my blood glistened in the cavity. It was a beautiful sight Master would have enjoyed.

As I waited, I stripped off my shredded clothes and washed away the dried blood and dirt. Then I cleaned him more thoroughly too. His skin was nearly translucent in the moonlight that filtered through the loft window.

Morning would be upon us soon, so I closed the blackout curtains and secured them. Then I fed from our new toy. After the battle and blood I'd given Master, I was ravenous. The human squealed a little at my rough treatment, and the sound helped soothe me.

I could have consumed a blood bag stored in the refrigerator but wanted to save that supply for Master since there were only a few left–rationed from Juicy before Cross and the wolves shut it down.

Fucking Brodier Ashley Cross. I'd known he was against us when he'd saved his favored feeder at the club but hadn't dared think he would choose to side with humans and wolves. By doing so, he'd made an enemy of every vampire. While he was old and was able to walk in the sun, he was not infallible. He had a weakness—a blonde with sweet-smelling blood that I vowed to tear into while he watched.

The thought helped ease some of my anger.

After I drank enough blood to regain my strength, I went to message the nest to let them know I had survived. Others were checking in as well, but I ignored them. I only cared that Adriel survived.

Me: I'm hiding with Adriel. Not sure if he'll survive.

A private text came through moments later.

Queen Bitch: I need you back here.

My hand tightened around my phone as I seethed. I always took commands from the master seriously. Not to do so could mean death or exile. But tonight, I'd take the risk. Adriel was more important.

Me: I'll return once Adriel heals.

Queen Bitch: Now. Or there will be consequences.

Me: Oh? And what consequences will Cross face for betraying us and taking what is mine from me? I stay with Adriel. We need him. Don't forget who he had worked for and why he can walk during the day while we cannot.

Queen Bitch: He no longer works with the fae.

Me: The fae have long memories.

Queen Bitch: You have two days, or I'll hunt you down and kill you myself.

She wouldn't. She needed me, and she needed Adriel. That didn't mean I wanted to listen to her nag.

Pulling a spare pair of cat ears from the nightstand, I placed them on Adriel. Better.

I curled him up into my arms and fell asleep.

THANK you for reading *Fangs and Fudge*! Everly's adventures continue with *Death and Donuts*, book 3 of the Ruin of Relics series.

If you'd like to continue where the epilogue left off and get a full behind-closed-doors look at Pet and Master's intimate bedroom life, you can download that sneak peek via BookFunnel at https://dl.bookfunnel.com/l7ovl442wz.

AUTHOR'S NOTE

We read reviews!

Readers of book 1 who left reviews questioned why Everly put up with Vena's antics. Hopefully, this book clarified their ride-or-die relationship.

Writing is an art, and artists need support to continue creating beautiful (beauty is in the eye of the beholder) works of art. Without readers like you willing to support us on this journey, we wouldn't have the freedom we do to continue creating the stories you love (or love to hate). Be sure to check out our other books written under our various pen names. You might discover another world to love!

When you leave your review, be sure to tell us who you're shipping for Everly. Are you #teamShepard or #teamCross?

We look forward to writing book 3, *Death and Donuts*, and continuing Everly's fun journey into the Shadow Trade world. Expect more Anchor and Vena romance and general hijinx as Everly figures out her own romantic life while keeping everyone she cares about safe from the growing vampire threat.

Happy reading!

Melissa and Nicole

DEATH AND DONUTS

BY MELISSA NICOLE

Love can be deadly.

Everly's cautious optimism for a normal summer shatters with the news of the dwarven prince's murder. By order of the dwarf king, the mountain is immediately shut down, trapping Vena's family inside along with the killer.

As Everly and her friends search for the truth behind the prince's sudden death to free Vena's family, tensions and passions rise, and Everly finds herself once again in a war for affection between Shepard and Cross. Not that being between two hot, alpha males is much of a chore...until Everly discovers why she was placed there.

All the clues point toward a terrifying truth–the vampires are out for blood, and no one is safe.

Death and Donuts is filled with laughs, steamy moments, unique dessert creations for creatures who have no culinary palette (Blood donuts? Gross!), and thrilling near misses in this new addition to the Ruin of Relics series.

MORE BOOKS BY MELISSA NICOLE

The Shadow Trade World

Ruin of Relics

(Sexy shifters and a hottie vampire!)

Blood and BonBons

Fangs and Fudge

Death and Donuts

*More to come!

Connect with the author

Website: melissanicoleauthor.com

Newsletter: melissanicoleauthor.com/subscribe

MORE BOOKS BY MELISSA HAAG

Did you know that Melissa Nicole is a co-authored pen name? Check out these amazing books by the "Melissa" part of Melissa Nicole!

Judgement of the Six Series (and Companion Books) in order:

(more shifters to make you "grr")

Hope(less)

Clay's Hope*

(Mis)fortune

Emmitt's Treasure*

(Un)wise

Luke's Dream*

(Un)bidden

Thomas' Heart*

(Dis)content

Carlos' Peace*

(Sur)real**

*optional companion book

**written in dual point of view

Connect with the author

Website: melissahaag.com

Newsletter: melissahaag.com/subscribe

MORE BOOKS BY NICOLETTE PIERCE

Check out these amazing books by the "Nicole" part of Melissa Nicole!

Black Moon Novels

(Paranormal romance mystery series)

Whiskers & Warrants

Kittens & Kidnappers

Jade Sommer Novels

(Contemporary romance mystery series)

Mostaccioli Murder

Penne Pyro

Fettuccini Fiasco

Rigatoni Ruin

Lasagna Larceny

Bucatini Bomber

Connect with the author

Website: nicolettepierce.com

Newsletter: nicolettepierce.com/newsletter/